Kappy King *and* *the* Puppy Kaper

Books by Amy Lillard

The Wells Landing Series

CAROLINE'S SECRET

COURTING EMILY

LORIE'S HEART

JUST PLAIN SADIE

TITUS RETURNS

MARRYING JONAH

THE QUILTING CIRCLE

The Pontotoc Mississippi Series

A HOME FOR HANNAH

Amish Mysteries

KAPPY KING AND THE PUPPY KAPER

Published by Kensington Publishing Corporation

Kappy King *and* *the* Puppy Kaper

Amy Lillard

ZEBRA BOOKS
Kensington Publishing Corp.
www.kensingtonbooks.com

ZEBRA BOOKS are published by

Kensington Publishing Corp.
119 West 40th Street
New York, NY 10018

All Kensington titles, imprints, and distributed lines are available at special quantity discounts for bulk purchases for sales promotion, premiums, fund-raising, educational, or institutional use.

Special book excerpts or customized printings can also be created to fit specific needs. For details, write or phone the office of the Kensington Sales Manager: Kensington Publishing Corp., 119 West 40th Street, New York, NY 10018. Attn. Sales Department. Phone: 1-800-221-2647.

Zebra and the Z logo Reg. U.S. Pat. & TM Off.

BOUQUET Reg. U.S. Pat. & TM Off.

eISBN-13: 978-1-4201-4298-3
eISBN-10: 1-4201-4298-4
Kensington Electronic Edition: January 2018

ISBN-13: 978-1-4201-4297-6
ISBN-10: 1-4201-4297-6
First Zebra Trade Paperback Edition: January 2018

10 9 8 7 6 5 4 3 2 1

Printed in the United States of America

To Ammo, the best beagle dog a girl could ask for.

Rest in peace, sweet beast. I'll forever miss your floppy ears.

Acknowledgments

So much goes into a book. So many people adding input, checking facts, and sharing ideas. It's a great and fantastic process. But I can honestly say that this book would not have been possible without the help of my best friend, all-around "Carl," and partner in crime, Stacey Barbalace. Thanks for always being there, helping me name characters, and putting up with me when I change them mid-stream because one of them stopped answering to the first name. Thanks for braving the wilds of Pennsylvania Amish country to track down yellow buggies, white pickles, and faceless dolls. Big Valley would have not been the same without you! Thank you! Thank you! Thank you!

Another big thanks to my family for all their love and support, even when they would rather have clean clothes and home-cooked meals. You guys are the greatest!

And, as always, thanks to my agent, Julie Gwinn, and to my editor, John Scognamiglio, for giving me the opportunity to bring Kappy and Edie to life. Here we go!

Chapter 1

Kappy King took one look at her front door and promptly marched back down the porch steps to her buggy. She didn't even bother to take the new bolt of sheer white organdy into the house. She tossed it onto the seat next to her and climbed in. Thankfully, she hadn't unhooked the mare when she arrived back at the house. Heaven only knew why. Maybe the Good Lord was directing her footsteps and He knew she would be needing the carriage sooner than she thought.

Sooner, indeed. This needed to be taken care of and fast. There was only one person she knew in the valley who would have the audacity to paint her front door blue without permission and that person was her across-the-road neighbor Jimmy Peachey.

She clicked the horse into motion and took a deep breath to calm her raging emotions.

Audacity wasn't the right word. *Clueless innocence, misguided helpfulness, unwanted good intentions.* All these described Jimmy and more.

He was as sweet as pie, stubborn as a mule, and cute as a button on a shirt. He was wily in his own way, despite the fact that he had Down syndrome. Kappy didn't know much about the ailment, only that it made Jimmy look a little different from other folks and act a little slower as well. But that didn't mean he wasn't smart. He was too smart by far, but in ways different from everyone around him.

And it had started off to be such a nice day, too.

The Peacheys weren't her closest neighbors, but they only lived less than a quarter of a mile from Kappy. Normally, she would have marched over there on foot, but since she had just returned from the bulk goods store and her horse was still hitched to her buggy, this way was much faster.

The tall stalks of corn rustled as she drove across the main road to the driveway on the other side. Mountains framed both edges of the valley as the clouds created shadows across the green. Blue Sky was one of five boroughs nestled between Stone Mountain and Jacks Mountain. The entire area was around thirty miles long, but only four miles wide. And most all of that was farmland: wheat, corn, and more. She supposed if she had walked it wouldn't have taken any time at all to get to Jimmy and Ruth's, but this way was much more acceptable. Even if she was coming to find out exactly why Jimmy had felt the need to add color to her door.

She shook her head. She knew why he had done it. She just didn't know *why* he had done it.

It was a common misconception that a blue-painted door in the valley meant a girl of marriage age and availability lived there. She supposed since she and Hiram Lapp had called off the wedding she was technically available, but she had already settled herself to being an old maid. Everyone in the valley thought she was odd anyway. Why not add old maid to the list?

The Peachey house seemed strangely quiet as she pulled up the drive. Cornstalks surrounded them on each side, land that belonged to Ruth and had been leased since the year Amos Peachey had passed. Ruth was nothing if not a shrewd businesswoman. But necessity had made her that way.

How long had it been now since Amos had died? Twenty years? Kappy couldn't remember. A long time ago, at any rate. Her family had been alive then and Ruth's daughter, Edith, had still been in the valley. Maybe fifteen. *Jah,* closer to fifteen, since Jimmy hadn't yet started school.

Kappy pulled her horse to a stop and set the brake on the buggy. She could hear the dogs barking from the barn as if on the hunt for something sinister. She shook her head at herself and got out of the buggy. She really needed to quit reading those detective novels. But they were just so interesting. She had never been anyplace but Kishacoquillas Valley, Pennsylvania. And she would probably never go anyplace else. But she could live a little through books. As long as the bishop never found out. She was certain Samuel Miller would not approve of a pipe-smoking Englishman who solved mysteries with the help of his good friend Watson.

Once again, Kappy was overcome with the sense of quietness. No, that wasn't right. It was more of a stillness, an expectancy, as if the farm were holding its breath, waiting for something else to happen.

She shook the thought away. That was ridiculous. Something else couldn't happen because the first something hadn't even happened yet. But as soon as she found Jimmy it would. And once she left he would know with great certainty that she did not need nor did she want her door painted blue.

"Silly tradition," she muttered as she stalked up the porch steps. Whoever came up with such a notion should be hauled before the church. Maybe even hauled into jail. It was just plain silly. Yet now that her door had been painted, she could only hope that not many people saw it or she would be the laughingstock of the community before church on Sunday.

Not that it would be the first time.

She ignored the quiet that didn't really exist, and the noise of thirty or so barking dogs, and knocked on the front door. She shifted from foot to foot waiting on someone, most likely Ruth, to come to the door.

She knocked again, uncomfortable just walking in as most

of her neighbors were prone to do. No one walked into her house uninvited and she couldn't see doing the same. If that made her an odd duck, then so be it.

No answer. Surely, someone knew she was there. How could they not with the dogs barking like crazy? Unless no one was home.

Kappy took a step back and eyed the door thoughtfully, as if the little bit of distance would provide some answers.

The paint on her door had still been tacky to the touch when she had pulled up to her house, which meant it hadn't been long since Jimmy had left. But how long? And had Ruth allowed him to cross the street by himself? She didn't think so.

The noise of the dogs grew louder, as if they had found another reason to bark. What was going on over there? She had been over to the Peacheys' plenty of times, and never had she heard the dogs acting like this. With one last look at the door—the nice, plain, *white* door—she skipped down the porch steps and around the back of the house.

Like her house, the Peachey place was a two-story white structure with a large barn off to one side. An open hay barn sat a little farther back, but now it held the yellow-topped buggy that belonged to Ruth Peachey. But that would mean . . .

Ruth was somewhere in the house or the barn. And since there was no answer at the house . . .

Kappy started across the side yard to the barn, a red jewel shining in the sun.

She stopped for a moment, thinking she'd heard something, then she shrugged it off and continued across the yard.

The barks grew louder with each step she took, and for a moment Kappy wondered if Ruth had gotten some new stock, dogs that weren't familiar with the noises of the valley.

It wasn't like they were friends or anything, she and Ruth. Just friendly-enough neighbors. Truth was, Kappy wasn't friends with many people in Blue Sky, but was that any fault of hers? Not in the least. She couldn't help what people thought of her. She couldn't control if someone believed she was a bit on the peculiar side. The Good Lord knew what was in her heart and that was all that mattered. Wasn't it?

Kappy resisted the urge to cover her ears as she stepped into the barn. The barks were almost deafening. Yet amid the woofs and howls, she thought she heard another noise, this one distinctively human. "Ruth?" she called.

Not a reserved person, she surprised herself by easing cautiously forward. "Ruth?"

Still no answer.

Light filtered through from the other side of the barn. The door was open, but Ruth's horse was nowhere to be seen, most likely put out to pasture for the afternoon.

"Hush!" she hollered toward the large pen containing Ruth Peachey's prized beagle pups. They were so loud she could barely hear herself think! The dogs quieted for a moment, then started back up again.

Kappy shook her head, then rounded the corner that led to the pasture. She stopped short.

Jimmy Peachey stood there, his feet nearly buried in the hay. Tears ran down his reddened cheeks. He twisted his hands in his straw hat, crushing it as he sobbed.

"I'm sorry. I'm sorry. I'm sorry," he chanted as he rocked back and forth.

His mother lay prone at his feet.

Kappy rushed forward. Jimmy didn't move, didn't stop chanting, as she knelt beside the woman. Ruth's storm-gray eyes stared unblinkingly at the rafters overhead.

The dogs continued to bark, blocking out all thoughts. Kappy moved by instinct, holding a hand under Ruth's nose to see if she was still breathing. No warm breath brushed her fingertips, and she saw no rise and fall of Ruth's chest. No movement of any kind.

Just the dogs barking and Jimmy chanting and rocking back and forth. Back and forth.

Kappy checked the woman's breathing once more, unwilling to accept her first answer. But there was no breath. And that could only mean one thing.

Ruth Peachey was dead.

Chapter 2

Kappy was on her feet in a heartbeat. "Jimmy, what happened?"

He shook his head, tears still streaming. "I'm sorry. So sorry."

"Where's the phone?"

Somehow he managed to pull himself together enough to point toward the front of the barn. She rushed into the tack room where Ruth had set up an office for her breeding business. Binders, ledgers, notebooks filled the shelves, but Kappy only had eyes for the phone sitting on the desk. The light on the answering machine blinked red, signaling that there was an unheard message. She grabbed the receiver and dialed.

"Nine-one-one, what's your emergency?"

"Come quick," Kappy said. "It's my neighbor. I think she's dead."

By the time the ambulance and the police arrived, Jimmy had stopped crying. Kappy threw a handful of treats into the dog pen, but it took the pups only a couple of seconds to devour the kibble and they were back to barking once again. She supposed it couldn't be helped. That was what dogs did. They barked, and beagles were the worst.

"Miss?"

Kappy whirled around, coming eye-to-shirt-buttons with

the tallest man she had ever seen. Or maybe it was his swarthy appearance that made him appear so . . . big. She craned her neck back to look into his dark eyes.

"Are you Kathryn King?"

"*Jah.*" Though no one had called her that in years.

"Miss King, I'd like to talk to you for a moment."

She nodded, though she wasn't sure why anyone had called the police to begin with. It wasn't like there had been a crime committed. Ruth had fallen and hit her head. Maybe she'd even had a heart attack first. After all, everyone in the valley knew that she had a bad heart. They'd needed an ambulance, not the deputies.

"I'm told you were the first one on the scene, is that correct?" He held a small plastic-looking stick over his cellphone.

"I guess. I mean, Jimmy was here."

He was taking notes, scribbling with the plastic stick on the screen. "Jimmy Peachey, right? Her son?"

"*Jah.* That's right."

"Did you see anything else?"

"Just Ruth." Kappy shuddered. She was certain she wouldn't be able to close her eyes tonight without seeing Ruth's unblinking stare.

"No one else was on the premises?"

"No. Why?"

He looked up from the tiny hand-held screen and gave her an indulgent smile. "No reason."

She nodded. "*Jah.* Fine, then." She moved past him, but stopped as he spoke again.

"Just don't go leaving the county for a while."

Just like the *Englisch,* making more out of something than need be. She waved him away with one hand and continued toward Jimmy.

Someone had given him a bottle of water. He cradled it in his hands, only half of it gone. Around his neck he wore a device Kappy knew would alert an ambulance or the police in case of an emergency. She wondered if perhaps they could have saved Ruth's life had they thought to use it to summon help.

No sense looking backward. God's plan was already in motion.

"Are you okay, Jimmy?" she asked.

He shifted, rocking back and forth as she had seen him do so often. But only when he was upset about something. His head was bowed and she wondered if perhaps he was praying. Right now praying sounded like a fine idea.

He squeezed the bottle, the plastic making crinkling protests as it took its former shape once again. He squeezed. *Crinkle*. Squeeze. *Crinkle*.

"Jimmy?"

"*Jah?*" He looked up as if only then realizing that she was there.

"Are you going to be okay?"

His red-rimmed eyes filled with tears. "My *mamm* is gone."

Kappy reached out to pat him on the arm, but stopped herself when she remembered that he didn't like to be touched. Her hand dropped back to her side. "Are you going to be all right here by yourself?" Was he even capable of staying on his own? She had no idea.

"I don't want to be alone."

"Is there someone we can ask to stay with you?" The only family she knew he had was a wayward sister.

He shook his head as the bishop pulled up. He was a heavy man with a large round belly that stretched the limits of the buttons on his sky-blue shirt. As was their tradition, he wore one black suspender diagonally across his chest, a necessary accessory as well to keep up his low-slung black trousers. He climbed down from his buggy and started marching over to where they stood. Well, as much as a man of his girth could march. He got halfway across the yard before one of the deputies stopped him.

The two men talked for a moment, but Kappy didn't hear what was said. There were too many people, too many dogs still barking. Now she knew what had them all agitated. Someone strange had come onto the property, and that person had killed Ruth Peachey.

The bishop nodded to the tall deputy, shook his hand, then wobbled over to where Kappy and Jimmy stood.

"Jimmy." Samuel Miller nodded in Jimmy's direction, then to Kappy. "This is a sad day. A sad day indeed."

Jimmy's tears spilled down his cheeks. "My *mamm* is gone."

Samuel's lips pressed together and he nodded, his gray-streaked beard billowing in the wind. "I know, Jimmy."

"I don't know what I'm going to do," Jimmy wailed.

As far as Kappy knew, Jimmy was at least twenty. He was old enough that he had bowed to his knees and joined the church, but he had never lived anyplace other than the home that sat behind them.

"Don't worry, Jimmy. The church will take care of you." She murmured the words, not really absorbing their meaning; they were just something she had been told her entire life. Had the church taken care of her after her parents' death? She supposed they had.

"You'll need to take care of him, Kappy."

"Me?" She looked from the bishop back to the crying young man. What was she supposed to do with him?

"*Jah,*" the bishop said. "Spend the night here so he doesn't have to be alone."

"But—" Kappy protested. "I have a business to run."

Which was true. Because she was the only *kapp* maker in the valley, all the women came to her for their head coverings. She needed to be at her house in case someone came by to purchase a new *kapp*. Well, maybe not in case they wanted to buy a *kapp,* but how was she going to sell *kapps* if she wasn't home making them?

"Then let him stay at your house."

"My house?" Her voice was strangely akin to the squeak of a mouse.

The bishop shrugged. "You have plenty of room."

It was true, but she still wanted to protest, to tell the bishop no, but she knew—no one told Samuel Miller no. And someone had taken her in. Her maiden aunt had, just after Kappy turned ten.

"Samuel—" she started, but he interrupted before she could say anything more.

"My wife has gone to her sister's in Lancaster. When she gets back, Alma can help. Until then, you need to rise to your Christian duty."

She couldn't take total responsibility for Jimmy. She wouldn't. But perhaps it was time to give back.

"*Jah.* Okay. Fine." She tried to make her voice sound gracious and caring, but she was afraid it just came out annoyed. If the bishop noticed, he didn't comment.

"You hear that, Jimmy? Kappy is going to let you stay with her for a while."

A while? Maybe she should have asked when Alma was due back.

Kappy was accustomed to being on her own. "A while" sounded way too long for her comfort.

Jimmy looked up, something akin to horror on his face. "Stay with her? You mean at her house?" He started shaking his head even before he stopped speaking. "No-no-no-no-no-no."

"Jimmy, you can't stay here alone." Kappy was surprised the gentle words came out of her mouth. She'd never been much good at the softer side of things. She blamed the death of her mother and then being raised by her crazy maiden aunt. No one was so bold as to actually call her aunt crazy, but she was. Kappy knew it, as sure as she knew her own name.

He continued to shake his head. "I can't go. What if *Mamm* . . . what if she comes back and I'm not here?"

Kappy wished she could take his hands or something, anything to get his attention off the ground and on to her face. That way she would know that he was listening to her. "Look at me, Jimmy."

He did as she commanded.

"I'm sorry. Your mother isn't coming back. Not until time for the funeral. You understand, don't you?"

He sniffed, but gave a small nod.

"You can stay with me at my house, or"—she took a deep breath and wondered why she was even going down this road—"I can stay here with you."

Jimmy seemed to think about it for a moment. "Do you have any dogs?"

She shook her head. "No."

"What about rabbits?"

"No. No rabbits."

"Do you have any gerbils?"

"No."

"Don't you have any pets at all?"

Not unless she counted her horse and the stray cat that came up from time to time. "Uh, not really."

"Then can we stay here?"

Kappy tried not to frown. "Of course," she said. But tomorrow morning, first thing, she would have to go back to her house and leave a note on the door in case anyone came by for a prayer *kapp*. And with the way her luck was going, everyone in the valley would need one while she was babysitting the neighbor.

Chapter 3

Kappy taped the note to the front door and stepped back to inspect her work. *Go around back. Leave your money in the jar by the door. Write special orders on the notepad on the table. Thanks.*

It would have to do. The door was still blue, but that couldn't be helped, either. Unfortunately, Jimmy needed her. And then she had needed him. The dogs had to be fed—along with the gerbils, the rabbits, and the ducks. Kappy had no idea there were this many animals on the property. But Jimmy had known just what to do. Still, she didn't have any doubts that he wouldn't be able to live on his own now that his mother was gone. It was such a tragic, tragic day. But she knew that God had a plan for Jimmy.

She started across the road back toward the Peacheys' place. She had left her buggy at Jimmy's, figuring she would be able to take care of her horse easier if she was in the barn closest. At least for the time being. She had no idea how long she would have to stay with Jimmy. Hopefully, just until the bishop's wife returned. Or someone got in touch with his sister. Surely, Edith would take him to live with her. After all, it was important to be surrounded by family.

She stepped cautiously along the edge of the fields, careful not to smash anything important. The man who farmed the land would surely not appreciate it if she took out a couple of rows of corn because she wasn't paying attention to where she was walking.

She had heard who had leased the farmland from Ruth, but she couldn't remember the name now. An Amish farmer, but the first year she had leased it to an *Englisch* man. Kappy wasn't sure why she remembered that. She had just come to live across School Yard Road with her aunt Hettie. Kappy couldn't have been more than ten, but it was as fresh in her mind as if it had happened just last week. A group of neighbors had gotten together and protested to the bishop. Preacher Sam had been newly chosen and had taken the side of the neighbors. Ruth was allowed to lease her land but only to Amish farmers. That decree had started the following year. Aunt Hettie had sold most of her farmland to Amos Peachey years before that, so Ruth's available acreage was larger than most in the valley held, just another reason why the neighbors wanted an opportunity to lease.

Farmland had been in short supply for quite some time. The Amish of Kishacoquillas Valley, or Big Valley as it was often called, prided themselves on being self-sufficient. But the less land there was to go around, the more the young Amish men from all three Amish sects in the area were having to turn away from farming and do their best to find other means to support themselves and their families.

She stopped and cupped one hand over her eyes to shade against the mid-morning sun. The farm just behind Ruth's was owned by Jay Glick. Jay was a farmer through and through, but his eldest son had to take up cabinetmaking and the next to the oldest had moved closer to Lancaster. Not that there was much more land in Lancaster. That son had lucked out and found a piece of property, and an *Englisch* farm was converted into an Amish one. Jay had two more sons. The youngest would inherit the family farm when the time came and the other son hadn't chosen a profession, instead working odd jobs around the district. Kappy wondered if the dwindling amount of land had contributed to his indecision. It was both a blessing and a curse that Blue Sky was nestled there between the two mountains. A blessing in the picturesque landscape and the close-knit communities, and a curse since no one could expand. The land was all gone.

"Kappy!" Jimmy stood on the front porch waving at her, his arm high in the air. "Kappy!"

She waved in return and started walking once again. Last night she had looked through Ruth's desk for some sort of phone book or even a scrap of paper with Edith's number written on it. Or even an address for the wayward Peachey daughter. Aside from the fact that Edith needed to know of her mother's passing, someone had to come take care of Jimmy. And the sooner that happened, the sooner Kappy could get back to her own life.

"It's time to feed the dogs again," Jimmy said when she got within earshot.

"Again?" Hadn't they just fed them the night before?

Jimmy nodded in his exaggerated way. "Food in the morning and after four. Fresh water twice a day."

Maybe he was a little more capable than she'd first thought.

"Do you know where everything is?"

"*Jah.*" He motioned for her to follow behind him as he jumped off the side of the porch. "I'll show you."

Kappy trailed behind Jimmy as he led the way to what had originally been a horse paddock. Now it had been enclosed with wire fencing to keep the tumbling puppies inside. A row of neatly maintained doghouses lined the far fence. Kappy counted eight in all, all painted pale blue like her door. At least she knew how Jimmy had come by the blue paint.

She hadn't had time to ask him about his intentions. Maybe he had been trying to do her a favor. After all, her door had needed a fresh coat of paint.

As he had the night before, Jimmy set out the many stainless-steel bowls, then used a plastic cup to scoop the dog food from the large waist-high container.

Dogs and puppies alike raced to the bowls, tails wagging as they devoured the food. Kappy couldn't help but smile at the sight of all those happy dogs with their floppy ears and long snouts. Ruth had quite a business going for herself.

After the dogs had been fed, Jimmy attached the hose to the spigot and filled the long drinking trough with fresh water. He wound up the hose and returned it to the barn.

"Do we have to feed the rabbits this morning?"

"Gotta pick up the poop first." Jimmy wrinkled his nose and grabbed a hand-held scooper and a large green bucket.

"Jimmy," Kappy started as he walked the large cage, cleaning up after the dogs, "do you know how to get in touch with your sister?"

He shook his head. "*Mamm* wouldn't let me talk to her." His tone nearly broke Kappy's heart. She could tell from just those few words that Jimmy missed his sister very much. "She's under the *Bann,* you know."

"I know." Edith had left after joining the church, which made her subject to a *Bann,* but with as much as Kappy missed her family, she couldn't imagine shunning any of her kin, *Ordnung* or no.

Jimmy shrugged. "She'll come back one day."

He said the words with such confidence that Kappy almost believed them to be fact. "We need her to come back soon." Tomorrow would be good. Or tonight.

"*Jah.*"

"Do you know if your mother had a way to call her or write her?"

Jimmy shook his head and placed the scooper on its hook by the back door. "She wouldn't talk to Edie. She was under the *Bann.*"

She had forgotten they had called his sister Edie.

Jimmy brushed past her and on into the barn. On the far side, rabbit hutches had been constructed. Bunnies of all colors and sizes waited. They watched, some even braced on the side of their pens as they caught sight of Jimmy. Their tiny noses twitched. It was obvious that they knew him and also knew that with him came food and clean water.

"Do you have a phone number for your sister?" She wasn't sure what made her ask.

Jimmy turned around from giving the rabbits fresh water. "*Jah*. It's in the house."

It might have been the hardest thing she had ever done, calling Edith Peachey and telling her that her mother had passed away.

"What?" The whisper barely reached Kappy from across the miles.

Kappy sat in the tiny room off to one side of the barn, surrounded by all of Ruth's records and binders, as she delivered the news. Most of the church members had to rely on phone shanties for their telephone conversations, but Ruth had gotten special permission since she and Jimmy lived alone.

"I'm sorry," was all Kappy could say in return. "Would you like to talk to your brother?"

"Jimmy's there?"

"Of course."

"No," Edie finally said. "I don't want to talk to him. It would just confuse him."

She didn't see how. "But you are coming home, right? I mean, back to Blue Sky?"

"I don't—"

Kappy couldn't listen to any more. "Jimmy needs you. He can't stay here by himself. And the funeral is the day after tomorrow."

"Day after tomorrow?"

"Or, well . . . as soon as the coroner has her body back."

"The coroner? Why does the coroner have her?"

Kappy shrugged even though she knew that Edie couldn't see her. "The police wanted to make sure of the exact cause of death since no one was around. Well, except for Jimmy."

"Jimmy was there?"

"Where else would he be?"

He picked that moment to walk in. "Is that Edie? Can I say hello? Will you tell her hello for me? Will you, Kappy, please?"

She handed the phone to him and tried not to be too interested in the conversation between them. She could only hear Jimmy's side about the gerbils, rabbits, and the beagle pups. Finally, he had talked himself out and handed the phone back to Kappy.

"Okay," Edie said with a great sigh. "Day after tomorrow. I'll be there."

The blond-haired woman dressed all in black was nearly unrecognizable as the young woman who had left over ten years ago. Not that it was any of Kappy's business. She was just glad that Edie Peachey had returned to Blue Sky.

Taller and thinner than Kappy remembered, Edie Peachey had blown in the night before wearing skintight pants made of a material patterned after some sort of animal hide and a formfitting shirt with the shoulders cut out.

Still, Jimmy had been so happy to see his sister. Kappy had gone to the room that she had claimed as her own to give them some privacy. But some part of her was reluctant to leave Jimmy alone with this stranger. Even if she was his sister.

Kappy looked around the downstairs at all the strange and familiar faces. Most everyone at the funeral she had seen or met at one time or another, but there were a few faces she didn't know. She could only speculate that they were some of Ruth's customers, a theory backed up in fact as she overheard a couple of them talking about their dogs.

But for the most part, everyone else was a member of their church. Alma Miller, the bishop's wife, had returned in time to make sure that everyone did their part. Alma had sparkling blue eyes, steel-gray hair, and was as round as she was tall. She couldn't sneak up on a soul for her shoes squeaked terribly with each step she took, a phenomenon that had been in place for as long as Kappy could remember.

"Is there pie?" Edie asked, sidling up next to Kappy. She had been standing with her back against the wall hoping no one noticed her, no one spoke to her, no one asked anything of her. Not even a quick question about pie.

Kappy waved a hand toward the table where the funeral pies had been laid out. "There's plenty."

Edie shook her head. "Not the nasty raisin pie. A good pie, like chocolate cream or peach."

"They always bring raisin pie to funerals, or have you forgotten?"

There was a stiff pie competition in Blue Sky. Raisin seemed to be the only flavor no one had claimed. Even then, everyone knew that Alma Miller's pie was the best.

Edie sniffed and tossed back her streaky blond hair. She had cut it so that it barely brushed the tops of her shoulders. "I remember. I just don't like it, that's all. And I really want a piece of pie."

Kappy sent her a chastising look, but managed to keep her thoughts inside. They were at a funeral, after all. She remembered, even if Edie had forgotten.

"What?" Edie shook her head. "I'm stressed out, and I like to eat when I'm stressed."

Kappy gave a small nod toward the table. "Then eat a piece of funeral pie."

Edie ignored that, so Kappy continued. "Why don't you ask? Maybe one of the church women brought another pie or something."

Edie shrugged as if it were no big deal and let her gaze wander around the room. "No one will talk to me. Shunned and all that."

Kappy had almost forgotten. Edie was under the *Bann*. But surely those rules could be bent a little in light of the day's circumstances.

"Have you seen Jimmy?" Edie asked.

"He doesn't have any pie."

Edie rolled her eyes. "I'm just worried about him. There are so many people. He never was good with crowds. Even church bothered him from time to time."

He had gotten over that in the past few years, but there were a lot of people in the house, and coupled with the stress of losing his mother . . .

"He's in the barn." A few of the male funeral goers had most likely overflowed to the large structure, but Kappy was certain a few was much better than the two hundred or so all milling around the Peachey household.

"*Pssst . . .* Kappy."

She turned to find Jimmy standing half in and half out of the kitchen doorway, as if that were enough to hide him from all the commotion. "*Jah?*"

"There are too many people here. I need to feed the dogs."

Kappy checked the plain wall clock over the mantle. "It's only three o'clock, Jimmy. The dogs aren't expecting to be fed for another hour."

Jimmy twisted his fingers together, unable to meet her gaze. "But what if we forget? There are so many people here. We might get confused."

"We won't," she said. "I promise."

"But—"

"Jimmy." She set her tone to low warning and he understood well enough.

He dropped his chin to his chest.

"How many people are out in the barn?"

"A lot. Maybe a thousand."

There were nowhere near a thousand people in the district, much less that many in the barn, but Kappy didn't bother to correct him. There were more than he was comfortable with and that was all that mattered. "Why don't you go upstairs and lie down?"

"But, Kappy—"

"No buts, Jimmy. It's going to be okay."

Jimmy didn't have time to respond.

"Kappy?" James Troyer, the district's mild-mannered deacon, hustled over to her. "That Jones fellow is here again."

"Jones?" She didn't know anyone by that name. Then she saw him, winding his way through the crowd, the tall deputy from the other day. He looked even more sinister today than he had then.

"Miss King." He nodded as he edged past, scooting between her and Edie as he reached for Jimmy.

The young man drew away from the deputy, his eyes wide with confusion and fear. "Don't touch me."

Jones kept coming.

"Kappy," Jimmy whined, cringing away.

"What's going on?" Kappy tried to get between Jones and Jimmy. People were starting to stare.

"I'm afraid we're going to have to detain Mr. Peachey." At least he wasn't reaching for Jimmy, but he had retrieved a set of handcuffs from his belt.

"Detain?" Kappy stared at the handcuffs. They looked heavy and like they meant business. "What does that mean?"

"It means we're arresting him." The uniformed deputy behind Jones took a step forward.

"What?" Edie screeched.

"Kappy!" Jimmy reached for her, but the deputy used the motion to his advantage, grasping Jimmy's arm and pulling it behind his back. He screamed, a keening sound, and started rocking back and forth.

"I don't understand." Kappy shook her head. How could they arrest Jimmy? *Why* were they arresting Jimmy?

"The coroner's report came back. Ruth died from head trauma."

Kappy nodded. "She fell and hit her head."

He shook his. "Not exactly. Someone hit her in the head, and then she fell."

Kappy frowned, the expression reflected on Edie's face as well. "I don't understand." Hadn't Ruth had a heart attack, fallen, and hit her head?

"It's simple, really," Jones said. "Ruth was murdered."

Chapter 4

"Murdered?" The word came from Edie, but echoed inside Kappy's thoughts.

"I'm sorry."

Jimmy continued to holler Kappy's name as the uniformed deputy escorted him through the crowd. Everyone had stopped to stare. She couldn't blame them. How many times was such a spectacle part of daily life? Much less at a funeral.

"Don't forget to feed the dogs, Kappy," was the last thing Jimmy said as he disappeared out the front door.

Kappy resisted the urge to go after him, but Edie had no such reservations. She hurried behind her brother, her heels clopping like horse hooves against the uncovered floors.

"This is ridiculous," Kappy said, turning back to Jones. "Jimmy wouldn't hurt a fly."

"Maybe we should go somewhere more private where we can talk." Jones cleared his throat and looked pointedly around them at the many staring faces of the funeral goers. No one had moved since the entire exchange had begun. And still they sat, watching to see the end of the encounter.

Kappy could feel their stares. It would be all over the valley in a matter of hours, but that didn't mean they needed to hear it all. But where was there privacy amid two-hundred-plus funeral attendees?

Jones seemed to read her mind. "Perhaps we can find a quiet space outside."

Kappy nodded and followed him toward the door.

The cheery sunshine seemed to mock the day. First the funeral and now this. There were definitely fewer people outside than inside. And most were staring at the sheriff's car that was pulling away from the house. Kappy thought she could make out Jimmy's form inside the car, rocking back and forth as he tried to soothe himself.

"Kappy, they took Jimmy." Edie hobbled toward them, her heels sinking into the grass as she picked her way across the yard.

"I know."

"I mean, they took him. They really *took* him." Edie turned her accusing stare to the tall deputy. "Why did you take my brother?" Her voice rose with each syllable. Sometime during the exchange she had started to cry, the tears leaving black marks trailing down her cheeks as her makeup smeared.

"Edie, I understand your concern, but perhaps you should give him a chance to explain," Kappy soothed. At least, she hoped he had a good reason for his actions. As Edie had already stated, Jimmy wouldn't hurt a fly.

Jones nodded. "He's your brother?"

"Yes," Edie returned. "And he did not hurt our mother."

Kappy shook her head, trying to clear her mind. "But . . . but why would you arrest Jimmy?"

Jones shifted his stance and for the first time Kappy noticed that he was wearing an *Englisch* suit. The last time she had seen him he'd had on a pair of blue jeans and a shirt with a collar. Was he allowed to wear anything he wanted to work? How was a person supposed to know he was a deputy? "I can't give you all the details, but Jimmy basically confessed when we talked to him."

"You talked to him?" Kappy asked. "When?" Had they waited until she left the house to try and question him?

"Basically?" Edie screeched. "What does that mean?"

"What's going on here?" Samuel Miller picked that moment to join them on the front lawn. He waddled toward them, his vest buttons pulled to capacity.

"I'm sorry, sir. Do I know you?" Jones asked. His tone was polite, but Kappy could tell that he resented the interruption.

Samuel puffed out his chest, straining his buttons even further. "I'm the bishop."

Jones looked to Kappy.

She nodded.

"I'm not able to discuss the particulars," Jones said.

"But you arrested my brother."

Jones nodded. "He confessed."

"Basically," Edie scoffed.

"The matter is not up for debate. He confessed. From here it's up to the district attorney." He nodded toward them all, then turned on his heel and headed toward his car.

"He can't stay in jail, Kappy." Tears filled Edie's eyes. She might have lost her Amish ways in the *Englisch* world, but she loved her brother. That much was obvious. "He'll never survive in jail."

She was right. Jimmy was too sensitive, too sweet. She had no idea what jail was like, but it was filled with criminals and thieves. He was neither.

Kappy raced to catch up with Jones. "Deputy," she said, laying a hand on his arm to stop him.

"Detective," he corrected, looking at her fingers on the sleeve of his suit coat.

"Detective," Kappy agreed with a nod. She drew in a deep breath before continuing. "Jimmy is special. Please, take care of him. He doesn't belong in jail."

He tugged his arm from her grasp. "I will," he promised, then ducked into his car and drove away.

"I don't understand. How can they just come get him and take him to jail?" Edie pushed her unnaturally blond bangs out of her eyes and sat at the table across from Kappy.

Shortly after the deputies took Jimmy away, the funeral wound to a close. Now Kappy sat across from Edie, wishing she was anywhere but there.

The kitchen table was still loaded with pies, bowls of prunes, and other leftover funeral food, but the dishes had been cleaned and put away, all except for a pile of silverware still sitting on the table. It would only take a few seconds to put it away, but for now it was fine where it was. Kappy was exhausted. Too exhausted to mess with it.

She had been to more funerals than she cared to remember in the years since her family had been killed, and every time the memories came flooding back. Sad, exhausted memories. Add to that the shock of Jimmy's arrest and the day was almost more than any one person should have to endure.

"Are you truly asking me? Because I don't understand any of this, either."

Edie shook her head and stared down into her coffee cup. She was silent for a moment before looking up and pinning Kappy with her sharp brown stare. "Say, why are you talking to me anyhow?"

"I see no reason not to." It was the truth. Edie had never done anything to her. Why shouldn't she talk to her?

"I'm excommunicated."

Kappy shrugged. "I can see no fault in your decision. Not if you're happy with it."

A shadow of something Kappy couldn't name passed across Edie's face, but it was gone almost as quickly as it appeared.

Truth was, Kappy had spent a great chunk of her life wishing she could talk to her family. She couldn't see not talking to someone who was sitting in front of her.

With a low growl, Edie grabbed a fork off the pile and pulled one of the pies toward her. Without the benefit of a plate, she started to eat straight from the pan.

"I thought you didn't like funeral pie," Kappy said.

Edie took another bite but didn't swallow before answering. "I don't."

"Then why are you eating it?"

"My mother died. My brother's in jail." She took another bite, then dropped her fork, the metal clattering onto the table next to her coffee cup. "What am I going to do, Kappy? I can't leave Jimmy in jail."

"No," Kappy agreed.

"I mean I was so happy to come back and see him again. Well, not really *happy*. You know, since my mother died. But I was excited to get to see him. I've missed him so much over the years. And now this." She leaned back in her chair and crossed her arms. She uncrossed them a heartbeat later, then leaned forward and braced her arms on the tabletop. "I can't leave him in jail, Kappy. I just can't. He doesn't belong there."

Truer words had never been spoken. But she remembered Jones's promise. "He'll be okay."

"But he can't *stay* there."

"And he won't." Would he?

Edie ran her fingers through her hair and chocked her elbows on the table. "You don't really think he killed *Mamm*, do you?"

"No." She didn't hesitate when she answered. There was no way Jimmy had killed Ruth.

But the image of him standing over her body telling her he was sorry was forever burned into her brain. Why had he been apologizing?

"He was the last one to see her alive," Kappy said.

Edie straightened. "How do you know that?"

Kappy took a cautious sip of her coffee. She didn't like it too warm. "I was the one who called the ambulance."

"What?" Edie knocked her chair over backward as she jumped to her feet. She took a moment to set her chair to rights before plopping down in it as if her body were too heavy to remain upright for long. "You called the ambulance? Why didn't you tell me this before?"

Kappy shrugged. "I didn't think it was important. I still don't."

"But that means you were there."

"*Jah.*"

"Don't you see? If you were there, then you could have seen something to help us clear Jimmy's name."

"What do you mean, clear his name?"

"We both know he's not guilty, and if the police think they have their man, they're not going to look any further for another suspect."

"I don't know." She had no idea how these things worked.

"Well, I do. And Jimmy will remain in jail unless we do something to help him."

"Like what?"

"Find the real killer."

"What?" It was Kappy's turn to jump to her feet. She didn't know the first thing about finding people. And why would they want to look for a killer?

"We have to do it, Kappy. For Jimmy."

She was right. But that didn't make it any easier to accept. Kappy snatched up the silverware and started to put it in the drawer. That took up all of thirty-five seconds. Now what?

She plopped back into her chair and eyed Edie across the table.

"For Jimmy," Edie said again.

Kappy nodded. "I'll tell you what I can."

She started with her trip to the bulk goods store and recounted coming back home to find that her front door had been painted blue.

"Jimmy painted your front door blue?" Edie laughed. "Why would he do that?"

Kappy shook her head. "Because Hiram and I broke up and I guess Jimmy thought that since I was available—"

"That he would paint your door blue to help you get a new suitor?"

"I mean, it's not even a real thing."

"He thought he was helping." Edie shot her an affectionate smile.

"*Jah*. I know he'd just done it. It was still tacky to the touch."

"Then what happened?"

"I hopped in my buggy and came straight over here."

"And your horse was still hitched to the carriage?"

"That's right."

"Jimmy couldn't have done it. Can't you see?"

"I wish I could."

"If your door was still not dry, then he must have just returned to the house. He probably wasn't even here when it happened."

"I suppose it's possible."

"It's more than possible." A self-satisfied smile spread across her face.

"Are you going to call the deputy and tell him?"

"Not yet." She shook her head. "I want to gather a bit more proof first." She leaned back once again, a thoughtful look on her face. "He's cute, huh?"

"Who?"

"Deputy Jones. Actually, I think it's Detective Jones. Did he come out here that first day?"

"*Jah*. He was here."

"And you don't think he's cute?"

Hiram's face appeared in front of her mind's eye. He was about the most handsome man she had ever seen. Kappy knew that a person was supposed to look deeper than the surface in order to find a mate, but she thought Hiram was about as handsome as they come. He was big and strong, not as tall as the detective, but he could hold his own if need be. He could bring in the crops and do all the other chores that were expected of an Amish man. But Hiram Lapp was a businessman through and through. He owned a shop called Sundries and Sweets that catered to *Englisch,* tourists, and Amish alike. The store carried a variety of goods including locally baked items, books, and handmade Amish dolls.

"He's kind of frowny."

Edie laughed. "You're right. It's his brow bone," she said, pulling one finger across her own forehead to illustrate. "I still think he's handsome, though."

Kappy pushed back from the table and stood. "I need to get home."

Edie frowned. "Why?"

"You don't need me here." She had done what the bishop had asked. Maybe even more than he requested. Jimmy was in jail, Edie was home, at least for the time being, and it was time for her to go back where she belonged.

"You can't leave." Edie was on her feet in an instant. "I don't know how to feed the dogs or the horses."

Kappy shot her a look. "I'm sure you can figure it out."

"Okay, the truth is I don't want to be here by myself. Will you help me feed the dogs?" Edie's tone turned soft. "And the horses, too?"

How could Kappy refuse? "*Jah.* Just this once. But after that I'm going home."

Edie's smile could have lit up the darkest night. "Whatever you say."

The pair worked in silence, feeding the dogs, pouring them fresh water, and stopping to pet them in between. Kappy had never owned a dog. Aunt Hettie would never allow one. But now, she wondered why she hadn't gotten one in all these years. They were adorable, especially the little ones, rolling all over each other and themselves, biting ears and barking at nothing. Every now and again, one would sit back on his haunches and howl at nothing.

Maybe when this was all over, she should look into getting

a dog of her own. Just one, she thought looking at the tumbling bodies. Maybe two.

"Why weren't we friends before . . . you know, before I left?" Edie asked as she walked the pen looking for poop to scoop.

Kappy stirred herself out of her thoughts of dog ownership and back to the present. "You didn't like me."

Edie shook her head. "I like everybody."

"Not me." Kappy finished winding up the hose and turned to face her new almost-friend.

Edie fell quiet. "I'm sorry."

Kappy shrugged. "I'm used to it now."

Edie Peachey hadn't been the first person to pretend Kappy was invisible. That was, until they needed a *kapp* made. But with the way she ran her shop, no one had to interact with her in order to do business with her. The entire setup allowed the whole of Blue Sky to simply pretend that she didn't exist. There were times when she enjoyed it, when she didn't have to answer to anyone but God and the bishop, but other times . . . well, it was just lonely.

"That's no excuse," Edie said. "It goes against everything I was taught and yet I did it anyway. Now that I'm out among the *Englisch* . . ." She shook her head. "It's not any better. It might even be worse."

"What's that supposed to mean?"

Edie held her arms out to her sides. "Look at me. I don't exactly fit in."

Before coming out to take care of the dogs, Edie had gone upstairs to change. Instead of funeral black, she now wore bright purple pants that looked a lot like tights and an oversized shirt with a kitten on the front. Lavender rubber flip-flops graced her feet, and her toenails were painted black. Black?

Kappy cocked her head to one side. "I don't understand. You left the Amish so you didn't have to conform and now that you're with the *Englisch* you want to be like them?"

Edie drew back. "It's not like that." But Kappy could tell she had never thought about it in those terms.

"We're done here. I'm going home now."

Edie dropped the scooper. "Don't go. Stay and we can watch a movie—" She stopped. "We could play a game."

Kappy shook her head. "I've been away too long." But the thought of returning to her empty house held no appeal. She felt antsy, anxious, as if something were about to happen. Or maybe she was just worried about Jimmy being in jail.

"Okay, so the truth is I don't want to be alone. There. I said it. We can talk about Jimmy. Maybe we can figure out how to get him out of jail." Those were perhaps the only words that could've kept Kappy from leaving. Not that they had any hope of coming up with an idea tonight. Still, they were both worried about her brother and that alone bonded them together as unlikely friends.

"*Jah*. Okay. I'll stay. But only for tonight."

Once the dogs were fed, the two continued with the gerbils, rabbits, the ducks, then finally the horses.

"I didn't realize *Mamm* had such a zoo around here."

Kappy nodded. "Isn't it something? She has all sorts of records and stuff in her office, though I think the gerbils, ducks, and rabbits are really Jimmy's."

Edie smiled affectionately. "He always did love anything with fur."

"Ducks have feathers."

"Don't ruin my reminiscing with semantics."

Kappy had no idea what she was talking about. Last year she had purchased a word-a-day calendar. It was the kind that had a removable sheet for each day and a word on it to increase her vocabulary. She had learned a lot of words in the past few months, but she still had a ways to go.

Edie walked around the corner toward the door that led out into the pasture. "So this is where it happened?" Her voice turned soft and wispy as if she were standing on sacred ground.

"*Jah*. That's where she was when I came in."

"Where was Jimmy?"

She pointed to the spot where Jimmy had been standing. "He was there."

Edie walked all around, using the toe of her flip-flop to overturn small piles of hay.

"What are you doing?"

"Looking for clues."

"The police have already done that," Kappy said.

Edie didn't bother to look up. "Maybe they missed something."

Kappy didn't know much about police work, but she supposed that was possible. "So what are you looking for?" She joined in the search, using her foot to brush the hay from side to side.

"Clues, I told you."

Kappy managed to keep the exasperation out of her voice. "What kind of clues?"

"Oh," Edie said. "I don't know. Anything. Something someone might have left behind. Like a shoe or a special coin. Or—"

"A button." Kappy bent down to retrieve this small item from the hay. She held it up to the light, then laid it in her palm and extended her hand toward Edie. "It's red."

Edie took a step closer, staring down at the object. It was no bigger than a dime. A shirt button, for sure.

"But Amish men don't wear red shirts in the valley," she said.

She didn't need to add that the women pinned their dresses, so the button had to come from—"An *Englischer*," Kappy whispered.

Edie chewed on her bottom lip, her expression thoughtful. "Kappy, didn't you say you drove your buggy over here that day?"

"*Jah*. Why?"

"Did you see anyone on the road? Maybe someone in a car?"

Cars passed Amish buggies all the time. How was she supposed to remember one car in a thousand? If she had known then that Ruth Peachey had just been murdered, she might've paid better attention. But as it was . . . "I don't remember."

Edie gave a little growl of frustration.

"I'm sorry."

"Never mind," Edie said. "It doesn't matter."

But it did.

"Maybe if the *Englischer* . . ." Edie didn't finish. "I mean, if the person who killed my mother lost this button, then we know they're not Amish."

Kappy thought about it a minute. The button grew hot in her hand. "What if they're Lancaster Amish and they came up here to get a puppy?" She shook her head. "It's not like we will ever find the piece of clothing this came from."

Edie plucked it from Kappy's palm and stuck it in the pocket of her purple pants. "It's still a clue."

"It's a button."

But Edie couldn't be deterred. "Tomorrow, let's go around and talk to the neighbors. Maybe someone saw something."

Or maybe not. "I'm not sure that's such a good idea. What if we alert the murderer that we're looking for him?"

"We'll never find out anything if we don't start talking to people."

"All right. You go around and talk to everybody. I'm going to sew some new *kapps*." After all, she still had a business to run.

Kappy turned to walk out of the barn with Edie right behind her.

"You have to go with me, Kappy. No church member is going to talk to me. Remember? I'm under the *Bann*."

"Why do you think they'll talk to me?" She had a bad feeling about this. When this was all said and done, Edie would head back to the big city, and Kappy would be left with the fallout.

"At least you're not excommunicated."

Kappy kept walking toward the house.

"Come on, Kappy. Please."

She didn't answer.

"For Jimmy."

Kappy stopped. The second victim in this tragedy, Jimmy Peachey. Just the thought of his innocent face made her heart squeeze in her chest. "Okay," she said. "I'll go with you, but I'm only doing this for Jimmy."

Edie grinned. "That's fine by me."

Kappy knocked three times on the door, then took a step back. How had she gotten sucked into this? It wasn't that she didn't want to help Jimmy. She did. She just didn't know how Edie had come to the conclusion that they could find out more than the police.

You did find the button.

But was it really a clue? Or just something else for them to chase?

"Knock again," Edie nudged.

"Give him a minute to get to the door." But she really wanted more than a minute. She didn't want to talk to Jay Glick at all.

Jay lived on the back side of the Peacheys, just a little farther down School Yard Road. Though Jay's house, unlike Ruth's, faced the road itself.

"He might be ignoring us."

It was possible. Jay Glick wasn't known for his friendly nature.

The door jerked open and there stood a glowering Jay Glick. He only opened the wooden door, leaving the storm door closed, but even the screen didn't soften his menacing expression. "Why are you bothering me, girl?" He glared at

Kappy first, then turned his attention to Edie. It took him only a minute to see past her too-tight *Englisch* clothes and dyed hair. His scowl deepened.

"We were hoping to talk to you about Ruth."

His expression didn't change. The scowl remained firmly in place. "What about her?"

"Did you know the police think she was murdered?" She was making a mess of this. Perhaps they should have written out some sort of plan before they started knocking on doors.

"Why would I know that?"

Edie took a step forward. "We were hoping that you might have seen something the day she was killed."

"Do you hear something?" He cupped one hand around his ear. "Nope. Pretty sure. I didn't hear a thing."

Kappy closed her eyes as she counted to five. "We, that is, *I* was hoping that you might have seen something the day she was killed."

Jay made a flicking motion with one hand. "The corn was just as high then as it is now. Much too tall for a man to see over."

True the corn was tall, but that didn't mean he couldn't have seen *something*. "Maybe around three o'clock?" Kappy pressed.

"I told you I didn't see nothing." He took a step back to shut the door.

"But you were home about that time?" Perhaps with a little time he would remember.

"*Jah*. I was here. But I didn't see nothing."

"Maybe we could talk to one of your sons. Maybe they saw something," Kappy called through the shrinking gap as the door closed.

"Nobody here's seen nothing," Jay said, then he was gone.

Kappy stared at the door for what seemed like a solid minute. Then she turned toward Edie. "That didn't go according to plan."

"You think?"

Kappy made her way down the steps. "You can't blame me. He hasn't changed one bit in twenty years. You knew as well as I did that he wouldn't be cooperative."

"Who's next?"

Kappy tapped her chin thoughtfully. "We could go over to Martha's and see if she saw anything." Martha lived on the other side of Ruth, though her house sat a little closer to the road. And since her land was planted with soybeans, she might have seen something.

"Kappy King." The words were spoken so softly she wasn't sure she had even heard them. "Kappy King."

Kappy looked to Edie. "Did you hear that?"

Edie nodded to a point behind Kappy. Anna Mae Glick poked her head around the corner of the house. "Come here," she whispered, motioning her over.

"What is it?" Kappy wasn't sure why they were whispering, but since Anna Mae had started it she felt obliged to continue.

"Jay's wrong. We did see something. I saw something."

"*Jah?* What?"

"A man in a blue shirt."

Excitement coursed through her. Another clue!

"You saw a man in a blue shirt?" Edie asked.

Anna Mae gazed expectantly at Kappy. As if she wanted something from her.

"You saw a man in a blue shirt?" Kappy repeated.

"I did. Running away from the barn. We all saw him."

"For Pete's sake! If you all saw him, why is Jay—"

Kappy elbowed Edie in the ribs to stop her words. "Which way was he going?" she asked.

She shook her head. "I wasn't paying close attention. How was I to know that he was a murderer?"

"Was he an Amish man?"

"I think so, *jah.*"

As far as clues went, it wasn't the best, but it was better than nothing. And better than any others they had uncovered. "Thanks, Anna Mae."

The tiny woman smiled. "Just trying to help." She flitted away, ducking onto the side porch and disappearing around front.

"Well?" Kappy asked.

Edie shrugged. "There's something strange about this."

"You're just saying that because she ignored you."

"Maybe." Edie propped her hands on her hips. "But it still seems weird."

"And it's still the best clue we have," Kappy pointed out. "Better than the button, don't you think?"

"If you say so," Edie grumbled.

"I say we go to Martha's. If the man was running toward her house, maybe she saw something, too."

"Maybe."

"Or would you rather ask Nathaniel and Ephraim if they saw anything?"

Nathaniel Ebersol and Ephraim Jess lived on either side of Kappy. Both men were old as the hills and had been feuding even longer. The bishop had long since given up on trying to get the two men to resolve their differences. Instead, Samuel made sure that the two were sitting on opposite ends at church and that they didn't go to the grocery store on the same day.

Edie seemed to think about it. "Like what?"

"The button is probably *Englisch,* right? So if it was lost that day—and I'm not saying it was—then perhaps they saw an *Englisch* car on the road."

"That's a long shot." Edie sighed.

Kappy knew what she was thinking. And she wanted the same thing, Jimmy out of jail as soon as possible. "But if they did see something . . . We have to follow up on every clue."

"Right." Edie gave a quick nod. "Let's talk to Martha first, then we'll see if those two know anything."

Martha's property sat behind Ruth's and faced the main road. It was a little closer to the street, and the quickest way there was to take Edie's car. Kappy wasn't an expert or even remotely knowledgeable about *Englisch* automobiles, but this one was a mess. One look at the backseat and Kappy wondered if there were any clothes left in Edie's closet at her apartment. Or maybe she just didn't own a suitcase. Whatever it was, the clothes were only outnumbered by the to-go cups and fast-food wrappers.

"Here," Edie said. "Let me get that." She brushed a stack of junk mail, two hamburger boxes, and a stray french fry onto the floorboard so Kappy could ease into the passenger seat.

She cast a dubious look around as Edie started the car. "You do have an apartment in the city, don't you?"

Edie put the car in reverse and backed out without once meeting Kappy's gaze. "Yeah, sort of."

"How does a person sort of have a place to live?"

"Well, I had a place to live, but I got evicted."

That would explain the box of shoes behind the driver's seat.

"Oh." Kappy hoped she had adopted a suitably understanding expression.

"It doesn't matter, though. The guy I was living with turned out to be a jerk."

Kappy's mouth fell open as she stared at Edie. "You were *living* with a man?"

Edie eased her car onto the side road and gave a small shrug. Still, she refused to look Kappy in the face. "We weren't supposed to be *living together* living together, but then he started to get other ideas. I was going to move out anyway."

"I see," Kappy murmured. But it was a lie. She barely knew anything about Amish men. How was she supposed to know about *Englisch* ones?

"*Englisch* guys are different," Edie groused. "They're not like Amish guys at all."

"I guess not," Kappy replied.

"So you and Hiram Lapp." Edie changed the subject so quickly it was nearly jarring.

"No. Not really."

"Then why did Jimmy paint your front door?" Edie asked as she turned into Martha's driveway.

"He's misguided," Kappy returned.

"Uh-huh."

Kappy didn't wait for Edie to turn off the car before she opened the door and got out. She didn't want to talk about Hiram. Not with anyone, but especially not with Edie Peachey, who had been living with a man up until she came to her mother's funeral. The thought was staggering.

She made her way up the porch steps and knocked on the door. "Martha?" she called.

The elderly woman opened the door almost immediately, as if she had been standing there waiting for someone to knock.

Martha Peachey was no relation to Ruth and Jimmy or if she was it was so far removed that everyone had forgotten. As it was, half the Amish in the valley held the last name Peachey. Some claimed kinship, others didn't. Either way it was no business of Kappy's.

"Why, Kathryn King! What brings you out today?"

Martha was the only person in the district, probably in the entire valley, who called her by her given name. She had been Kathy until her younger brother was born. When he couldn't manage that, she had been dubbed Kappy by everyone around. Some wondered if it was perhaps an omen of things to come since she was the only *kapp* maker in the area. Kappy didn't think much of the theory, only that she felt a keen sense of loss when anybody called her by her real name.

It had been nearly sixteen years since her parents and her two brothers were killed in a car-buggy crash, and still she missed them every day. She often wondered how different her life might have been had her mother been there through her run-around years. But there was no going back, only forward.

"Hi, Martha. I was wondering if I could talk to you for a bit."

Martha smiled, showing her perfect dentures. No one knew exactly how old Martha was, but if Kappy had to guess on wrinkles alone, she would say one hundred and twelve. Martha talked about times long past as if she remembered it all, though there was no one to dispute her tales. Most everyone close to that age had long since passed while Nathaniel and Ephraim wouldn't agree if their lives depended on it. But if Kappy took into account the fact that Martha was an old farm girl, she could be only eighty or so, and just badly wrinkled by all the years in the sun. She was stooped and thin and walked with a cane . . . most days. "You know you're welcome here anytime. Come on in."

Kappy made a quick, flicking gesture toward the car. "I can't stay long. I was just wondering if you happened to see anything the other day. The day Ruth Peachey was found."

Martha's rheumy eyes narrowed. "What are you doing, Kathryn?"

"I'm checking to see if perhaps you saw anything odd the day Ruth Peachey was killed."

"Why are you riding around in that car? You thinking about jumping the fence?"

"No, Martha. Of course n—"

"Who would make our *kapps* if'n you do?"

"But I'm not."

She squinted at her. "You sure?"

"*Jah.* Positive."

"I hope so, because that would be terrible for everyone."

Kappy shifted in place. "Martha, I came to ask you about Ruth Peachey."

Martha shook her head sadly. "Tragic. Just tragic. But you

know the Lord works in mysterious ways. One day we'll know His will."

"*Jah,* but until then we're trying to find out who killed her."

Martha drew back. "Killed her? You mean—"

Kappy nodded. "*Jah.* Ruth was murdered. And Jimmy is in jail."

"Oh, no, no, no." Martha shook her head. "That boy doesn't belong in jail."

"I know. That's why I'm trying to find out if anyone saw anything strange the day Ruth was murdered."

Martha tsked, clicking her dentures. "Well, let's see, that would've been Thursday."

"Tuesday. Ruth was killed on Tuesday."

"That's right. My memory's not always what it used to be."

Kappy nodded politely.

"Tuesday," Martha mused. "Oh, yes. On Tuesday, that's when I saw the woman in red."

Chapter 5

Fifteen minutes later, Kappy waved good-bye to Martha and climbed back into the car with Edie.

"What'd she say?"

Kappy shook her head. "I don't know what to believe as truth and what she's made up in her own mind."

Edie put the car into reverse and backed out. "What do you mean?"

"Do you have any idea how old she is?"

Edie shrugged. "She was old when I was here."

"Exactly. She barely can remember what day it is, much less—"

"Are you going to tell me what she said or not?"

"If I tell you, you can't get your hopes up."

"Of course not."

Edie pulled onto the main street and headed back toward School Yard Road.

"You have to promise."

Edie let out a sound that was half sigh, half growl. "I promise."

"Martha said she saw a woman in red running across the fields around the time Ruth was murdered."

Kappy was nearly flung into the windshield as Edie slammed on the brakes. "Are you kidding me?"

"I don't know much about driving, but I don't think you're supposed to stop in the middle of the road."

"Oh, right." Edie set the car into motion once again. "This is exciting," she said as she turned toward Ruth's house.

"No, it's not."

"How can you say that? We have a red button and a woman in red. It all goes together."

"And an eyewitness who can barely see three feet in front of her face."

Edie waved a dismissive hand and turned down the drive. "Everybody knows the short vision goes first. And who can't see red at a distance?"

"Someone who's color-blind."

Edie put the car in park and turned to face Kappy. "Is Martha color-blind?"

"I don't know. I guess not."

Edie gave a satisfied nod. "I rest my case." She got out of the car and marched toward the front porch, not bothering to wait on Kappy.

"Don't you want to go talk to Ephraim and Nathaniel?"

"Maybe later. Right now I want to write all this down before we forget."

Kappy shook her head. Forgetting wasn't the problem. If it was true or not—that was what they needed to know.

After a quick meal of sandwiches made from leftover funeral roast with applesauce on the side, Edie stood and stretched.

"I want to go to town and see Jimmy."

"You don't want to talk to the neighbors across the street?"

"Nope. I think Jimmy's our best bet. I mean, he was in the barn. He would have had a better chance of seeing something than Ephraim and Nathaniel."

Kappy stood and gathered up her plate and glass. "And here I thought you wanted to go visit him because you missed him."

Edie pulled a face. "I do miss him. And I want him to know that we're doing everything we can to get him out of there as soon as possible."

They set their dishes in the sink.

"I still think you should let the police handle this," Kappy said. She knew her words would fall on deaf ears, but she had to say them all the same. "It's their job to find the killer."

Edie shook her head, her bangs brushing from side to side. "They think they found the killer already. You just have to trust me on this. I know more about the *Englisch* world than you do."

Kappy couldn't argue with that. Not one bit.

"Come on," Edie said. "Once we're done with our visit, I'll buy you an ice cream in town."

In all the years she had lived in Blue Sky, Kappy couldn't remember one trip to the jailhouse. And yet here she was.

The building itself was squat and brick. It held a weathered look like the rest of the buildings in the area. Most of them had gone up somewhere around the turn of the century—the twentieth century—and a hundred years of wind and rain had taken the sharp edges away.

"I'm here to see Jimmy Peachey," Edie said to the brunette behind the desk.

"And you are?" she asked without looking up.

"Edith Peachey."

The brunette jerked to attention, her mouth hanging open and her eyes wide. "Edie? Is that really you?"

"Yes." Then the identity of the woman seemed to strike home. "Heather?"

The brunette nodded. "That's me. How are you doing? How have you been?" She stood revealing a large baby belly under her close-fitting pink shirt.

Kappy briefly wondered if she was a police officer like Jack Jones and wore regular clothes and a badge or if she was merely an employee who answered the phones and let in visitors.

Heather shot a quick glance in Kappy's direction. Her golden-brown eyes seemed to take in all of her appearance at once, and Kappy resisted the urge to make sure her prayer covering was on straight. Like Heather would know. Still, there was something a little unnerving in her perusal.

Heather turned her attention back to Edie, handing her a clipboard over the tall desk. "If you'll just fill this out for me, I'll get you back as soon as possible."

Edie started to fill out the form, then gestured toward Kappy with the end of the pen. "Can you get Kappy one, too?"

Heather gave an apologetic smile. "Sorry. Visitation is just for family members. I hope you understand."

"Yeah, sure."

Kappy went to sit in the short row of orange plastic chairs lined up against the far wall. There were only four of them, making her think that visitors were not exactly welcome in the lobby of the sheriff's office.

Edie finished filling out the form, and before she had a chance to join Kappy she was escorted back to see her brother.

Kappy sighed. She should have just stayed at home. She could be making *kapps* right now instead of staring at the cheap paneled walls of the squatty little office.

The thought had no sooner crossed her mind than the door opened and Jack Jones strolled in. He looked about the same as he had every other time she'd seen him. Somehow he still managed to have stubble on his jaw even though it was barely one in the afternoon. His dark hair was mussed as usual, as if he simply rolled out of bed without a second thought of a comb.

He was talking to a woman no taller than Kappy, with honey-colored hair pulled back in a bob at the nape of her neck. She had a badge pinned to her belt much like Jones did, and there was no doubt this woman was a deputy.

Kappy was on her feet in a second. "Detective Jones. Jack Jones," she called.

He stopped and turned to face her, his expression surprised. Because she had remembered his name? Or because she was there at all? She didn't know.

"Miss King." He nodded more to himself than to her, and she was certain because he was proud he had remembered her name in return.

He turned to leave once more, but Kappy stopped him with a hasty tug on his sleeve.

Jones looked down at her hand and back up into her eyes, his stare almost a warning. "Yes?"

Kappy let go of him as if his shirt were on fire. "Jimmy Peachey is innocent."

"And you came all the way here to tell me that?"

She shook her head, then gave a little shiver as her *kapp* strings tickled the back of her neck. "I came with his sister, so she could visit. But I think you should know. He's not capable of doing what you say he did."

He turned back to the woman at his side.

"We can talk about this later," she said. "Give me a call sometime this afternoon." Then she turned on her heel and walked away.

Jones shifted his attention back to Kappy. "The evidence says otherwise."

Kappy crossed her arms to show she meant business. "The evidence is wrong."

"I appreciate your concern."

But she knew it to be a lie. "I found a button in the barn," she blurted out to keep him from walking away. This might be the only chance she got to talk to him and she wasn't going to waste it. "It's red," she continued. "And the neighbor . . . The neighbor said she saw someone wearing red running across the field."

"Was it the one-armed man?"

Kappy frowned at him in confusion.

"Sorry." Jones shook his head. "That's all well and good, but it doesn't help me with the case."

"Don't you see?" Kappy asked. "This just shows you that your case against Jimmy is wrong. I think the lady in red is the murderer."

For some reason Jack Jones seemed to find that amusing. His grin deepened, then he took one look at her face and adopted a more solemn expression. "I'll take that under advisement."

Kappy had no idea what that meant. But it sounded like he was doing nothing.

"Thank you, Miss King." And before she could protest further, Jack Jones walked away.

"I'm telling you, Kappy, it was the saddest thing I've ever seen."

After Jones had left her standing in the lobby at the sheriff's office, Kappy was suddenly filled with the need to prove Jimmy's innocence. As much as she hated to admit it, Edie was right. The police thought they had their man and they weren't going to search any further. But once Edie finished her visitation, there was nothing left to do but go home and take care of the dogs.

Kappy busted open a fresh hay bale and spread the straw around, while Edie used the yard broom to sweep it into the doghouses.

"But he seemed okay, right?" Kappy asked. "They're not hurting him or anything, are they?"

"They seem to be treating him fine. And he told me as much. But it was so sad seeing him in an orange jumpsuit like a common criminal." She shook her head.

"We've still got Ephraim and Nathaniel to talk to," Kappy soothed. It wasn't much in the way of an investigation, but it was more than Jack Jones was doing.

"I suppose. I mean, what do you think they could have

seen—" Edie broke off as the sound of an engine approaching cut through their conversation. "Who do you suppose that is?"

Kappy could only hope it was Jack Jones coming to tell them that he had changed his mind. Even better, that he was bringing Jimmy back home.

But a strange car sat in the driveway.

A gray-haired man got out, looking around as if inspecting the place. He caught sight of them and turned his attention to them. "I'm looking for Ruth Peachey."

Edie stepped in front of Kappy, saving her the trouble of answering. "She's not here. Can I help you?"

The man nodded and took a folded piece of paper out of one pocket. He opened it and waved it toward them as if they could see what was written there. "I contacted her last week about some beagle pups."

Kappy and Edie shared a look. This was one thing she hadn't thought about. And she was certain Edie hadn't, either.

"Beagle pups?" Edie said the words as if she'd never heard them before.

Kappy stepped around her. She approached the man, her hand out. "Can I see your paper?"

He frowned, obviously a bit confused, but handed her his notes. She scanned the writing, noting the small doodles in the margin. It seemed the man wanted four puppies, and other than an estimated price for each one, Kappy couldn't make out much else. She folded the paper and handed it back to him. "Are you still wanting four of them?"

The man nodded. "If they're still available."

"Of course." Kappy graced him with a smile, but it died quickly on her face as Edie grabbed her arm and jerked her backward. "Will you excuse us for a moment, please?" Edie's expression had morphed into one of stiff politeness as she pulled Kappy back toward the barn. "What are you trying to do?"

Kappy pried Edie's fingers from around her arm. "I'm trying to sell dogs."

"You can't sell that—"

"Why not? That's what they're here for, right?"

Edie pressed her lips together and gave a small sigh. "I guess so. *Mamm* was a dog breeder." She stopped. "We don't know what to charge him."

Kappy nodded. "*Jah*, but I have his quote on the paper and Ruth kept ledgers in her office. Let me go see what I can find. You take him around back and show him the puppies."

Edie cast a skeptical glance over one shoulder, back toward the man who stood in the driveway, car still running, confusion still branded across his brow. "Are you sure it's okay?"

"What do you mean?"

"I mean, we don't know that man from Adam. How do we know he's not going to come in and—" She stopped, obviously unwilling to continue with her train of thought.

One thing her parents' and brothers' untimely deaths had taught her: Anything could happen at any time. One minute they had been there and the next they were gone. Just like Ruth.

"You have to have faith, Edie." Then the thought struck.

"What's that?" Edie asked. "Why do you have a look on your face?"

"When the police were here, no one said anything about theft."

"Because nothing was missing." Edie's words grew slower as her sentence drew to an end. "That means—"

"—the person who killed her was not a robber," they both said at the same time.

They smiled at each other. Somehow it felt as if they were one step closer to solving the mystery and getting Jimmy out of jail. Whoever killed Ruth wasn't there to steal from her, so what business did they have?

A not-so-discreet cough drew their attention back to the man in the driveway.

They turned to face him.

"The dogs?" he asked.

"Right," Kappy said.

"My partner is going to check the records and double-check on which ones are ready to go. In the meantime, would you like to come look at the puppies?" Edie asked.

The man reached inside his car and cut the engine. "I thought you'd never ask."

While Edie showed the stranger the pens and how Ruth had cared for the dogs, Kappy pored over the ledgers. In the twenty minutes it took her to find Ruth's records on which dogs were ready to go first, how to determine which dog was which, and the lineage of all the puppies on the property, Kappy also learned more about beagles than she ever thought she would know. And there was still a lot about Ruth's business left to discover.

She used what little knowledge she'd gained to help the gentleman pick out his four puppies—all of which had been tattooed at the local vet to enable them to track the dog in case it ever got lost.

"A dog with a tattoo," Edie said. "Who would've imagined?"

Kappy shrugged. "I guess it's as good a way as any." She actually thought it was pretty clever of whomever thought to tattoo a dog to keep a record. Especially when people pay as much for dogs as the man who had just left.

"Maybe I should get a tattoo," Edie mused, pulling up her shirtsleeves and examining the skin on her upper arm.

Kappy drew back with a frown. "Why would you want to do that?"

Edie shrugged. "Why not?"

"I know you've heard this your entire life, but you do not need to mark yourself."

Edie rubbed her arm thoughtfully. "But if I get one that's unique. Maybe Ruth's and Jimmy's birthdays on a full-bloom rose?"

Kappy shook her head. It was really no business of hers. And yet . . . "You shouldn't try so hard to fit in."

"It's hard," Edie said. Her words were softly spoken and heartfelt. "You have no idea how hard it is out there. No one fits in. Everyone stands out. But you can't fit in unless you stand out. Everyone thinks they're special and it's chaos."

Kappy finished making the notation in the ledger as to which puppies the man had bought and how much he paid. "Then come back." She set her pencil down and calmly met Edie's gaze.

"Are you kidding?" Edie shook her head. "How can I come back here?" She made a sweeping gesture with one arm. "It's just so . . . rural."

Kappy shut the ledger then stood. "*Jah*, that's what happens when you live next to farmers."

"So what-all is in there?" Edie asked, pointing to the ledger still lying on the desk.

Kappy knew she was trying to change the subject and she allowed her new friend this much. But soon, and it wouldn't be long, Edie would be on her own to determine her place in Blue Sky. That was, if she stayed.

"Everything you need to run the business, it seems."

Edie gazed around at the numerous volumes surrounding them. "Like what?"

"Like breeding schedules, vaccination records, customers' contact information, all that sort of thing." She pointed at each set in turn. "Then there's books on beagles themselves, Ruth's notes, and a whole bunch of other stuff I haven't even looked at yet."

"Oh," Edie said. But the word sounded small. "Jimmy can't do this by himself, can he?"

"No," Kappy said, though she wasn't sure if Edie wanted an answer or not.

She watched the expressions cross Edie's face, but Edie didn't ask the one question that Kappy knew was weighing on both their minds. Once they got Jimmy out of jail—and they would get Jimmy out of jail—what was Edie going to do with him then?

But Kappy said nothing. It wasn't her business, after all.

She closed the ledger and shelved it once more, then she stood and dusted off the front of her apron and dress. "Come on," she said. "I'll help you feed the dogs, then I'm going home."

"What's so interesting over there that you want to leave here?" Edie asked. She took another scoopful of the duck feed and spread it around. Kappy had lost count of the number of scoops she'd fed the birds so far, and hoped that ducks weren't one of those animals that were prone to overeating. If they were, Edie and Jimmy were going to have the fattest ducks in Blue Sky.

"It's not a matter of interesting," Kappy replied. "It's a matter of that's where I belong."

"It must be nice."

Kappy pulled the blue plastic swimming pool closer to the water spigot, rinsed it out, and started refilling it once more. The ducks quacked their approval. "What do you mean?"

Edie sighed and started to spread another cup of food for the ducks.

"I think they've had enough now, Edie."

"What? Oh." She tossed the cup back into the container just inside the barn. "I mean, it must be nice to know where you belong."

"And you don't think you belong?" Kappy asked.

Edie gave her a sad smile. "I know I don't."

The words were so filled with melancholy that Kappy almost told her that she would stay another night. But Edie didn't need her. Not like Jimmy had.

"You belong where you belong," she said instead and started to roll the hose back up.

"I wouldn't mind if you stayed. I've sort of gotten used to having you around."

"*Danki*," Kappy replied, "I think, but I need to get home for a while."

Edie nodded. "Of course. I think I'll just look through *Mamm*'s ledgers. Maybe I can find some sort of clue as to who would want her . . . dead."

It was the one thing they hadn't talked about. Who would want Ruth gone? And why?

It was true that Kappy was something of an outlier, living on the fringes. And because of this, she didn't know a lot of what went on in the district, but she couldn't imagine anyone having a problem with Ruth. The woman had a true and kind heart. The whole thing didn't make any sense, and frankly, she was a little tired from trying to figure it all out.

"That would be good," Kappy said. But she wasn't sure what Edie would find. The books were filled with schedules, births, and vaccine records. Kappy was fairly certain Ruth hadn't penciled in her own demise.

Chapter 6

It took Kappy the better part of the evening to clean her house. Then she went to the barn to get June Bug, her mare, settled in once more. She checked her garden, picked everything that was ripe, and gathered all of the apples that had fallen from her tree. She still had time to make a batch of chocolate chip cookies she was sure they wouldn't let Jimmy have at the jail.

She grabbed one of the cookies for herself and nibbled on it thoughtfully as she watched the sun go down. She was happy to be at home. But it was quiet. Really quiet.

Over the last couple of days, she had sort of gotten used to having someone around, whether it was Jimmy, Edie, or even both. But this was how it should be. Edie would go back to the *Englisch* world, and Jimmy . . . well, she wasn't sure what Jimmy would do, but she would be here, on her own once more.

She nearly jumped out of her skin as a knock sounded at the door.

"Kappy?"

"If you want a *kapp,* you have to go around back," she hollered in return.

"Kappy, it's me. Edie."

She marched over to the door and wrenched it open. "Edie! What are you doing here?"

Edie stepped inside without waiting for an invitation. "Something smells good."

Kappy shook her head, trying to get a handle on the situation. "I baked cookies."

"Can I have one?"

She shrugged. "Of course." But Edie was already on her way to the kitchen.

Kappy followed behind, feeling like a lost puppy. Which was strange considering that of the three of them—her, Edie, and Jimmy—hers was the future laid out the clearest. She would stay right there in Blue Sky, never get married, and live in the same house until she died.

The thought sank like a rock in her stomach.

"I think we should go over the clues," Edie said. She had propped one hip onto the counter as she devoured her treat.

"What clues?" Kappy asked.

Edie stopped. "We have clues. There's the red button."

"That could have been there for months."

"What about the woman in red?"

"I'm not even sure she actually exists."

"But . . . but . . ." Edie held herself rigid, then deflated like a balloon. "We have to get him out of jail, Kappy."

They could go talk to Jack Jones again, but he hadn't seemed too impressed with the information she had presented to him earlier.

"We need more information," Edie said. "Some real clues."

"How are we going to get that?" Kappy asked.

"I don't know, but when I think of something, I'll let you know."

Kappy usually enjoyed Sunday mornings. Especially church Sundays. Off Sundays were spent cleaning and resting while the rest of the district visited family and friends. But church Sundays were special, one of the few days that she felt a part of the community. She finished pinning her prayer *kapp* in place and critically studied herself in the mirror. *Not bad for an old maid,* she thought.

She licked one finger and smoothed down the baby hairs next to her ears, turning from side to side to make sure she got them all. Then she took a step back to assess the rest of her reflection. Sky-blue dress, crisp white apron, black tights, and black shoes all polished up and ready to go. That was one thing Aunt Hettie had taught her: Always look your best. No one could find fault there.

Today's church service was to be held at Jay Glick's house. Since he was so close, there was no need to hitch up June Bug and drive the carriage. She took one last look in the mirror, as satisfied with what she saw as she could be. Then she started for the door.

The day was cooler than the one before. Thick gray clouds had blocked out the sun. She grabbed an umbrella from the front closet before locking up the house and heading down the lane. At School Yard Road, she looked back toward Ruth's house. If she had been alive still, Ruth would be heading to church as well, Jimmy at her side. But that wasn't to be. Edie had jumped the fence, Jimmy was in jail, and Ruth had been murdered in her own barn.

The thought made her stumble. Ruth had thought she was safe, there on her own property, taking care of business, and doing what she had always done.

Kappy gave a small shudder. It could've happened to any of them. So why Ruth? She pushed that thought aside.

This was the Lord's day and she should be thinking pure thoughts, not trying to find an answer to a mystery that might not ever be solved.

The *clip-clop* of horse hooves sounded behind her, mixed with the whir of carriage wheels on the roadway. She glanced back over her shoulder, briefly noting that Samuel and Alma Miller were coming up behind her. Behind them she spied another buggy and another. Everyone was going to church.

Across the valley, Hiram had climbed into his buggy for

church today as well. As much as she hated to admit it, she missed him. Not the times when she felt like less, as worthy as Laverna. But the times when they sat on the porch and talked, just sat with each other and enjoyed the day the Lord had made and all of the beautiful creations around them. Why couldn't life be a little simpler? But if she was asking questions like that, she should ask why couldn't he love her the way he loved Laverna. Neither one had a ready answer.

Once upon a time Kappy and Laverna had been the best of friends. Kappy had been so excited for her friend when she came and told her that she was marrying Hiram Lapp. Okay, maybe she was a tiny bit jealous, but Kappy knew that marriage wasn't part of God's plan for her. But Laverna and Hiram would make a wonderful, beautiful couple.

Yet it wasn't meant to be. Two years into their relationship, Laverna had died. Hiram had been heartbroken and Kappy had done everything she could to help him overcome the loss. But the more time she spent with him, the more she grew to care for him. Those feelings turned from friend to more, and when Hiram had asked her to marry him the year before she had readily agreed.

But she had been too caught up in the happiness and joy to see that the two of them would never work. She was odd little Kappy King, raised by an eccentric old-maid aunt with no other family to speak of. And Hiram was from one of the most prominent families in the valley. At least among the black-toppers.

Too many differences stood in their way, starting with the fact that he was Renno Amish while she had been raised Byler Amish. She was just glad she became aware of it before her heart was completely broken. She loved Hiram. And probably always would. But that didn't mean she would be able to be the wife to him that he deserved.

Samuel waved as he guided his bright yellow carriage around her. Kappy returned the greeting, pulled out of her reminiscing, and kept up her steady pace to the Glick house.

A while back, Jay Glick had built a large barn in the back of his property. The bottom part was used for miscellaneous work, some blacksmithery, among other things. But the top part was perfect for holding a church service.

Many of the members of the congregation were already milling around in front of the barn, waiting for the signal that it was time to go inside.

Kappy didn't suppress her smile as she walked up the driveway. A church day was always a sight to behold, even though she'd seen it every other week for as long as she could remember. It still felt special. Their yellow buggies lined up in a row, contrasting beautifully with the green grass and the red barn. Large hay bales covered in white plastic snaked down one side of the fields, while the men and women chatted with one another before the service started.

She wasn't sure how it began but most every woman and girl in the district wore blue to church, the colors ranging from pale, powdery blue to the color of a cloudless summer sky. But the men captured her attention even more. How handsome and pious they looked in their crisp white shirts and form-tailored black vests. Or maybe she just loved that everybody put their best foot forward. On church day, more than any other day, everyone seemed equal, at least in looks.

Greetings were called to one another. The young girls had gathered at one side of the yard, whispering behind their hands about the young boys who had clustered together on the other side. Neighbors milled among themselves, checking the sky and trying to determine how soon it would rain or if it would rain at all. The most Kappy got was a quick nod from James Troyer, the deacon, before he moved on into the barn to prepare for today's service.

After years of such treatment, Kappy should be used to it, but she wasn't. It still stung, even though she had accepted her place as the district's eccentric, just like her aunt before her. But the fact that she somehow all these years remained on the fringes of her community just brought to mind Edie.

She supposed it could be worse. She could be shunned like her new friend, not that she had done anything to deserve such treatment. But there was one good thing about being a fly on the wall.

Kappy moved behind a group of women all clustered around and talking. These were the women who would be preparing meals to take to Ruth's had Edie not been under the *Bann*. They probably would've done the same thing for Jimmy, if he'd been out of jail. But as it was they were off the hook for their church duties.

"And they've really arrested him?" one of them asked. Kappy thought it was Rose Menno, sister to Alma Miller, the bishop's wife.

"Put handcuffs on him and took him away." Maggie Troyer gave an emphatic nod.

"How do they think that boy could've done that?" Alma said. "I just don't understand."

Maggie looked this way and that, then leaned closer to her friends. "They say he just snapped. That can happen with his kind."

"I suppose," Rose murmured. But Kappy didn't believe a word of it and she couldn't believe that they did, either. She pressed her lips together and moved on, unwilling to listen to any more of such an *inane* conversation. It was so ridiculous that she couldn't even take joy in the fact that she'd found a way to use today's word from her word-a-day calendar. Maybe she would try again tomorrow as well.

She moved a little closer toward the men, hoping to pick up news, any kind of news. Maybe someone else had heard of a man running across the field, though they would've had to have been passing by in their buggy in order to see it.

But the men offered no help, and church was announced. It was a good thing, too, for no sooner had they all gotten into the barn than the bottom fell out of the sky and the rain came down.

* * *

Despite the fact that she had an umbrella, Kappy was soaked by the time she got home. Her shoes squished with every step she took, and although the umbrella helped a bit, she was certain she'd have to replace her own prayer *kapp*. The fabric just couldn't stand up to the rain.

She watched each step she took, careful not to slide into a big puddle, and got a surprise when she looked up.

Edie Peachey was sitting on her front porch.

Kappy swung her gaze to the side, just then noticing Edie's car parked in front of the house. That would teach her to stare at the ground while she was walking, even if it did mean saving her shoes from another coat of mud.

"What are you doing here?"

"What are you doing walking in the rain?"

Kappy was reluctant to admit that no one would bring her home. Not that she had asked. She hadn't asked. They hadn't offered. Now she was wet.

An understanding light dawned in Edie's eyes. "Oh."

"And I repeat," Kappy said as she tromped up the steps, "what are you doing here?"

A bright flash of a smile crossed Edie's face. She stood as Kappy fished her keys out of her bag. "I think I may have found something." She held up one of Ruth's ledgers.

Kappy would've been excited if she hadn't been so wet. "Come on in and you can tell me about it." She finally managed to jiggle the door open and stepped into her foyer. It felt good to be home, a little like the weight of the world had been lifted off her shoulders. She had realized how tense she had been sitting at church, eating the meal, trying to hear snatches of conversation and if anyone else was talking about Jimmy and Ruth and Edie and the murder. It seemed it was all anyone could talk about, and yet there was no new information passed around. Mostly just sentiments that they couldn't believe that Jimmy was capable of hurting his *mamm*.

"I started looking through *Mamm*'s books last night," Edie said as Kappy started to work on her wet laces. "Did you know she had a logbook for all her phone calls?"

"I think I remember seeing that in her office." One shoe down, Kappy began to work on the other.

"I looked into it and on last Tuesday Kenneth Delaney called Ruth four times. He left a message with each call."

Kappy set her shoes on the floor next to the door and resisted the urge to rip off her soaked stockings. "I don't know who Kenneth Delaney is."

"He's the man who came to buy the four beagles on Saturday. Don't you think it's strange that he would call her four times on the day she was murdered, then show up the following Saturday?"

Kappy nodded and reached for the pins in her prayer *kapp*. She could almost feel the fabric disintegrate beneath her fingers. *Jah*, time for a new one for sure. "I'll admit that it's strange," she said. "But it doesn't prove anything."

Edie gave a half-shrug. "I don't think it proves anything, either. Except that he was in contact with my *mamm*. Don't they say that criminals always return to the scene of the crime?"

"I would hardly call this returning."

"You know what I mean."

It was Kappy's turn to shrug. "How am I supposed to know?"

"Right."

"I'm going to change." Kappy plucked at her wet dress and apron.

Edie nodded, as if she had just noticed that Kappy was soaking wet. "Okay. Go ahead. I'll be right here."

Damaged prayer *kapp* still in hand, Kappy made her way to the back bathroom. As quickly as she could, she stripped out of her wet clothes and donned the dry day dress she had hanging on the back of the door. She grabbed a coat hanger from the laundry room and hung her dress up over the bathtub. It was already starting to drip when she headed back to the kitchen where Edie waited.

"So? What you think?" Edie asked.

"I think it's interesting," Kappy said with a small frown. "But not enough to take to Jack Jones."

"Why not?" Edie asked. "Delaney could be another suspect."

"Or he could be an innocent man who just tried to contact Ruth, then came by later to buy dogs."

Edie threw back her head and growled. "There has to be something here. There just has to be."

Kappy could understand her frustration. Jimmy had been in jail for days now. And though Kappy was trusting in God to make sure he was safe, she knew it would be a lot easier on Edie if they could get him home. "Is there anything else in the ledger?"

Edie tossed the books onto the kitchen table, then slid into the nearest chair. She flipped open the nearest book and started riffling through the pages. "She has everything written down here. A feeding schedule, if something changed, if she switched their food, and all of her appointments. It's almost like a journal of the day."

Kappy eased into the chair opposite Edie's. "So what's written on last Tuesday?"

Edie quickly scanned the page. "Not a lot. She fed the dogs, gave a couple of them a bath, then set Jimmy to painting the doghouses."

That explained a lot. "Go on."

"She had an appointment with a Dr. Carlton Brewer, and then the hunting guy."

"Who's the hunting guy?"

"Kenneth Delaney."

"But he didn't show up." Kappy drummed her fingers on the tabletop.

"What makes you so sure he didn't show up?"

She sighed. "You don't think he came, killed Ruth, then

came back again on Saturday to actually buy the dogs he could've taken with him while he was there?"

Edie slumped back in her chair. "But why didn't he mention that when he came on Saturday?"

"Why don't people do a lot of things?" Kappy returned.

Edie nodded. "I guess you're right." Her tone conveyed her reluctance to give in.

"So our next suspect would be this Carlton Brewer. How are we supposed to find out who he is?"

"I don't suppose you have a laptop tucked back anywhere that the bishop doesn't know about?" Edie asked.

Kappy shook her head. "No, but I have a phone book." She pushed back from the table and went over to the cabinet to fetch it.

"You have a phone book?" Edie asked. Her face was crinkled with confusion. "Why do you have a phone book if you don't have a phone?"

Kappy retrieved the book and started back to the table. "It has addresses in it, too, you know."

Edie didn't look quite convinced, but let it go. Not many Amish residents of Blue Sky or even the whole valley for that matter, had phones near their houses. Ruth was one of the lucky ones with a phone in the barn to take care of business, but most had to walk to a phone shanty near the main road in order to make a phone call.

"Remember to look for his last name first," Edie advised.

Kappy shot her a look. "I know how the phone book works."

Edie threw up her hands in surrender but smiled. "Just checking."

With a shake of her head, Kappy went back to her search. "Carlton Brewer DVM out on Mills Road." She pressed her finger to the spot where he was listed and met Edie's gaze. "DVM?"

"That's a vet."

"An animal doctor? That makes sense," Kappy said.

"Maybe we should pay him a visit."

Kappy grabbed her arm as Edie started to stand. "It's Sunday. He's not going to be working today."

Edie collapsed back into her seat once more. "Does it have his home address in there?"

Frustration came off her in waves. Kappy could only imagine how she would feel if her brother were locked up in jail for a crime he didn't commit, but getting upset wasn't going to correct anything. They had to keep level heads in order to figure this thing out. "Why don't we tell Jack Jones? Let him investigate."

Edie jumped to her feet. "Are you kidding? He's not going to investigate this. Not unless we hand him some solid evidence."

"Like an appointment book?" She pointed to the ledger still open there on the table.

Edie shook her head. "Not enough. We need more than that for him to go after a doctor."

"Okay, fine. But I don't think anybody needs to 'go after' this Dr. Brewer. How about we go over there tomorrow? Maybe poke around and see what we can find out. Maybe take one of the puppies with us."

"And there's not a home address listed?"

"We're not bothering this man at home," Kappy said. "How suspicious would that look?"

Edie stopped pacing. "Right." She chewed on her thumbnail. "Okay. Fine. Tomorrow we'll take one of the dogs over there and see what we can find out."

It wasn't a lot, but it was something. At least another lead in the case that seemed determined to go nowhere.

"I guess I should go." Edie pushed up from the table and started to gather the books she'd brought with her. They hadn't found any more clues as to who might be responsible for Ruth's murder, but not for lack of trying. "It's almost time to feed the dogs."

Kappy sat back in her seat. "Do you want me to go out there with you?"

Edie frowned. "To feed the dogs? If you want to."

"No," Kappy scoffed. "To the vet's office. You don't need me. He's not Amish. He'll talk to you."

Edie stopped rearranging the tomes in her arms and pinned Kappy with her gaze. "Of course I want you to go with me. I thought you were my partner in all this."

Partner was not the best term. That seemed to indicate they had an equal stake in finding Ruth's murderer, and it was so very obvious that it would mean more to Edie than it would to Kappy. That was only natural, of course.

"Unless you have *kapps* to make or something." She looked away as if to allow Kappy an opportunity to tell her no.

She did have coverings to make. She even needed to make one for herself. But she had a feeling that Edie needed a friend more than she needed to make *kapps*. Or maybe Kappy herself was the one who needed a friend. Whatever, she wanted to go, as strange as the feeling was.

"I'll go with you." Her tone was as offhand as she could make it. Still, Edie grinned from ear to ear.

"Fantastic," she said. "I'll pick you up first thing."

Kappy nodded. "I'll be waiting."

A knock sounded at the door. Kappy jumped and pricked her finger with the needle. "If you want a *kapp,* go around back," she hollered, then stuck her injured finger in her mouth. Ow, that smarted.

"I don't want a *kapp.*"

Then she remembered: It was Sunday. No one would be out shopping. Besides, she knew that voice. It sounded suspiciously like Edie.

"Just a minute." She set the prayer *kapp* aside. She needed to finish it tonight. She needed a new one for tomorrow when they headed over to the vet's office. Normally she wouldn't be sewing a *kapp* on a Sunday, not even for herself, but this was something of an emergency.

She stood and brushed stray threads from her apron and headed for the door. She could never remember having this much company. It was a little unnerving, but after she and Edie figured out how to get Jimmy out of jail, she knew things would slow down and once again life in Blue Sky would return to normal. At least for her.

She opened the door to Edie standing on the other side of the threshold, a foil-covered casserole pan in her hands.

"You should have asked who it was before you opened the door." She stepped past her and into the house.

"I recognized your voice." Kappy shut the door and started after Edie. "By the way, what are you doing here?"

"Well, I decided I would make a casserole for supper. Then I realized it was too big for one person, so I thought I would come over here and share with you." She smiled as if it were the grandest idea ever concocted.

"I see. And if I don't really want to eat a casserole with you?"

Edie set the pan on the table and whirled around, hurt flashing in her brown eyes. "You don't want to eat with me?"

Kappy shook her head. "I didn't say that. What *if* I don't want to?"

"But you want to, right?"

Kappy pinched the bridge of her nose. "What kind of casserole?"

"Chicken and rice. It takes two cans of soup to make it. That's why there's so much. But it's good in the morning for breakfast, too."

Kappy shook her head. "You're not going to be here for breakfast."

Edie just smiled. "Come on. It will be just like a slumber party."

"No way."

"Sourpuss."

But Kappy grinned as Edie went into the kitchen to get a serving spoon and plates.

"Maybe another time," she said as Edie came back to the room.

"Oh, I know. You have *kapps* to make, right?"

"A ton of them."

They smiled at each other and a friendly sort of antagonistic peace settled across the table.

Edie scooped up a bite of casserole and surveyed the room at large. "I can remember coming here when I was a little girl and buying prayer *kapps*."

"That was when Aunt Hettie made them."

Edie snapped her fingers in remembrance. "That's right. I remember her. She always smelled like peppermint and beef jerky."

Kappy laughed. "You have a good memory."

Edie smiled a bit to herself. "She's memorable, you know. I mean, she was a little strange, but that's why I liked her."

Kappy nodded in agreement. She had loved her aunt on a strange level. Aside from the fact that Hettie King had taken her in when she had no one else, there was something about her that was a little on the special side. As if her peculiarity stemmed from an advanced relationship with God. As if she were somehow more than the rest of the people who lived in Blue Sky. Whatever it was that had affected her aunt, it seemed to have rubbed off on Kappy as well. Most times she didn't mind at all. And other times . . .

"What made you leave?" Kappy hadn't planned on saying those words. Somehow they jumped from her mouth without her brain knowing they were there. And once they were spoken they couldn't be taken back.

Edie took a small sip of water and cleared her throat. It was obvious that she was stalling for time, trying to come up with a suitable response, but Kappy figured she could allow her that much.

"I never felt like I belonged here." Then what she said seemed to dawn on her. "I mean, some folks belong here and some folks *belong* here. I didn't belong here either way."

Kappy shook her head, trying to get her thoughts back in order. "You didn't feel like you belonged here so you went off to live with strangers?"

Edie rolled her eyes. "When you say it like that, it sounds completely dumb."

"It doesn't seem like the smartest plan."

Edie shrugged, then pushed her plate away. "It's done now."

But Kappy knew she meant her decision, not just her dinner. "And you're happy living among the *Englisch?*"

The ghost of a shadow brushed across Edie's face. "*Happy* is such a strong word."

Her heart constricted in her chest. "Content?"

Edie shrugged. She picked up her fork and turned it over, twirling it in nothing at the edge of her placemat. "It's hard when you don't belong in the place where you were born, and you were born in a place and don't belong anywhere else."

So coming back wasn't an option.

It was sad, really, when the decisions a person made in their life sometimes weren't the best ones to make. But if there was one thing Kappy knew, it was that God had a plan for everybody. He had a plan for Jimmy. He had a plan for Kappy. And He had a plan for Edie. They just had to hold on until His plan was revealed.

Chapter 7

It was after dark when Edie took her clean casserole pan and headed back across the street. All in all, it was a good evening. Kappy hadn't gotten her new prayer *kapp* made but vowed to do it first thing in the morning.

She washed her face and brushed her teeth, then used the tiny stairs to climb up into the big four-poster bed where she slept. Kappy wasn't sure where such a monstrous piece of furniture had come from. She'd never seen anything like it at any of the other Amish houses in the valley. Just another piece of tangible proof that her aunt was different from most by far. The bed was big and fancy and since it had been in her aunt's room when she had died, Kappy knew that the bishop had seen it. But he said nothing. So Kappy had said nothing and continued to sleep in the ornate bed.

She settled the covers around herself, turned onto her side, and punched her pillow into place. Tomorrow morning they would go visit Carlton Brewer, a local vet there in the valley. And hopefully, he would have some clues they could take to Jack Jones. Maybe some small piece of information that would tell them who had killed Ruth and why.

She supposed the *why* wasn't all that important, but the *who* was monumental. The *who* was the most important thing, for that was what would lead to Jimmy's release. And once Jimmy was released, Edie would leave the valley.

Kappy rolled over and sighed. As much as she hated to admit it, she was going to miss Edie when she went home.

And Jimmy, too. Maybe she should ask him if he wanted to live with her. Edie had insinuated that she wouldn't stay in Blue Sky, and Kappy was smart enough to figure out that Jimmy wouldn't make it in the *Englisch* world. If Edie couldn't, Jimmy didn't stand a chance. If he stayed with Kappy, then those times like . . . well, like now when the house seemed so quiet that every creak and every sigh could be heard, she would have company. But it had been so long since she had shared her living space with another.

She rolled over and punched her pillow a bit more.

Or maybe she would just get a dog.

Kappy was waiting on the front porch when Edie drove up the next day.

"Are you ready to go?" Edie called out the window.

"What took you so long to get here?" She grabbed her bag and headed for the car.

Kappy tossed her purse onto the floorboard, briefly noting that Edie had cleaned the trash out of her car. Most of it, anyway. She glanced in the back. The box of clothes remained, but the fast-food wrappers were missing. And so was the dog. "I thought you were going to bring a dog along."

Edie waited until Kappy slid into the passenger seat and buckled her seat belt before backing out of the driveway. "I was. I am. I just couldn't figure out which one."

She turned onto the lane that led to Ruth's house. "Plus I thought you might help me catch one."

"Catch one? They bark at me whenever I get close." It was next to impossible to feed them without stepping on one or two of the crazy hounds. But Kappy loved to watch them eat, their little ears spread out on either side of them as they ducked their heads into their food bowls.

"I don't think they like me," Edie said. She parked the car and got out, then headed for the barn.

Kappy followed obediently behind.

"Do you have any blue jeans?" Kappy asked.

Edie was dressed as colorfully today as she had been every day that she had been back in Blue Sky. Today's jeans were the color of sunflowers and rolled up a bit at the bottom. Her shirt was black and had some sparkly design on it, and once again she had on those seen-better-days purple flip-flop shoes.

"I don't like blue," Edie threw over one shoulder as she approached the dog pen.

She didn't like blue? Who didn't like blue?

But Kappy supposed that blue was just another reminder of Blue Sky and the Amish of the valley.

"Watch," Edie instructed as she let herself in with the dogs. She walked around, calling to them, but they barked and bounded away out of her reach. The puppies and the big dogs alike seemed almost afraid of her or . . .

"It's your shoes," Kappy called. "They don't like your shoes."

Edie stopped and propped her hands on her hips. "What are they, fashionistas?"

That definitely wasn't on Kappy's word-a-day calendar. "I'm not sure what that means."

"Never mind." Edie waved it away with one hand.

"Take off your shoes," Kappy returned. "I think you're scaring them."

"For real?" Edie asked.

"*Jah.*"

With a shake of her head, Edie slipped off her flip-flops and tossed them back toward the pen's entrance. She took a couple of cautious steps toward the dogs. They barked, but didn't run.

"I can't tell," Edie called back. "It's hard to walk in here with all the poop."

Kappy shook her head. "You're supposed to scoop that twice a day."

Edie stared at her, mouth agape. "You were serious about that?"

"Very." Kappy laughed, then retrieved the pooper-scooper from its place just inside the barn. She handed it and the recycled pickle bucket over the fence to Edie.

She wrinkled her nose in distaste. "If you say so," she said.

"I do. If you're going to be a puppy breeder, this is part of the job."

They both stopped.

Edie had made her intentions clear. Once she got her brother out of jail she was leaving. Her days as a puppy owner were numbered.

"At least for now," Kappy qualified.

Edie nodded, then ducked her head and got down to work.

Once the pen was clean and a puppy singled out for the trip to the vet, Edie looked down at her dirty bare feet.

"Now what shoes am I going to wear?"

The puppies had carted off her purple flip-flops long ago and the pieces had been nearly too small to pick up. They really didn't like those shoes.

"You don't have another pair of shoes?"

Edie pouted. "Those were my favorites." She washed her feet in the back spigot, then let herself in the back door. A few moments later she came out the front wearing a pair of flip-flops identical to the first pair except for the color. These were green.

Kappy cleared her throat.

"What?" Edie asked.

"Nothing."

Kappy lifted the puppy into her arms and got into the car. He really was a cute little thing with long black ears and sad eyes. His tail was tucked between his legs, but he settled down in her lap as Edie came around to the other side of the car and got in.

"Are you ready?"

"I am, but I'm not sure Elmer here is."

Edie started the car, but gave Kappy a look. One of her *What are you talking about?* looks. "Elmer?"

"That's what I've been calling him. He has to have a name, doesn't he?"

"I guess so." She gave a one-armed shrug, then started toward town.

The Brewer Animal Clinic sat just off the main road between the bait shop and the bank. Kappy supposed she had passed the place a dozen times, but had never had need for the services and hadn't paid it any mind.

Elmer braced his front feet on the dashboard as Edie cut the engine. His tail wagged back and forth, the little white tip like a sweeping light.

Edie smiled at the pup. "You don't know what you're in for, do you, little fella?"

Kappy scooped the pooch into her arms and kissed him on the top of the head. "Don't listen to her," she crooned. "She doesn't know."

Edie just laughed as they made their way into the small office.

The unmistakable smell of animal and cleaner met Kappy's nose as they entered. Elmer must have sensed that something was up. He scrambled in Kappy's arms, trying his best to get closer to her.

"Can I help you?" The middle-aged receptionist asked. Kappy had seen her once or twice, in the grocery store and maybe even once in Sundries and Sweets, but she didn't know the woman's name.

Kappy adjusted her hold on the squirmy puppy as Edie went to the counter. "Yes, ahem, we have a puppy and we would like an appointment with the doctor."

"O-kay. Is there anything wrong with the puppy?"

"Oh, no." Edie shook her head. "We just want to make sure he's healthy."

"Right."

Kappy resisted the urge to roll her eyes. That had to be the dumbest excuse she had ever heard. They should have made a better plan before getting in the car and coming over here.

"Fill this out and I'll get you back as soon as I can." She handed Edie a clipboard over the counter and waved them away to the waiting area.

Edie and Kappy found seats between the other two people waiting. Kappy wished she had brought a leash for Elmer. At least then she could place him on the floor like the other dogs in the waiting area.

"What exactly are we waiting for?" Kappy leaned close to Edie as she asked. The puppy squirmed against her as her motion decreased his space.

"Our turn . . . ?" Edie replied, tapping the records form with the end of the ballpoint pen.

"No, why are we waiting here? Isn't there a way to find out what we need without taking Elmer back there?"

Upon hearing his name, the puppy wiggled his way up and started licking the underside of Kappy's chin.

Edie frowned. "They're not going to hurt him. Besides, he needs the rest of his shots. He's the only one that *Mamm* didn't bring on her last visit."

"Okay. If you're sure."

Kappy shifted in her seat and repositioned Elmer back into her lap as Edie studied her. "You like him, don't you?"

"Who? El—the dog?"

Edie laughed, shook her head, and went back to the form.

"So what if I do like him?" Truth be told, she more than liked him. And she had never had a dog before.

Thankfully, Edie didn't answer. She filled out the form and returned it to the lady behind the counter.

Kappy kept her hold on Elmer and looked around the office. "It doesn't look like the office of a killer," she whispered to Edie.

"What does the office of a killer look like, exactly?" Edie whispered in return.

Kappy glanced around once more. "Not like this."

A large fish tank filled with colorful fish sat against the far wall. Cheap paneled walls were covered with notices on how to protect your dog from heartworms and other diseases. A bulletin board hung next to the reception desk and contained pictures of lost cats as well as reader notices and special requests. The linoleum floor showed more than its fair share of wear, but the place was clean and as far as Kappy was concerned that was very important.

"I'm just saying a man who cares about animals this much . . ." She shook her head, unable to find the words she needed. "I just can't see that sort of person being capable of murder." Her voice rose a little louder than she had intended. The two people in the waiting area looked up and frowned as if they weren't sure they had heard what they thought they had heard, then they went back to their magazines.

"Human beings," Edie said, "whether they love animals or not, are capable of all sorts of evil acts. They just have to be pushed too far. That's all it takes."

"That's the thing." Kappy's voice returned to a whisper. "What's his motive? What would push him that far?"

Edie sniffed. "I don't know yet." She reached toward a magazine sitting on the chair next to her. She flipped it open and pretended to study it even though the magazine was upside down.

"You don't know because there's not one." Kappy sat back in her chair. In her lap, Elmer had started to tremble. "Maybe we should just take him home."

"Wasn't it your idea to come here?"

Kappy shrugged. "I changed my mind."

"Elmer King," the nurse or receptionist or whatever she was called from the doorway leading to the exam rooms.

Edie elbowed Kappy in the side. "That's you."

"Oh." She jumped to her feet, still cradling Elmer close.

Beside her, Edie stood as well.

"This way," the woman said.

They followed her down a short hallway past two doors before entering a small exam room.

"The doctor will be in momentarily."

The receptionist laid her clipboard on the small counter, then shut the door as she left.

Like the waiting area, the exam room was filled with more posters on caring for pets, as well as ones showing all the bones in a dog's body.

Elmer whined to get down and Kappy obliged him, setting him on the floor so he could snoop around and sniff all the new smells. She took a step closer to the poster examining the bones. Interesting stuff. And she wondered, had she not been Amish, maybe she would have been an animal doctor. Or maybe even a scientist.

Edie propped her hands on her hips and looked around the room. "What exactly are we trying to find?"

Kappy checked to see where Elmer had wandered off to, then turned her attention to Edie. "I don't know. Just anything, I guess. Something suspicious maybe." She gave a small shrug.

Edie gave the room another once-over. "Nothing suspicious here."

Perhaps this trip was just a waste. It wasn't like the vet would have an appointment book that said *Today I killed Ruth Peachey*.

"I say we get Elmer his shots, then head back home," Edie said.

All Kappy could do was nod in agreement.

A small knock sounded at the door a split second before it opened. Elmer jumped as if he'd been goosed, turning around and barking at this newcomer.

Kappy rushed across the room and scooped him into her arms as a very old man shuffled into the room. He wore a white coat with Dr. Brewer stitched above the pocket. Underneath he wore a yellow shirt and brown slacks. This was the doctor? Carlton Brewer had to be nearly as old as Nathaniel and Ephraim.

"Well, hello there—" He looked down at the clipboard the receptionist had left on the counter. "—Elmer."

In her arms Elmer squirmed to get down, barking the whole while.

"I'm Dr. Brewer." His voice was frail and thin, his hands trembling as he reached out in greeting.

Kappy managed to contain Elmer in one arm and shake Dr. Brewer's hand. His grip was weak, soft. *Jah,* their trip was definitely a waste. There was no way this man could have killed Ruth Peachey. Kappy wasn't sure that he could lift more than an ink pen.

"Let me just take a look here." He took Elmer from Kappy and set him on the table. She caught Edie's glance over his bent head as he listened to Elmer's heart. Edie's expression reflected her own. They had hit another dead end.

"Is this one of Ruth Peachey's dogs?" He looked from Edie to Kappy then back.

A moment of panic flashed across Edie's face, then she took a step forward. "Um . . . why do you ask?"

The doctor rolled Elmer over, pointing to the writing on his belly just off to one side near his right leg. "He's got a tattoo."

Busted. And they thought they could get in and get out without anyone knowing why they had come.

"Well . . . yeah," Edie said, obviously stalling. "She's my mother. Uh, I mean she was." Clouds of sadness floated across Edie's expression, then she pulled herself together. "This is my friend and she wants to buy this dog, and so I wanted to make sure that everything was okay with the dog, right?" She turned her sharp gaze to Kappy.

"*Jah,* that's right." Kappy flashed the doctor a quick smile. If the doctor was suspicious, he didn't let on. "That was a sad, sad situation with Ruth." He shook his head. "There was none better than Ruth Peachey."

Edie mumbled something inconsequential, but it seemed to satisfy the doctor. He finished his exam, declared Elmer was in perfect health and once he got the last of his shots would be ready to go live with his new owner. He shook their hands once again, called for the assistant to come finish the vaccinations, and bid them both a farewell.

"Well, that was a waste," Edie said as they gathered their things and prepared to leave the exam room.

"Look at it this way: If we hadn't come, we would forever be wondering."

"That's true," Edie agreed.

Kappy gathered Elmer into her arms once more and together they walked to the reception desk. The woman they had spoken with earlier already had their chart and was tallying the cost of today's visit.

"I suppose Dr. Brewer has been practicing for a long time," Kappy said. She wasn't sure what made her voice the words, and once they were out she wished she could call them back. She had all but called Dr. Brewer ancient.

"Over fifty years," the receptionist said with a quick smile. "I'm surprised he comes in anymore at all."

"It would be a shame if he retired," Kappy murmured. He might be as old as dirt, but he seemed like a nice man. He obviously loved animals, handling Elmer with the utmost care and offering him a treat after the exam was complete.

"What would you do then? Would he sell the clinic?" Edie asked.

The receptionist chuckled, her ponytail swinging from side to side as she shook her head. "No, the young Dr. Carlton Brewer would take over."

Chapter 8

"Wait," Edie said. "There's a young Dr. Brewer?"

The receptionist smiled. Kappy noted that the name on her badge said BONNIE. "That's right."

"And he's a veterinarian as well?" Edie pressed.

"Oh, yes. He took over the practice several years ago. The elder Dr. Brewer only comes in on Mondays and Friday afternoons."

"And the young Dr. Brewer?" Edie asked.

"He works the rest of the time." She smiled and pushed their statement across the counter toward the two of them.

Kappy could only give it a cursory glance. She was too busy assessing the information she had just received. Ruth was killed on a Tuesday, and if she had an appointment with a Dr. Brewer, chances were it was the young Dr. Brewer and not the fragile man they had just met.

"Does the doctor make house calls?" Edie asked.

Kappy juggled Elmer in her arms as Edie took the necessary bills out of her wallet. She pushed the money across the counter toward the receptionist.

"Just the young doctor." She smiled at them. "Let me get you a receipt."

Kappy nodded, then caught Edie's stare.

Now what do we do? Edie mouthed.

"Is by chance the young doctor here today?" Kappy asked.

Bonnie counted out her change and shook her head. "Not today. But he does live around back if you ever need him for anything else."

Kappy wasn't sure if anything else also included a murder investigation, but she really wanted to talk to the young Dr. Carlton Brewer.

"Thank you." Edie flashed her a quick smile, and together she and Kappy walked Elmer out to the car.

"Are you thinking what I'm thinking?" Edie asked.

"I am if you're thinking we should go around the back and see if we can find the young Dr. Brewer." With any luck he would be outside mowing his grass or even watering his garden or something where they could get a good look at him. Maybe even talk to him for just a moment.

Edie thoughtfully tapped her chin. "We have to have a reason . . ." she said. "So we take Elmer back there to show him how big he's gotten and just bring up Ruth from there."

Kappy frowned. She wasn't sure that would actually work, but she couldn't come up with anything better. "Let's go."

Once again Kappy wished she had brought a collar and leash for the little pup. He didn't weigh hardly anything, but he wanted down so bad to sniff the ground and see what was new around him that her arms began to ache as she held him in place.

She would definitely have to invest in a leash when she took him home—She reined her thoughts to a quick stop. She wasn't taking Elmer home. She might like him and she might have even been contemplating getting a dog the night before, but the reality was . . .

Well, the reality was she lived alone, she had no friends except for Edie, who would be leaving soon, and she lived alone. Wait. She'd already said that. It wasn't like Elmer would fill in the spots when she came home alone. But she knew he would fill other voids.

"There he is." Edie cocked her head in the direction of the large Victorian-style house. It was painted pale yellow and looked similar to Amish houses other than the color and the ornate trim that seemed to drip from every flat surface. A man sat on the front porch in the rocking chair, a glass of tea on the table at his side and a cell phone pressed to his ear.

"Should we go talk to him?" Kappy asked.

"We've come this far," Edie replied.

The man caught sight of them and seemed to understand their intentions. He held up one finger as if to say he would be off the call shortly and didn't protest as they climbed the porch steps.

"I'll call you back," he said into the receiver. "Yes, that's right. Okay then. Bye."

He tapped the phone off, then turned to Edie and Kappy with a smile. "Is that one of Ruth's puppies?"

"Yes." Edie spoke as Kappy took one giant step forward and pressed Elmer toward the young Dr. Brewer.

He accepted the dog without complaint, scratching him behind the ears.

"I take it you're her daughter." He didn't look at either one of them as he said the words.

Edie inched closer. "I am."

"I'm sorry for your loss. It's such a shame."

"Yes," Edie said. "Did you come out to the house last Tuesday?"

Nothing like jumping in feet-first.

If he thought her question strange, his expression showed no indication. "I did."

Kappy's heart gave an excited thump. Maybe they were onto something now! He was certainly stronger and more capable of a physical confrontation than his father.

"Are you aware you may be the very last person to see her alive?" Edie asked.

Dr. Brewer stopped rocking. "How so?"

Elmer continued to sit in his lap, content and not wriggling to get down. Maybe Kappy just wasn't a dog person.

"She had an appointment with you and then a little over an hour later she was found dead."

He shook his head. "That would've been the case if I'd made the appointment. I had a flat tire on the other side of Jacks Mountain. I didn't make it to Ruth's house until after the police were there."

"I was there," Kappy said. "I didn't see you."

"I didn't stop. I drove by, saw all the commotion, and figured whatever Ruth needed we could take care of another time. I had no idea she was dead."

Kappy and Edie shared a look. His alibi was plausible, even believable, and they might even be able to verify it. Or it could all just be one big lie.

"Can anyone back up the story?" Edie asked.

A frown marred the doctor's handsome face. "Are you questioning me?" He stood and handed the puppy back to Kappy. She accepted the dog, which immediately began to squirm to get down.

"Just merely trying to find out what happened to my mother."

"I thought they had arrested Jimmy."

"That's true," Edie said. "But just because he's arrested doesn't mean he's guilty."

"I'm sure the police had their reasons. I'm sorry. I know this must be hard on you."

He didn't sound sorry to her.

"My brother did not kill our mother. He loved her very much." Tears welled in Edie's eyes. Her lips pressed together in a line that Kappy recognized as anger.

"Most murders happen between people who love each other."

Kappy had never really thought about it. Actually, she didn't know much about murders at all, but his statement almost made sense.

"Regardless," Edie said, "I don't believe Jimmy is guilty."

Dr. Brewer flashed them a quick smile that didn't reach his ice-blue eyes. "Neither am I."

Less than five minutes later, Edie and Kappy were asked not so politely to leave Dr. Brewer's house.

"That didn't go as planned, huh?" Edie said. She grabbed a tissue from the center console and dabbed at her eyes.

"I'm sorry," Kappy said. She could only imagine how Edie felt, trying to protect her brother while the whole world thought him guilty.

"I'm just worried about him." She wadded up the tissue and started the car.

"Of course you are," Kappy said. "I would be worried about you if you weren't."

"I just don't understand how everyone can think the worst of him." She pulled the car onto the main road and headed back toward their houses. "I mean he's not that different, is he?" She cast a quick look at Kappy.

"I don't know. Not to me." And that was the truth. He was different, yes. But weren't they all? But just because he was different didn't mean he was dangerous or capable of violence.

"If the cops could have seen him taking care of the dogs that first day, petting the rabbits, feeding the ducks, and all his other chores, they would know he couldn't hurt his mother."

Edie gave a quick nod but kept her eyes trained on the road ahead. "You don't think he just . . . snapped?" The last word was nearly whispered.

It was a question Kappy didn't want to answer. "I suppose anything is possible." All one had to do was look at a newspaper these days and that was evident.

"I know," Edie said. "But what do you think?"

"I don't think he snapped," Kappy said. "When I got on the scene he was crying, trying to wake her up, and praying to God for her to be okay. I don't think someone who snapped could recover that quickly. *Jah?*"

"I don't know."

They rode in silence for a few miles, each lost in her own thoughts. At least Kappy was. They seemed to be chasing themselves around in her brain a lot like Elmer chasing his tail. But one thing always came back. She didn't believe Jimmy was guilty. That meant someone else out there was. But who?

Edie pulled into Kappy's drive, the corners of her mouth turned down into a frown.

"Do you want to talk to the neighbors?" Kappy asked.

Edie shook her head. "I think I'm going to lie down for a while. I feel a headache coming on."

It was no wonder, with everything that Edie had been through.

"If you're sure," Kappy said. She got out of the car and set the puppy in the passenger seat.

"Go ahead," Edie said. "I think you should keep him."

Kappy shook her head. "No, no, no. I don't need a dog."

Edie gave her a sad smile. "No one needs a dog," she said. "But everyone *needs* a dog."

Kappy opened her mouth to protest once again, then took one look in those sad brown eyes and scooped Elmer into her arms.

Kappy was just finishing up the breakfast dishes when a car horn sounded outside. Elmer started barking, pushing himself backward across the wood floor with his efforts.

"What in the world?" she muttered as she dried her hands. She only knew one person who would show up this early and honk the horn outside.

"Edie Peachey, what are you doing?" she called once she had stepped out onto the front porch.

"Let's go, Kappy. We have clues to find."

Kappy looked back to her front door and to the car where

Edie waited. She should make some *kapps* to replenish her stock. Or she could go with Edie to help her clear Jimmy's name. And as quiet as the house was last night after Edie left . . .

The choice was clear.

"Give me a minute to get my purse." Kappy ran back into the house and grabbed her bag, did a quick check of the stove to make sure everything was off, let Elmer into the backyard, then slipped on her shoes and headed out to the car.

"Where are we going?" she asked once she had slid into the passenger seat.

"To talk to your neighbors." Edie's mood had greatly improved from the day before, and Kappy was grateful. She had been worried about her friend.

"Do you want to walk?" Kappy asked.

"In this heat?" Edie shook her head.

"So where are we going first?"

"I thought we would head over to Ephraim's. He still lives there, right? He hasn't—"

"He's still there."

Ephraim Jess lived on the other side of Kappy, nearer to the mountain. He was maybe the oldest man in the district. The exception possibly being Nathaniel Ebersol, who lived on the other side of Kappy.

Edie's car engine must have alerted him that he had visitors. Edie had no sooner pulled to a stop than Ephraim hobbled out onto the porch. Shading his eyes, he peered at them.

"I never noticed it before, but he looks like Ichabod Crane," Edie said in a near whisper.

"Who?" Kappy asked.

Edie shook her head. "Never mind." She turned to Kappy. "Are you going to go talk to him?"

"Me?"

"He's certainly not going to talk to me."

Kappy gave a quick nod. "Right." She got out of the car and waved to Ephraim.

"Kappy King? Is that you?" His squint grew more pro-
nounced.

"It is." Kappy drew to a stop at the bottom of the stairs.

"What are you doing out and about at this time of the
day? I always thought you were something of a hermit."

She gave a quick cough. She didn't need him telling her
how she kept to herself most days.

"Did you hear about Ruth Peachey?" she asked.

He cocked his head to one side and smacked his lips
thoughtfully. "I was at the funeral. You sure you're feeling all
right today?"

"I'm fine. I was talking about the murder."

He drew back. "Murder?"

"The police took Jimmy away for killing his mother."

Ephraim tsked. "That boy couldn't hurt a flea."

"I know that and you know that, but the police think
they've found their killer."

He thought about it a moment. "Why are you here telling
me all this?"

"I thought maybe you saw something the day Ruth was
killed. Any strange cars on the road, anything weird? Maybe
a woman in red?" She was reaching, but she had to have
something more to take to Jack Jones.

"Have you been over to talk to your *other* neighbor?"

Kappy hoped her expression remained impassive. That
was what she was going for, anyway. "Not yet. Why?"

"Just watch him. He may be acting suspicious. Be careful,
you hear?"

She started to ask him if he really believed Nathaniel could
be guilty of Ruth's death but decided against it.

"I understand, but did you hear anything? Did you see
anything that day?"

Ephraim propped his hands on his hips and studied the
porch ceiling. "Well, now, let's see . . . Strange cars? No.
Most cars are strange though, *jah?*"

"What about people?"

He smacked his lips again. "None that I can recall." He lowered his chin and met Kappy's gaze.

"*Danki*," she said. "If you happen to think of something, feel free to stop by and let me know."

"I will."

Kappy turned to go back down the porch steps and to the waiting car.

"Are you headed over to the *other* neighbor's now?"

Kappy wanted to shake her head. The men had been arguing for more years than anybody could count and wouldn't even say the other's name. "That's the plan." She said the words without even bothering to turn and face him.

"Just be careful with that one. He's not trustworthy."

"I'll keep that in mind." She made her way down the stairs and across the yard.

Chapter 9

"Well?" Edie asked as Kappy buckled her seat belt. Edie half turned in her seat, her gaze searching Kappy's face as if for some clue to what was said.

Kappy shook her head. "He doesn't know anything. And he also told me that he thought Nathaniel was guilty."

Edie's mouth dropped open. "Of *Mamm*'s death?"

"You have been away a long time."

Edie put the car into reverse and backed out of the drive. "I guess so. I don't remember them being quite so . . . hostile to each other."

"It gets worse every year."

They continued toward Nathaniel's house in silence.

"So I guess if he was trying to blame Nathaniel that he didn't see anything himself?" Edie asked.

"That's about the way of it," Kappy said.

Disappointment flickered across Edie's face. She pulled into Nathaniel's drive and put the car in park. Hands still braced on the steering wheel, she let out a great sigh.

Kappy didn't need her to say what was on her mind; she already knew. Nathaniel was the last hope they had. If he hadn't seen anything, then chances were no one else had. They would never find out who the woman in red was, or if she even existed. The red button would forever remain a potential clue to an unsolved mystery.

Kappy shot her a sympathetic look, then got out of the car.

Nathaniel Ebersol had something of a green thumb. He grew plants and flowers of all kinds and sold them to *Englischers* and Amish alike. Kappy started up the walkway surrounded on both sides by bubble-gum pink petunias and sweet potato ivy. The amount of plants he had in his yard and on his porch made the house look more like it belonged to a Mennonite, but apparently the bishop turned a blind eye to Nathaniel's fancy yard.

Unlike Ephraim, Nathaniel was nowhere to be seen. Kappy climbed the porch steps and knocked on the front door. No sounds from inside the house greeted her. She listened for rustling sounds or shuffling footsteps, but only silence met her ears. She knocked again.

"Nathaniel?" she called. No answer. "Nathaniel?" Louder this time. "Nathaniel!"

"Quiet down there, girl. You're apt to wake the dead with all that carrying on."

Kappy whirled around as Nathaniel came around the side of the house.

Like Ephraim, Nathaniel was as old as Methuselah. He walked with a slight limp, hobbling from side to side as he drew nearer.

"I thought you weren't home," Kappy said.

Nathaniel stopped. "You thought I wasn't here so you yelled louder? Did you think I'd hear you all the way to where I was?"

"Uh, no?"

"Then why were you yelling?"

She opened her mouth to answer but had no words. She shut it again, scrambling for the exact reason for her visit. "I came to talk to you about Ruth Peachey."

Nathaniel scratched his forehead near his hairline, knocking his hat askew in the process. "Ruth passed."

Kappy gave a small nod. "I know that. But have you also heard that she was murdered?"

Nathaniel took a step back.

Apparently not. Kappy didn't remember seeing him at the funeral. He might've been there, just keeping his distance from Ephraim.

"I had not heard that."

"The police think Jimmy killed her."

Nathaniel took yet another step back. "Jimmy Peachey is the kindest boy I know. A little odd, *jah*. But he's got a good heart. He would never hurt anyone, much less his own *mamm*."

Kappy readily nodded. "*Jah*, that's true. But he's been arrested and is in jail."

Nathaniel's gaze wandered away from Kappy to the car parked in his drive. "Who's that? They with you?" His blue eyes snapped back to hers.

"That's his sister, Edie."

She could almost see the thoughts tumbling, one on top of another, mixed in with the questions that most people wanted to know. Was Edie back for good? Was she going to stay *Englisch?* And how could they get Jimmy out of jail?

"I haven't seen Edie in a long time," Nathaniel mused.

"She's trying to help Jimmy."

Nathaniel gave a quick nod.

"I was wondering," Kappy started, trying to get the conversation back on track, "if perhaps you saw something the day Ruth died."

"Something?"

"Anything strange," Kappy clarified. "A car you've never seen before? A man you've never seen before? A woman dressed in red?"

"I didn't see any woman, but I did see a man running across the fields."

Kappy perked up. This might be the break they needed. "A man in a blue shirt?"

"No."

"A red shirt?"

"No."

"Amish man?"

"If you give me a minute I can tell you," Nathaniel groused.

"*Jah*, okay then." Kappy tamped down her excitement, doing her best to hold it in check as Nathaniel gathered his words. "It was an Amish man in black trousers and a green shirt. He was running across the fields. I would have never noticed it but I was coming home from the store. The grocery ad had just come out and, well, that's the day I usually like to go shopping."

Kappy nodded politely. "A green shirt, you say?"

"Like a spring apple."

"And that's all you saw?" Kappy asked.

"*Jah*. That's it."

It wasn't a lot, but at least it was something. "*Danki*, Nathaniel."

He tipped his hat, and Kappy made her way back to the car.

"Well?" Edie asked.

"He gave us a clue."

Edie's face lit up with excitement. "Yeah? What is it?"

"He says he saw a man running across the fields the day that Ruth was murdered. A man in a green shirt."

Edie's expression fell. "He saw a man in a green shirt. Anna Mae Glick saw a man in a blue shirt. That's not a very good clue."

"I never said it was a good clue."

In fact, there had to be hundreds of men wearing green shirts in the valley. Most men preferred some shade of blue above all else, but that didn't mean it was part of the *Ordnung*.

"That really doesn't help us at all," Edie said.

Kappy hated the disappointment in her voice. They had done everything they could. Some things were better left to God.

"Do you want to come over and see the puppies?" Edie asked.

Kappy shook her head. "I really need to get some coverings made. I haven't worked in days."

The second layer of disappointment descended on Edie's features. "Maybe later then."

"Maybe later," Kappy repeated. But they both knew their impromptu investigation was at a dead stop. And without another clue to take to the police, life in Blue Sky would go back to normal. For everyone except Jimmy.

"You have company," Edie said as she pulled her car to a stop in front of Kappy's house.

A black buggy sat in the middle of her drive. The horse was still hitched and the shiny roan gelding unmistakable.

"Hiram," Kappy whispered.

"I thought you said you two broke up," Edie said.

"We did."

"Hmmm."

Kappy chose to ignore that.

"Thanks for going with me," Edie said. She didn't even bother to put the car into park as she waited for Kappy to get out. "You know you're welcome to come by anytime."

Kappy nodded, her thoughts torn between Jimmy and Ruth's murder and Hiram and whatever he wanted from her today.

"I guess I'll be seeing you then," Edie said.

"*Jah.*" Kappy shut the car door and turned toward Hiram. She was barely aware of Edie backing up the drive and heading home. All of her attention was captured by the handsome man sitting on the porch swing. She started up the steps, her heart pounding.

"I didn't expect you to be out." Hiram's tone was almost accusing.

Kappy gave a small shrug. "Edie wanted me to go with her somewhere."

Hiram frowned, the motion not dimming his handsomeness even one bit. "She's under the *Bann*." He stood as she unlocked the door. "Are you going to invite me in?"

Part of Kappy wanted to invite him in and never let him go home and another part wanted him to stay on the porch and as far away from her as possible. The conflict of emotions was almost more than she could take.

"Why don't you come in?"

He followed her into the house. Kappy was relieved that she had straightened up the night before. Most times there was fabric and *kapp* strings, pencils, patterns, and yardsticks strewn about as she worked. Hiram had fussed about her untidy habits more times than she could count. And even though she was glad her house was more than presentable today, she knew it didn't change anything. She would always be a little messy and Hiram would always be neat as a pin.

Kappy made her way through the house and let Elmer inside.

"What is that?" Hiram stared, mouth open, as Elmer skidded to a stop in front of him. Elmer's tail wagged back and forth like it was caught in a strong wind. Then he stopped, sat, and raised his snout to howl.

"A dog."

"I know it's a dog. Why is it in your house?"

She gave a quick shrug. "Edie gave him to me."

"And you let him run around in the house?" Hiram was nothing short of appalled.

Kappy bit back a sigh and whistled for Elmer as she made her way to the back door once again.

He stopped his cry and trotted happily to the door.

Maybe it was better this way. At least she and Hiram would have less distractions as they talked. Or maybe that was why she had let him in to begin with.

Kappy put Elmer out once again, then turned back to Hiram.

He shook his head and she could almost see the questions forming in his mind. Which one would he ask first? "You aren't afraid he'll run away?"

She didn't have a fenced-in yard, but he seemed to want to stay close. That would work until she could make other arrangements. "I'm afraid he won't stay gone," she teased.

Hiram sucked in a breath. "So what are you doing running around with Edie Peachey?"

Kappy cleared her throat. "Would you like something to drink? I can make you some tea." She started toward the kitchen.

"No, *danki*."

"Oh." She stopped and returned.

"I was hoping we could talk."

Those were the words she had been dreading the most. "There's nothing to talk about, Hiram."

"I disagree. I think there's a lot to talk about."

She shook her head. Her throat clogged with emotions. Love, regret, longing, despair. "He's just a dog."

"You can't keep hiding from this."

She let out a small bark of laughter, then covered her mouth to keep any more from escaping. "I'm not hiding from anything, Hiram. This is just the way it is."

He shook his head and reached for her hands. She shoved them behind her back and out of his reach. "At least sit down and hear me out."

Reluctantly, she gave a small nod and eased into the living room. She perched on the edge of the rocking chair, purposefully not taking a seat on the couch where he could sit next to her. Distance. That was what she needed right now.

He frowned as if he knew the motivation behind her actions and sat on the end of the sofa nearest her.

"You can't keep running from this, Kappy."

She sighed. They had been over this too many times to count. "We're just too different."

"I disagree."

"I know." She ran her hands down the front of her dress. "But disagreeing doesn't change that."

Hiram shook his head, then chuckled. "That's what I mean. I know you're different. I love that you're different."

But she knew the truth. He loved Laverna.

"Are you going to tell me why you're out running around with Edie Peachey?"

She bristled a bit at his tone. It wasn't like they were married. Or if they ever would be. He didn't have the right to question her.

"Don't get that look," he said. "I'm just watching out for you. She is excommunicated and all."

"I know," she said. "But I see no reason not to talk to her."

Hiram sat back in his chair. "She has sinned against the church."

"Let he without sin cast the first stone," Kappy retorted.

"That's not exactly how it works."

"Well, it should." She had grown accustomed to Edie in the last few days and had discovered that she even liked her. Kappy hadn't had a friend since Laverna died. She'd never thought she would have one again. Surely, the Lord had something to do with putting Edie in her path, offering them friendship and the cause to bind them together. He knew what He was doing.

"Why are you hanging out with Edie?"

"She's my friend. She always was."

Hiram shook his head. "Edie was never anyone's friend. She hated us all. She hated everything about Blue Sky."

It was true. No one was shocked when she left for the *Englisch* world. But she was back now. "Well, that may be. But she's my friend now." And that was the truth. Somehow she and Edie had become fast friends, bonding over a mutual desire to get Jimmy out of jail.

"Once we're married—" Hiram started, but Kappy didn't let him finish.

"We're not getting married. I thought I made myself clear."

"I know what you said," Hiram returned. "But I also know that you and I are meant to be together."

She resisted the urge to close her eyes and let those words

settle around her like a warm blanket in wintertime. How she wished that were true. "I think you should go," she said.

Something flickered through his eyes. He pressed his lips together then stood. "This isn't over, Kappy."

She stood as well. "*Jah*. It is." Because there was nothing left to say. They were just too different for anything other than friendship to exist between them.

She walked him to the door, her hands shaking.

Thankfully, he didn't try to kiss her. He just wrapped one of her cold hands into his own and squeezed her fingers, a gesture of support and affection.

But if she was being honest with herself—really, truly honest with herself—she would admit that she wanted Hiram to love her as much as she loved him. As much as he had loved Laverna. That was something she'd never get, and she wasn't willing to settle for less.

"I'll see you," he said.

"*Jah*," she returned, then watched him get into his buggy and drive away.

She eased onto the porch and sat down in her swing. She should be inside making *kapps*, replenishing the stock that she had sold over the last week that she had been busy with Ruth's death and subsequent murder. But she didn't think she could concentrate. Plus, her hands were shaking.

Her gaze wandered over the fields of rippling corn, the patchwork fields dotted with white houses and red barns. Blue Sky was such a peaceful place to be. Or it had been, until Ruth was killed. Now it seemed as if Kappy's life had been turned onto its ear. So much had happened in the last few days.

She mulled it all over in her mind, turning each aspect of the last few days around and around, trying to find something they had missed. But there was nothing. They were at a dead end, no pun intended. They could go no further. Ruth was gone, Jimmy was in jail, and they were out of possible witnesses.

She absolutely hated the thought of poor, sweet Jimmy locked up behind bars. So she could only imagine how Edie felt about it, coming home for her mother's funeral only to have her brother dragged away for the crime.

The wind softly rustled around her. Clouds moved over the mountains and cast shadows below. The faraway sound of an engine mixed with a quick *clip-clop* of horse hooves on asphalt. How she loved the valley. The quiet, peaceful, rustling valley.

I wonder what Edie's doing?

Without another thought, she pushed up from the swing, called for Elmer, and headed for the Peachey house.

It was a short walk on such a beautiful day. Kappy strolled down the driveway, then the short distance to Ruth's driveway and up the small incline to the house. Elmer loped along at her heels. Only one car passed as she walked, a small red vehicle with four doors and a flat back end. She grabbed Elmer into her arms to keep him from giving chase. In a second, they were gone. They didn't look suspicious, but the red brought to mind the button that Edie so adamantly believed was a clue.

Kappy smiled, set Elmer back on his paws, and shook her head just a bit. Poor Edie. She was so determined to find the real killer that she saw clues where there were none. What they needed was something good. Something solid. Like an enemy. Maybe someone Ruth had feuded with. But that was impossible. Everyone loved Ruth Peachey.

Yet someone had killed her.

If Sherlock Holmes were here, he or Watson would deduce that the chances were greater that Ruth was killed by someone outside the community. It made more sense that way for sure. Especially with strangers from all over the place coming to her house to look at the puppies. And if they arrived in the car . . . Well, look how quickly the red car had disappeared. Just a few moments ago it was there, and in a flash it was gone. Along with all her hopes. There was no way they

would be able to track down the killer who could be anywhere.

Then the idea struck. She took off running around to the
barn. Elmer chased behind her.

"Edie? Edie! Where are you?"

Edie came out of the small barn office, her green flip-flops
slapping against her heels. She wore skintight black pants
and a green-and-black zebra-print T-shirt that hung off one
shoulder. The slouch showed one hot-pink bra strap. Her
eyes lit up when she saw Kappy. "What are you doing here?"

"I came to visit, but I thought of something on the way
here."

"What is it?" She had to shout over the barking dogs.
Elmer ran up and down the fence, happy to see his family
once again.

"Have you looked through Ruth's appointment book?"
Kappy asked.

"I glanced through it a little more, but it's not that interesting."

"I think it may be the key to solving who killed her." As
she said the words aloud, Kappy's excitement grew. "If we
can figure out who all came by that day. And cross-reference
it with her call log and her appointment book—"

"—then we can narrow down who killed her," Edie finished with her. "Kappy, you're a genius."

Kappy smiled, but shook her head. "Not really. It just
took some time to think about it."

"Let's go look." The words had no sooner left Edie's
mouth than the barking changed from one of greeting to a
warning that someone was out front. Someone who didn't
belong there.

"Are you expecting company?" Kappy turned to Edie.

The blonde shook her head. "Are you kidding? No one
within ten miles of the place will even speak to me." She
started toward the barn door.

Kappy followed behind, nearly as anxious to see who it

was as she was to get started on searching through Ruth's ledgers.

A shiny black buggy had pulled up Ruth's drive. For a moment Kappy thought it might be Hiram coming to look for her again, but quickly pushed that thought away as a gray-haired gentleman got out.

"Do you know him?" Kappy asked out of the corner of her mouth.

"How am I supposed to know him?" Edie returned. "I don't even live here."

But Kappy didn't know him, either. She knew most everyone in the valley, regardless of their church affiliation. But this man she'd never seen before.

He walked toward them, his expression open, though there was a sadness about his eyes.

"You must be Ruth's daughter." He reached out a hand toward Kappy.

"I'm Ruth's neighbor. She's her daughter." Kappy pointed to Edie, who gave a small waggle of her fingers in lieu of a wave.

Shock overtook his features but then disappeared as quickly as it came. "It's nice to meet you." He shook Edie's hand and turned back to Kappy and shook hers as well.

"I'm sorry," Edie said. "But you seem to have me at a disadvantage. Who are you?"

He flashed them a charming smile that somehow didn't quite reach his eyes. "My name is John David Peight. I live over close to Belleview." He inclined his head in that general direction.

"I see," Edie continued. "And how do you know my mother?"

The expression on his face drooped a bit at the edges, yet even then Kappy was sure he was one of the most handsome men she had ever seen, Hiram included.

"I guess you could say your mother and I were friendly competitors." As he spoke he reached into his pocket and pulled out a plain white business card. Kappy read the simple black lettering over Edie's arm. *Peight Pups—If you need a dog we have it.*

Edie studied the card, then turned her attention back to the man in front of them. "You're a dog breeder?"

"*Jah,* that's right. One of the best there is."

Chapter 10

Edie's hands trembled as she handed the card back to John David.

"You can keep that."

Edie tucked the card under the edge of her bra strap, then somehow managed to face the man. "So you breed beagles as well?"

"Among other hounds. They're my specialty. Bloodhounds, black-and-tan hounds, beagles, bassets. Mostly hunting dogs."

"I see," Edie said. She whirled around to face Kappy. "Can I speak to you for a moment please?" She cast a furtive glance at John David. "Alone."

If he thought the request was odd, John David didn't utter a word.

Edie snagged Kappy's sleeve and dragged her toward the entrance of the barn. "He breeds beagles," she practically hissed.

"I know. I heard."

"Do you know what this means?"

As far as Kappy was concerned it meant a lot of things. "That Ruth is not the only beagle breeder in this area?"

"It means that he could be our killer."

Kappy slowly turned to look at John David Peight. He didn't look like a killer. Not that she really knew what a killer looked like. But if she did, she wouldn't think one would resemble the man standing in the driveway right then, doing his best to pretend that they were not looking at him. His single suspender was smooth black and without any frays, his pants almost creased in the front. His shoes were clean with only a thin coat of dust covering them. His shirt was tucked in neatly with barely a wrinkle, despite the heat the day had brought.

"For a killer he's very neat."

"Just because he's a killer doesn't mean he has to be messy."

Kappy turned back to Edie. "Just because he's a beagle breeder doesn't mean he's a killer."

"Think about it. Ruth's dogs are the best. You've seen them. You see what she can charge for them. This man comes in, wants to breed hunting dogs, and he can't get anywhere because my mother's taking all the business. So what does he do? He sneaks in, hits her on the head, and kills her so he can take over."

And Kappy thought *she* read too many mystery books. "The theory is sound except for one thing."

"What's that?" Edie asked.

"He hasn't shown any violent tendencies."

Edie blew her bangs out of her face. "*Pfft* . . . like that matters. He can be like Dr. Jekyll and Mr. Hyde."

"Who's that?"

"Never mind. But I say we keep an eye on him."

"No accusations?" Kappy asked.

"None for now."

Kappy nodded. "Agreed." They turned and together walked back over to where John David stood.

"So you and my mother were friends?"

"I wouldn't say friends," he said, his eyes guarded, his wary smile tacked firmly in place.

Edie cast Kappy a look.

She shook her head. "I'm sorry, John David. But does this visit have a purpose today? We're very busy."

"Oh, *jah*, of course. I'm sorry. I just wanted to come out and give you my condolences."

"Thank you," Edie murmured. "Did you also know my brother has been jailed for the murder?"

John David's lips pressed together. "I had heard as much, but I've been hoping it was just a rumor. Jimmy is a good kid. And there's one thing I know for certain, he would never hurt Ruth."

At least they all could agree on that.

"I thank you for coming by, John David," Edie said.

"You have my card," he said with a nod. "If you need anything, don't hesitate to call."

Edie shot him a most charming smile. "You bet I will."

They watched him climb back into his buggy. He gave them a quick wave, then he was gone.

"So what do you make of that?" Edie asked as John David's buggy disappeared down the lane.

"I don't know," Kappy answered truthfully. She knew Edie was ready to try and hang John David without any more information than what they had. But she wasn't a hundred percent sure he was guilty. He was hiding something, that much she knew. But whether it was good or bad remained to be seen.

"Well, I'm moving him to the top of my suspect list."

"Based on what?" As far as Kappy was concerned, there were no suspects in this case. Unless she counted the man in the green shirt and the woman in red, both of whom might be merely figments of all people's imaginations. Not to mention the man in the blue shirt.

"His shirt, for one. Didn't you notice?"

Kappy's heart gave a hard pound. "What about his shirt?"

"It was apple-green just like Nathaniel said."

Kappy waved away her half-baked theory. "They have whole bolts of that at the dry goods store, Edie. It's not like only one person can get their hands on it. The whole community will have a shirt made out of it by the end of the month. And why would he wear that shirt over here, knowing that he wore it the last time he came over?"

Edie chewed on her thumbnail. Kappy could practically see the thoughts tumbling around in her brain, ideas and speculations. She was sure it was a mess in there. "I don't know, but there's something about him I don't like."

"I agree, but I still don't think he's a murderer."

Edie stopped chewing. "You agree with me?"

Kappy nodded. "*Jah*. He's hiding something, that much I'm sure of, but the rest . . ." She shook her head. "Just because he's hiding something doesn't mean he's the killer."

Edie's shoulders slumped. "I know. But I need somebody to be guilty fast. I need to get my brother out of jail."

"We have to get the right person in jail, otherwise we're doing no better than the police right now."

"I just don't know how they can say he's guilty."

"Jack Jones told me that he confessed."

"What? Jimmy confessed to killing our mother?"

"Apparently, but you know how hard Jimmy can be to understand from time to time, and he was crying so hard when I was here. I don't even know when they talked to him. I stayed with him those first couple of days, but I had to go home a couple of times for different things. They must've come when I wasn't here."

"I knew it." Edie pounded her fist into the palm of her other hand. "They set him up."

"I don't think so. I think it was just bad timing. Why would anybody want to accuse Jimmy of anything?" And she had seen the look in Jack Jones's eyes when he had to have Jimmy arrested. She could tell that it bothered him. If he had any other choice he would have taken it. But with a confession . . . Even Kappy knew enough to know that a confession meant an arrest.

"Hello?"

Kappy and Edie both turned as Jay Glick, the neighbor who lived behind Ruth, came walking around the side of the barn. He carried a foil-covered plate in one hand.

"Hi," Edie said.

Jay's eyes skimmed right over Edie and settled on Kappy.

"Hello to you, Jay Glick," Kappy said. His shun was obvious to her, but she wasn't sure Edie had noticed.

Kappy's mind was still going in circles trying to figure out the connections and why anybody would want to arrest Jimmy. The most valuable thing he had were his rabbits, and that wasn't saying much.

"Anna Mae said I should bring you this pie."

Edie's eyes lit up like the Christmas lights they strung down Main Street each year. "Pie?"

Jay kept his eyes on Kappy.

"Shoofly?" Kappy asked. Anna Mae Glick was known for her shoofly pie.

"Chocolate shoofly. She found the recipe in the back of a magazine at the doctor's office. She's been chomping to try it ever since."

"*Danki,*" Edie said. She reached for the pie, but once again Jay pretended she wasn't around and passed it off to Kappy.

This time Edie did notice, and her brown eyes filled with hurt. It was one thing to know that people would shun her but quite another to live it.

"Hard to believe that Jimmy was capable of such violence."

"Jimmy didn't do anything." Edie charged toward Jay, but Kappy held her off, distracting her by handing her the pie.

"I'm not convinced Jimmy did it."

"What about the man in blue?"

"I thought you didn't see anything that day," she said, even though Anna Mae had said otherwise.

"Maybe I did, maybe I didn't."

"What about him?" Kappy asked.

"How does he fit into all this?"

"How would I know?"

"Has the daughter decided what she's going to do with the land?"

"I don't know," Edie replied. "Why don't you ask her?"

Kappy shook her head. "It's too early to make a decision yet."

"It's never too early," Jay returned.

Kappy gave a discreet cough.

"I'm willing to pay market value and cash. You won't get a better offer. And with Jimmy's troubles, he's going to need a good attorney."

Neither one of them had thought about that. They had been more interested in clearing his name from the source instead of in court. But Jay was right. Jimmy would need an attorney. Kappy wasn't sure how "good" worked where lawyers were concerned, but if Jimmy had confessed even though he was innocent, he would need the best. And in the *Englisch* world, the best meant money.

She turned to Edie, but she shook her head. "I'm not selling. Especially not to him."

Kappy turned back to Jay. "No decision has been made yet."

"Oh, yes, there has," Edie interjected.

Jay gave a quick nod. "So you'll be in touch?"

"When a decision is made, you'll be the first to know."

Edie threw her hands up in the air. "I love being invisible. It brings me such joy."

"Hush," Kappy chastised, then waved as Jay started back across their joined properties. "You might need that money."

"He's not the only buyer in these parts," Edie groused.

"But if you need a quick sale, sounds like he's your man."

Edie crossed her arms and frowned. "Why would I want to sell Jimmy's house to a man who wouldn't even speak directly to me?"

"Because he's right. Jimmy's going to need good representation to clear his name. And lawyers like that cost a lot of money. Do you have money?"

Edie deflated like a balloon that had been pricked with a pin. "No, I don't have any money at all."

Kappy nodded. "Just keep your options open. That's all I'm saying. You don't have to sell to him. But don't burn the bridge."

Edie glared after Jay's departing back, her look so fiery, Kappy was surprised he didn't burst into flames on the spot. "If you say so," she said. "There's something about that man I don't like. Not one bit."

Kappy walked into Sundries and Sweets the next day and her heart gave a little flip in her chest. Hiram stood behind the counter looking so handsome, as usual. It was a shame, really, that she loved him so much and yet she knew his heart still belonged to Laverna. It was even more heartbreaking that she and Laverna had been such good friends. Kappy would love nothing more than to marry Hiram as she had promised, but she couldn't bring herself to share him with Laverna's memory. Maybe one day . . .

As if sensing her stare, he looked up. A light of recognition sparked in his eyes. He smiled. "Kappy."

"Hi," she breathed. She had to get herself together. If she was going to talk to him about something so important, she needed to make sure she had her mind on business and not on how beautiful his green eyes looked today. She cleared her throat and tugged on her sleeves. She could do this. "Can I talk to you for a minute?"

"*Jah.* Of course." He traded places with the young girl standing behind the counter. It was Emma, his youngest sister. She was fifteen and finished with school, but this was the first year she had helped out in the store. "Let's go into my office."

He stood to one side, and Kappy preceded him through the door into the small area he'd claimed for office space. Like everything about Hiram, it was neat, clean, and organized. Not one scrap of wayward paper littered his desk. All files were put up neatly in the filing cabinets, all the books shelved, spines even. Not even dust dared settle in Hiram's domain.

"Have a seat. What do you want to talk about?" His expression grew hopeful.

A pang of regret shot through Kappy. She hadn't thought that her coming here might give him false hopes. "Do you know a man named John David Peight?"

Hiram gave a brief nod. Of course he knew him. As a store owner, Hiram knew everybody around these parts. "He's new to the area. Been here about six months."

Kappy's brows shot toward her hairline. "That long?"

Hiram graced her with an indulgent smile. "If you would get out more, I think you would be surprised at what goes on in our little community."

It was perhaps their second oldest argument. But Kappy had a tendency to keep to herself. It'd always been that way and she couldn't see changing now. "*Jah*, well, he came by Ruth's house yesterday."

"Really? I would think he and Ruth would be in competition with each other. As much as would be allowed."

"That's what I thought, too. And it made me wonder."

Hiram shook his head. "Please tell me you're not still digging around."

Kappy sat back, surprised. "I have to help Edie get Jimmy out of jail."

"No, you don't." Hiram's eyes grew guarded. "It's not your business."

But somehow it was. Maybe because the bishop had asked her to look after Jimmy. Maybe because Edie was in such need of a friend. Or maybe because Kappy herself needed

Edie almost as much. Whatever it was, it had somehow gotten intertwined with her business, and she couldn't let it go now. "I think John David Peight might have killed Ruth."

"What?" Hiram jerked back, an incredulous smile on his face as if he couldn't tell if her words were a joke and he should laugh, or if they were true and he should be aghast. "Why in the world would you say such a thing?"

"You said it yourself. They were in competition with each other, right? And Ruth's dogs are fantastic. I've read her ledgers. I've seen what she charges for pups and how she breeds them and raises them and how much care she gives them. She's got the best dogs around, hands-down. What if he wants part of her business and he can't get it any other way?"

Hiram shook his head. "I understand that Ruth's dogs are superior, but John David Peight would never harm her."

"How do you know that? You said he's only been in the area for six months. That's not long enough to get to know somebody like if you had known them your entire life."

He reluctantly nodded. "That's true, but John David Peight is not that kind of man."

"He has the greatest motive."

"Have you been reading those mysteries again?"

Anger rose up inside Kappy. She jumped to her feet. "What I read is none of your concern."

Hiram stood as well. "It is when you come in my office and accuse people that you don't know of crimes they didn't commit."

"I didn't accuse him of anything. I said he might have. I said he had motive."

"That's as good as saying he did it, Kappy. And I wouldn't suggest you go around saying that in this town. Not if you want to uphold your reputation."

Her reputation? It was this he was worried about. She didn't have a reputation for anything but being odd. He was the upstanding one. He was the one with something to lose.

"All of this started when Edie Peachey came back to town. Ever since then you've been acting strange."

"This is not Edie's fault."

"I don't think she's a good influence on you."

She started to protest and he held up both hands to stay her response.

"I'm just saying, Kappy. She's under the *Bann* and should be shunned. Yet you're running around with her trying to solve the mystery that's better left to the police. Maybe you should give that more thought instead of whether or not John David Peight is guilty."

"You know, I thought you were different. But it seems I was wrong." He was just like everyone else in the town, judgmental and only concerned with himself. Oh, they might go around talking all about community and working together. But when it came down to helping out a poor orphan boy, everyone was willing to leave it to the police whether they had his best interest at heart or not.

She turned on her heel and marched from his office. "Kappy," he called after her. But she refused to stop. And he didn't come after her.

Kappy stewed all the way home. Her conversation with Hiram just drove home their differences. And the realization made her want to pray and eat ice cream, not necessarily in that order. One thing was certain, praying would be beneficial, but eating ice cream not so much. Perhaps the only way to keep that in check was to stop by and see about Edie.

She pulled her buggy into the opposite drive, taking her to Edie's house instead of her own. Two other cars were parked in front aside from Edie's maroon-colored sedan. Edie herself was standing just outside the barn, one arm folded protectively across herself as she chewed on her thumbnail. *Stressed* was not quite a strong enough word for her harried appearance. *Fearful* seemed more on target.

Kappy set the brake and hurried over to her friend. "What's going on?"

Edie startled as if she'd been poked with a cattle prod. She'd evidently been so wrapped up in her own thoughts that she hadn't heard Kappy come up at all. "What are you doing here?"

"I came by to check on you."

"Thank goodness, Kappy. I don't know what to do."

"Who are these people?"

"Some kind of inspectors. You won't believe it. They came because they think Ruth was running a puppy mill."

Kappy couldn't help herself: She let out a bark of laughter. "A puppy mill?" Ruth's puppy farm was a far cry from a puppy mill. The dogs had plenty of room to run and play, a clean pen, fresh food and water, anything that a dog could desire as they waited on their new owner. "And they just showed up? Like a random inspection?"

Edie continued to chew on her nail as she shook her head. "Somebody complained."

"I don't understand. They're here because someone turned you in for having a puppy mill?"

Kappy knew. She had seen newspaper articles about not-so-on-the-level Amish dog breeders. For some reason lots of *Englischers* believed that if an Amish person raised puppies that it had to be in substandard conditions. Saying that would be like saying that all *Englisch* people treated their dogs like royalty. Neither statement was accurate. But who would tell animal control that Ruth had a puppy mill?

She looked up and caught Edie's gaze. "Are you thinking what I'm thinking?"

"John David Peight?" Edie said.

"*Jah.*"

"But he was just here yesterday. He saw what kind of operation we have."

Kappy nodded. "He sure did and he's jealous. This is his way of getting back at you and Ruth."

"But having an inspection isn't going to do anything but show that we raise our puppies correctly. Humanely and cleanly."

Kappy nodded. "That's true. But if you have to stop every week or so and do an inspection . . ."

"You think he's trying to make me tired so I'll go out of business?"

"Right. If he can make things hard on you, maybe you'll just quit."

"But I can't quit. I owe Jimmy this."

It was as if a lightbulb went off in Kappy's brain. "You don't think?"

"I don't think what?"

Kappy cleared her throat, then nodded toward the group of four inspectors who approached. They wore tan-colored battle pants like soldiers and T-shirts with MIFFLIN COUNTY ANIMAL WELFARE printed across the back. On the front was some sort of badge stitched over the pocket to make sure everyone knew they meant business.

"Miss Peachey?" The woman of the group took a step forward and tucked her clipboard in the crook of her arm. "Everything seems to be in order."

Edie wilted with relief. Kappy had no worries on the matter, but she could see how Edie would be a little unnerved having strangers come in and poke around while she was working so hard to take care of her mother's business.

"You'll receive a copy of the inspection in the mail. Nothing needs to be changed at this time."

"Thank you," Edie said, reaching out a hand to shake.

Kappy took a step forward. "What happens the next time someone calls and makes a complaint?"

The woman flashed her a hesitant smile. "We'll hope that doesn't happen."

"But what if it does?" Kappy pressed. "Are you going to come back out and do another inspection?"

The woman gave a quick nod. "That is our job."

"So essentially, if somebody called every day, you would have to come out here every day."

"I suppose. We've never had anything like that happen."

First time for everything.

"Take care." The woman nodded to them both, and together with her three counterparts, they walked back to their cars.

Kappy and Edie stood side by side as they started the engines and backed down the drive. Once they were out of sight, Edie turned to her. "You don't really think they will come again tomorrow, do you?"

She remembered the hooded look in John David Peight's eyes. "I wouldn't put it past him."

"I can't believe you ate that whole pie in less than a day." Kappy shook her head.

They were standing in Edie's kitchen, still mulling over a way to get Jimmy out of jail. As much as she hated to admit it, it was looking bleaker by the moment. It seemed that John David Peight had everybody fooled into believing that he was a completely innocent, upstanding citizen in the community.

Well, maybe he was. But right now he was Kappy's number-one suspect.

"What can I say?" Edie responded. "I like pie."

"And you're a stress eater."

Edie gave a shrug. "Maybe."

"Maybe my foot," Kappy said.

"You want to run over with me and give Anna Mae her pie plate back?" Edie asked.

She didn't have anything better to do except sit around and mull over new ways to get Jimmy out of jail. And she would much rather do that with Edie than alone. "Sure."

Edie grabbed the pie plate and together they started across the field. "I wonder why Anna Mae can make me a pie, but Jay won't talk to me?"

"It is strange. Or maybe they made the pie for me." Kappy laughed.

"He brought it to my house."

"That's true. Maybe he was just trying to get some information. You know? About finding out if you were selling."

"He could've done that without pie," Edie said. "Not that I'm complaining or anything. The pie was delicious."

They walked between the field of hay and the field of corn. Both rustled in the wind as they made their way across.

"Do you think this is where the man in the green shirt was running?"

Kappy shook her head. "I'm not even sure there was a man in a green shirt. Or even a man in a blue shirt."

"What about a woman in a red dress?"

"It could've been a wayward kite."

They seemed to think about that a moment. All three neighbors were adamant they had seen something that day, yet the things they had seen were so incredibly different, who knew what was the truth?

Their trek across the fields landed them in Jay Glick's backyard. A laundry line was bowed under the weight of more than one load. It slapped and snapped in the wind as they came up behind the chicken coop.

"Maybe we should have gone around front," Edie said.

The place seemed almost deserted, then Anna Mae bustled out of the back door and down the porch steps, another basket piled high with wet clothes cradled in her arms.

"Hello," Edie called, waving to the other woman. Anna Mae stopped and shaded her eyes to see who her visitors were.

"Kappy King, is that you?"

"Yes, Anna Mae. It is."

"And I'm chopped liver," Edie quipped. She was trying to be funny, but Kappy could hear the hurt in her voice.

"We're just bringing back your pie plate," Kappy explained.

Anna Mae smiled. She was as tiny as she could be, small in stature. Yet despite her diminutive size, she was bursting with energy, flitting about like a hummingbird. She set down the laundry basket and fluttered over, careful not to look in Edie's general direction. "Oh, the pie. Did you enjoy it?"

Kappy looked to Edie, then back to Anna Mae. "Edie did."

"Best I've ever eaten."

Anna Mae's chest puffed out with pride, but still she didn't acknowledge Edie's words. "*Danki* for bringing my pan back."

Edie smiled. "You're welcome."

Anna Mae's gaze stayed trained on Kappy as she waited expectantly.

"You're welcome," Kappy parroted.

From beside her Edie made a growling noise, then blew her bangs out of her face.

Anna Mae flitted back toward the house, then turned to Kappy once more. "I would invite you in, but—" Her words trailed off. Kappy knew what she was trying to say. She couldn't find an excuse not to, but because of the rules she still couldn't. Edie was under the *Bann* and most people preferred to pretend she was invisible. That was Blue Sky for you.

"That's okay," Kappy said. "We need to be getting home anyway."

Anna Mae smiled with relief and fluttered back over to her laundry line.

"Let's walk down the road instead," Edie said. "I keep getting grass and straw inside my shoes."

Kappy looked down at Edie's green flip-flops. Most Amish women walked around barefoot, but she supposed after so many years away, Edie's feet weren't used to it.

"Whatever you want," Kappy said.

They waved to Anna Mae once more and headed around the house.

"Is that Jack Jones's car?" Edie asked.

In the driveway sat a four-door car that looked an awful

lot like a police car without any markings on it. It was silver and understated and vaguely familiar.

"I don't know," Kappy said. "Maybe." But it wasn't the kind of car that stood out. It might only look like his and not be his at all.

"Why would Jack Jones be here?" Edie asked.

"I sort of told him I thought Jay Glick might be guilty of harming Ruth."

"What?" Edie screeched. "Why would you do something like that?"

"I thought he needed to know so I called the station a couple of days ago."

"But I don't think Jay did it. Why would he hurt my mother?"

"I know. That was before John David Peight came up."

"Maybe you should tell Jones about him."

Kappy shook her head. "We can't go around accusing everyone."

Edie sighed. "I guess we can't."

They turned in front of the Glick house and walked down the lane toward School Yard Road. They had no sooner gotten out of sight of the house than a car came up behind them. Edie moved behind Kappy and they walked in single file down the side of the road. The car pulled even with them and slowed. It was the silver car from in front of Jay Glick's house. The window rolled down and Jack Jones leaned toward the passenger side. "You girls need a ride?"

Kappy slid into the backseat while Edie got in the front passenger side. The inside of the car smelled like vinyl cleaner and stale coffee. Only occasionally Kappy would catch a whiff of what had to be Jack's aftershave, proving that he did shave from time to time even though his face held constant stubble.

"Out for a walk today?" Jack asked.

"Something like that," Edie replied. "What about you? What brings you to our neighborhood?"

He gave a nonchalant shrug, but Kappy could see the tension in his shoulders. "Just dotting i's and crossing t's."

Whatever that meant.

"Investigating, Deputy?" Edie asked.

He shot her a quick smile. "Detective," he corrected.

"Right," Edie said, though Kappy had the feeling the next time the opportunity arose she would call him deputy again. There was just something about the two of them that seemed to make sparks fly. She wasn't certain if it was Jimmy's arrest or if perhaps Edie had a thing for the tall detective.

"Were you talking to Jay Glick about Ruth's murder?" Kappy had learned a long time ago that the best way to get a straight answer was to ask a straight question.

Jack caught her gaze in the rearview mirror. "Maybe."

Edie turned in her seat. "Really?" she gushed. Her tone had gone from bristly to soft and sweet. "So you believe us?"

Jack turned into Edie's driveway. "I didn't say that. I'm just making sure."

"I thought you had a confession," Kappy probed.

Jack frowned. "I'm not at liberty to discuss the particulars of this case with anyone." Which was a cop's nice way of saying, "Don't ask any more questions. I'm not answering anything else."

Edie turned in her seat and captured Kappy's gaze. They were both thinking the same thing. Jack Jones was investigating once more. And that was more than they could have hoped for.

He pulled his car to a stop in front of Ruth's house.

Kappy and Edie got out.

"Thanks for the ride, copper," Edie said.

He gave her a small salute, and Kappy wondered if this was perhaps *Englisch* flirting. She had no idea. She'd never seen such action in motion.

"Anytime," Jack replied.

Kappy blocked the door before Edie could shut it, leaning

in to make sure Jack heard. "If you're out investigating, go check out John David Peight. He might be your man."

"I thought we had agreed not to go around accusing everyone," Edie said as Jack pulled away.

"I'm not accusing. I'm just giving a suggestion." She gave a small shrug as if to back up her words.

Edie smiled and shook her head. "You sure are mouthy for an Amish girl."

"Hasn't anyone told you?" Kappy asked. "I'm no ordinary Amish girl."

Chapter 11

Sunday morning promised to turn into a beautiful day. The weather report had called for rain, but for now the skies were blue in Blue Sky. Fluffy, white clouds that had no intention of raining floated lazily in the sky.

Kappy stared at the basket of sewing that had yet to be completed. But that would have to wait until tomorrow. There was no work on Sunday, only that which was absolutely necessary. And she was positive Samuel Miller would put *kapp* making in the not-necessary category.

She sighed and pushed herself up from her rocking chair. Surprisingly enough, her house was clean. Maybe because she had hardly been home this last week. Not that she could clean house on Sundays, either. But she could at least wash the dishes. Had there been any.

What did she normally do on off-Sundays? Up until a few weeks ago she had spent them with Hiram, visiting with his family or just spending time with each other, reading the Bible and making plans. They'd had so many plans, but all those were for naught.

"I wonder what Edie is doing," she muttered to herself. Only one way to find out: Walk over there and see. There was no rule against walking to a friend's house on Sunday. Kappy hooked Elmer to his leash and headed out the door.

The short walk did a lot to raise her spirits. Kappy wasn't sure why she felt so down on such a beautiful day.

Ruth's dogs barked as she started up the short drive that led to the house. Elmer tugged at his leash, anxious to be reunited with his beagle friends.

"Hey!" Edie waved from the porch. "What brings you out today?"

Kappy shrugged. "It's the off-Sunday."

"Good." Edie smiled. "You can help me clean out the barn."

Kappy unhooked Elmer and let him run over to the fence. The other dogs met him there, barking out their welcome. "It's Sunday."

"And a perfect day to get a few things done around here."

"Only work that is absolutely necessary can be performed on Sunday."

"Only if you're Amish."

Kappy held out her arms. "Amish."

Edie stopped. "Right. Does that mean I can't count on your help?"

"I'd be happy to help you tomorrow."

"But not today."

"Everyone needs a day of rest, Edie. Even you."

"A day of rest, huh?"

"It's the perfect day for it."

Edie looked up at the lazy clouds in the blue, blue sky. "Okay. A day of rest it is. As long as you promise to help me tomorrow."

"You got it."

They settled down in the rocking chairs on the front porch, a pitcher of lemonade and a package of cookies on the table between them.

"See?" Kappy asked. "Isn't this nice?"

They rocked back and forth, just enjoying the day.

Well, sort of. As much as Kappy wanted to relax, she

couldn't help thinking about all the things she should be doing. All the things she would be doing if it hadn't been Sunday.

"Yeah, nice." Edie sounded as thrilled as she felt. Not at all.

Kappy took another drink of her lemonade and wondered how long they would have to sit like this. It wasn't that she didn't want to sit with Edie. It just felt weird, like they were wasting time better spent on something else.

But it was Sunday.

"So, you and Hiram," Edie said.

"I told you. We broke up." Hiram was one thing she didn't want to talk about.

"Why?"

"We just aren't suited for each other."

"Uh-huh," Edie said. "Now tell me the real reason."

"That is the real reason." Well, the real reason she gave everyone. "Do you remember Laverna Fisher?"

Edie thought about it a moment. "Blond hair, green eyes."

"Really pretty."

"Yeah, I remember her."

"She married Hiram." Kappy took a bite of her cookie, pretending it was no big deal.

"She did? Are you kidding?"

"Why would I kid about something like that?"

Edie nodded. "Right. So she married Hiram. And I assume something happened to her."

Kappy dusted the crumbs from her lap. "She got sick a couple of years after they got married. And she just died."

"Hiram must have been heartbroken."

"He was. And when someone you love dies so quickly and unexpectedly . . ."

"You think he's still in love with her."

Kappy gave a sad smile. "I know he is."

"And that's why you broke up with him."

"It's silly of me, I know, but I want him to love me the way he loved her."

"It's not silly," Edie said. "Everyone should have love like that."

"What about you? Have you had that kind of love?"

"No, but I'm counting on it. One day. Hopefully, soon." She took a drink of her lemonade.

They rocked for a few more minutes. Back, forth, back forth. Their chairs squeaked in the same rhythm. She could be sewing. If it wasn't Sunday. Edie could be cleaning out the barn. Maybe even looking for more clues.

"This is relaxing," Edie said. "Don't you think so?"

"Oh, *jah.*"

Edie leaned her head back and closed her eyes. "Totally relaxing."

"Completely."

Edie rolled her head to the side and opened her eyes. "I won't tell if you won't."

Kappy pushed up from the chair and reached out a hand to help Edie do the same. "Deal."

A strange commotion woke Kappy the next morning. It sounded like . . .

Boom! Boom! Boom!

Someone was pounding on her front door.

It was too early for visitors, too early for company, and that could only mean one of two people. Hiram or Edie.

"Kappy! Kappy! Open the door! Kappy!"

Edie.

Kappy wiped the sleep from her eyes and stumbled out of bed.

"Kappy! Open up!"

She opened the door, and Edie flung herself inside. "I thought you'd never let me in."

"I was thinking about not," Kappy said. She was still exhausted from all the work they had done the day before. They had rearranged the barn, organized Ruth's office, and cleaned through the downstairs closets. Of course, helping

Edie didn't get any new *kapps* made. But there was always this afternoon.

"Something terrible happened."

That woke her up. "What? It's not Jimmy?"

Edie shook her head and, for the first time, Kappy noticed that her hair was standing up all over her head. "I don't know what it is, but there are people everywhere at the house."

"Ruth's house?"

"No, Martha's house. Of course Ruth's house!"

"What is it?" She really needed to get fully awake before she started having these types of conversations.

"These people showed up first thing this morning and started talking about inspections and health care and all sorts of things with the dogs. They're all over the place looking for problems. Half of them seem legit, but the other half—" She shook her head. "I think they're just there to start trouble."

"And you left them there alone?"

"What was I supposed to do?"

"Get back over there, for one."

Edie's expression changed into one of sheer panic. "You have to come help me, Kappy. I can't do this by myself."

"Of course you can."

"Please, Kappy. Please come help me. I need your support."

She must be getting soft in her old age. Twenty-five seemed to be her downfall. "All right. Okay. Let me get dressed. I'll be right there."

Edie threw her arms around Kappy and squeezed her tight in an unexpected hug.

Kappy held her breath, unaccustomed to such affection. Awkwardly, she patted Edie on the arm. "Get on now. I'll be right there."

"Okay." Edie released her and headed for the door. Kappy watched her sprint across the yard. "Where's your car?" Edie didn't go anywhere on foot. She preferred to drive to the mailbox.

Edie didn't slow her steps. "It's at home. The crowd was so thick; this was the only way I could get here."

And Kappy knew this was much bigger than she'd thought. She hustled into her bedroom to get dressed.

Crowd was too small of a word for the multitude of people at Ruth Peachey's house. Amish funerals were big and Ruth was much loved, but Kappy was certain there hadn't been this many people to come see her off.

"You see what I mean?" Edie cried.

They stayed as close to the cornstalks as they could, hoping to not draw any attention to themselves. Kappy had no idea whether they knew who Edie was or not, but it wasn't worth the chance.

"Who are all these people?" Kappy asked.

"Animal-rights activists, I guess."

"Animal what?" Kappy nearly tripped over her own toes.

"Animal rights. You know, like ethical treatment, proper food and shelter."

She managed to right herself and keep walking. "Animals have rights?"

"Of course," Edie said.

They were halfway to the house now. Kappy checked out the signs that the people were holding. PUPPIES HAVE RIGHTS, TOO! one read. YOU SHOULDN'T TREAT A DOG THAT WAY! said another. Along with YOU WOULDN'T PUT YOUR MOTHER IN A PEN! and HABID.

"What does that mean? HABID?"

"Humans And Beasts Integrating Destinies," Edie replied. "I Googled it."

Kappy stumbled again. *Integrating* had been one of last month's words from her word-a-day calendar. But destinies? And Googled? "So they're here to protest the dogs?"

"Not exactly. They're here to protest *the treatment* of the dogs."

"Ruth's dogs are treated better than most people."

Edie pressed her lips together and gave a stern nod. "I know," she said. She didn't have time to say anything else.

"Look! An Amish girl!" They could only be talking about her.

The protesters swarmed, running toward her, practically surrounding her and Edie. She turned to look at her friend. But Edie had raised both arms in the air and started chanting, "Down with puppy mills! No more puppy mills!"

No help there.

The protesters tugged on her sleeve, yelling for her to set the puppies free. Didn't they understand if they were let loose they wouldn't be fed?

Kappy did her best to ignore the protesters and just kept walking. Thankfully, they were so jumbled together that they were stepping on one another and preventing their own from reaching her.

Edie kept chanting, even as she led the way to the porch.

The angry protesters were unable to make it up the narrow steps and Kappy and Edie made it into the house. They shut the door quickly behind themselves.

Edie turned the lock and leaned back against the door, her expression one of concerned relief. "I'm not sure how long I can hold them off."

Kappy shook her head. "Why are they even here?"

Edie pushed herself upright and headed for the kitchen. "My guess is they found out that the animal welfare was out here doing an inspection and they decided to target us."

Kappy followed behind her. Something tickled her arm and she reached up, just then realizing she had a small tear in her sleeve. Those people meant business. "You don't suppose . . . ?"

Edie opened the fridge, then glanced back at Kappy. "I don't suppose what?"

"Maybe John David Peight called them."

Edie shut the fridge and sank into the nearest kitchen chair. "But that would . . ."

"Stall Ruth's business? Give her puppies a bad name? Give her farm a bad name?"

All that and more.

"He just didn't seem like that kind of guy," Edie said.

Kappy gave a quick nod. It was true. John David Peight seemed like a very nice man. But money and reputation could make nice men do mean things.

"Well, who else would want to sabotage Ruth's business?" Kappy asked.

Edie tapped her chin thoughtfully. "He is definitely at the top of the list," she said. "But what about the vet? He was sure acting strange."

As true as it was, acting strange wasn't a crime. But she couldn't think of anyone else who would want Ruth out of business.

A sharp rap sounded at the back door a moment before it opened.

Kappy and Edie were on their feet in seconds.

"It's just me." Anna Mae Glick bustled through the mudroom and into the kitchen. "I heard all the commotion," she explained. "Jay has gone down to the phone shanty to call the sheriff."

Why hadn't they thought of that?

"Good plan," Edie said.

"*Danki,*" Kappy said, then eased back into the chair.

All they had to do was wait.

Edie drummed her fingers against the tabletop. Anna Mae slid into one of the chairs, even though no invitation had been issued. Kappy wished she'd stayed at home.

"How long have they been out there?" Kappy asked.

"They were here when I got up this morning."

"Did you get to feed the dogs?" Kappy asked.

She stood and made her way over to the front window. The shades were drawn, the dark green blocking out the view from the front yard. Kappy peeked around one side. It seemed the protesters had grown in number. Some had even brought lawn chairs. Lawn chairs! Were they planning on staying that long?

"I couldn't get to the pen," Edie answered.

"And they say they are doing this for the puppies. The poor beasts haven't even been fed today."

Come to think of it, she hadn't fed Elmer this morning, either. She'd hustled over here instead. Now she looked out at the yard, wondering how she was ever going to get back to her house.

She let the shade fall back into place and moved away from the window.

"Hopefully, the sheriff will be here soon," Anna Mae put in. She had been so quiet Kappy had forgotten she was sitting there.

"You wouldn't happen to have any pie on you?" Edie settled her gaze on Anna Mae.

Anna Mae didn't even blink, didn't acknowledge Edie in any manner.

"Great," Edie scoffed. "She can sit down at my table, but she can't talk to me." She turned to Kappy. "What is wrong with people?"

Kappy looked from Anna Mae, whose expression never changed, back to Edie. "I don't know."

It was another fifteen minutes before Kappy heard the abbreviated sound of a police siren. Kappy ran to one side of the big front window while Edie ran to the other. They both peered outside, careful not to let the protesters see them.

The members of HABID dotted the yard and spilled over, blocking the lane that led to the Peachey house. A familiar silver car inched its way through the crowd. The protesters moved out of the way only long enough for the car to inch forward, then they closed behind it as seamlessly as oil spilled on water.

The car stopped in front of Ruth's house, and Jack Jones got out. Kappy wasn't sure if she was happy to see him or not. The last time they had run into the detective deputy, he said he was investigating Ruth's murder. Yet no arrests had been made. None but Jimmy. She wondered if he was doing it out of sheer obligation rather than on a hunch that she and Edie might be right.

Three short, rapid knocks sounded at the door. Edie jumped back from the window and looked down at herself.

"Kappy," she hissed in an urgent whisper. "Answer the door."

"Me answer the door? It's your house."

Edie shook her head. "I can't answer the door like this." She wore another pair of her too-snug pants, these pink and covered with the face of a chubby cartoon kitty cat. Edie's too-big T-shirt was red and boasted an overlarge depiction of the same white cat with a red bow on her ear.

Kappy didn't understand her reluctance. It was perhaps the tamest outfit she had seen Edie wear to date. "Why not?"

"These are my pajamas!"

Kappy laughed. "You ran to my house in your pajamas?"

"Don't pick fun. I panicked."

"I would say so."

Another knock sounded at the door, this one louder. "Answer the door." Edie gritted her teeth and jerked her head in that direction.

"All right." She still didn't know why Edie could run across her yard, the road, and Kappy's lawn and back again in her pajamas, but she couldn't open the door for Jack Jones while wearing them.

She moved toward the door as Edie disappeared up the stairs.

"Detective Jones," Kappy said, as if his visit was a complete surprise.

"I hear you're having a little bit of a problem." He jerked a thumb over his shoulder at the crowd still chanting in the front yard.

"You could say that."

"May I come in?"

Kappy stood to one side, allowing Jack entry.

"Where's Edie?"

Kappy shut the door and locked it before the protesters could swarm the porch, then turned back to Jack. "She's upstairs. She should be down in a moment."

He gave a quick nod and shoved his hands into his pockets. Kappy clasped her hands in front of her and the two stared at each other for a moment.

"Jimmy's innocent," she said.

"I believe you said that before."

She had, but she couldn't let an opportunity pass. She and Edie were coming up with blanks with every clue they had. They needed professional help. They needed Jack Jones on their side.

"How is the investigation going?"

He gave a shrug without taking his hands out of his pockets. The motion resembled a jerk or spasm more than anything. "I'm not at liberty to discuss any new developments."

Kappy examined his words, somehow coming up with the meaning. He wasn't going to talk about it.

"Are you the sheriff?" Anna Mae appeared from the kitchen.

"I'm one of his deputies." He extended a hand to shake. "Detective Jack Jones." Anna Mae shook his hand, then turned to Kappy. "I believe my work here is done." She turned on her heel and disappeared through the kitchen. A moment later they heard the back door shut.

"What was that all about?" Jack asked with a frown.

"Her husband called you out here."

He stared in the direction where Anna Mae had last been. "Is that Jay Glick's wife?"

"*Jah*," Kappy said.

The look on his face was pure speculation. Kappy liked that word. It was yesterday's word-of-the-day. And though she hadn't been able to use it in conversation, she was still proud that she had managed to put it in her thoughts.

"Deputy Jones," Edie greeted him as she swayed down the stairs. "So good of you to drop by."

"Detective," he corrected. "I happened to be in the area when the call went out. But you're welcome . . . I guess."

From outside came the sound of another stuttering siren.

"What's that?" Kappy asked.

"That's probably the marked cruiser," Jack said. "They'll get the protesters off your land." He swung his attention to Edie. "Any idea why they picked you?"

"Not a clue." She shook her head and Kappy noticed the glint of light on her lips. Had she put on makeup?

And today's outfit? She should've left her pajamas on. Her orange pants were rolled up to mid-calf, showing off her lower leg, her green flip-flops, and her black nail polish. The shirt she'd picked out was purple with orange polka dots on one side and orange stripes on the other, and Kappy found she couldn't look at it for very long or the pattern started to move. The nicest thing she could say about it was the colors matched. Sort of. She shifted her attention to Jack.

"HABID doesn't come out for just minor offenses," Jack explained. "It looks like you've been targeted."

"You mean like someone called and told them we were running a puppy mill?" Edie asked, her eyes wide and innocent.

"Most probably."

"But why would someone do that?"

Wait. Hadn't they already covered this? What was Edie doing?

"Did your mother have any enemies that you are aware of? Maybe a rival? Or longtime feud with someone?"

Edie flipped her hair over her shoulder "No. Not that I know of."

She was flirting! Edie was flirting with Jack Jones!

Kappy took a step forward. It seemed that neither one of them realized she was still in the room. "What about John David Peight?"

That stirred Jack to attention. "I talked to him myself. There is no evidence against the man."

"Only that if he destroyed Ruth's business he would probably double his," Kappy said.

"I'm sorry," he said. "He's off our list of suspects."

"What about Carlton Brewer?"

"The veterinarian?"

Edie took a giant step between Kappy and Jack. "If we're going to discuss the finer points of this case, why don't we all sit down at the kitchen table? I think we would be much more comfortable." She beamed him her brightest smile. "I'll fix us something to drink."

"And some breakfast," Kappy muttered. Edie had rushed her out of the house so early she hadn't had time to eat. Her stomach growled in agreement.

"I can't discuss the case," Jack said again. "But I wouldn't mind a cup of coffee."

"Coffee it is," Edie said, leading the way to the kitchen table.

Jack took the seat, and Kappy was about to slide into the chair opposite him when Edie spoke.

"Kappy, can you come here a moment?"

Kappy gave Jack a quick smile, then joined Edie in front of the stove.

"I don't know how to make coffee on this thing," she urgently whispered.

"You never learned to make coffee?"

"I never learned to cook at all. I hated being Amish, remember? I was the one who left."

"And you can't light a stove?" Kappy asked again. She could hardly believe what she was hearing.

"I thought I'd made that clear," she said. "Now make some coffee."

"So you can flirt with the detective?"

Edie tossed a quick smile over her shoulder, then ducked her head back close to Kappy. "He is cute, don't you think?"

"I wouldn't go that far," Kappy said. She supposed Jack

Jones did have some sort of dark charm. He had a nice smile, if only he wouldn't frown so much.

"Well, I think he's cute and I want to give him some coffee."

"I'll make a deal with you. You find me something to eat and I'll make coffee." Her stomach growled again, punctuating the sentence.

"Deal."

Ten minutes later, the coffee was ready. Kappy poured everyone a cup, then looked forlornly at the cheese sandwich Edie had prepared for her. She supposed it was better than nothing and sat down to eat.

"What is going on out there?" Edie asked as she slid into the chair next to Kappy. Her gaze was trained on Jack.

From outside what sounded like shouting through a bullhorn could be heard along with the occasional rip of the siren.

"I'm sure that the uniformed officers are getting everyone off your property."

Edie heaved a sigh of relief. "Oh, good. I've got to get out and feed the dogs."

"And scoop the poop," Kappy added.

Edie shot her a withering look, but Kappy just shrugged.

Jack gave her an encouraging smile. "It shouldn't be long now, and you can go about your daily routine."

A knock sounded at the front door.

Edie jumped to her feet, and Jack stood as well. "Better let me get that," he said.

"Of course," she murmured, but followed behind him to the front door.

A uniformed deputy sheriff stood on the other side of the threshold. "We've done what we could, Jack."

"But they're barely off the yard," Edie protested.

Kappy stood and, sandwich in hand, joined the others at the door. The protesters had been pushed out of the yard, but as Edie had observed, only just. They stood on both sides of the road while some even stood in the lane. They still held their signs. Some sat in lawn chairs and all still chanted about the evils of puppy mills.

"That's the thing," the deputy said. "Some man is out here telling them that the three feet on either side of the road belongs to the county. I've got a call in to find out, but until then I'm not sure I can make them move."

"I told him he didn't need to call." Jay Glick strode up the porch steps to stand next to the deputy. "I know that land belongs to the county. Ruth only had an easement for the lane there. She and Martha have use of it as the driveway, but it doesn't belong to them."

"If that's the case," Jack started, "we can't make them move any farther."

"Are you kidding?" The flirty gleam in Edie's eyes died a quick death that very instant.

"I'm afraid so. Unless they get out of hand and threaten you or each other, then they have every right to protest on public property."

"But . . . but . . ." Edie stuttered.

"I'm sorry." Jack flashed her that sweet smile of his. When he did that, Kappy supposed he really was cute.

"Thanks for nothing, Jack Jones."

He stepped over the threshold and onto the porch. It was a good thing, for Edie closed the door, effectively shutting the three men on the other side.

Edie whirled on her, throwing her hands up in the air in frustration. "Can you believe that?"

"I suppose so," Kappy said. She didn't know the first thing about easements, only that they existed.

Edie turned back to the door. Even though it was still closed, she hollered out to Jack Jones. "And go check with Carlton Brewer. Something's not right with that man!"

Whether Jack heard her or not, Kappy had no idea. She took another bite of her cheese sandwich while the world went crazy around her.

Chapter 12

"I want to go visit Jimmy," Edie said sometime after lunch.

And Kappy needed to go feed Elmer. But how were they going to get out amid all the protesters? They managed to get into the backyard to feed Ruth's dogs, but trying to leave on the lane was a different matter altogether.

The crowd hadn't thinned any since Jack Jones left that morning. Two uniformed deputies had stayed behind, their cars parked to one side of the road, lights flashing as if to remind HABID the police were there still.

Kappy peeked out the front window. It would be next to impossible to get Edie's car through the throng. But Jack had gotten in this morning. And back out. She snapped her fingers. "I've got it. We call Jack, have him come get us, and take us over there."

Edie's face brightened. "Do you think it will work?"

"We'll never know unless we try."

"I think I have his card." Edie hopped up from the couch and went to fetch her purse, a big yellow monstrosity that looked like it was made out of lemon peels.

She dug around for a moment, then held the card over her head as if it were a winning lottery ticket. "Here it is." She grabbed her cell phone and dialed the number.

"How are you keeping your phone charged?" Kappy asked.

"Hello?" Edie said. She mouthed *car charger,* then turned

her attention back to whoever answered on the other side. "Is this Jack Jones?"

Edie paused as if waiting for an answer.

"Jack, this is Edie Peachey. I would like to visit my brother, but with all the protesters outside, I can't get through. Would you be able to come pick up me and Kappy and take us to the jail?"

Kappy held her breath as she waited. It was one thing to choose to stay at home all day and quite another to be forced into the practice. She was more than ready to get out of the house.

"Oh, good," Edie gushed. "We'll be ready." She tapped the phone off.

"He'll do it?" Kappy asked.

Edie nodded. "He's on his way."

Not only did Jack Jones pick them up and take them to the jail so Edie could see Jimmy, he got clearance for Kappy to go in, too.

"Are you getting enough to eat?" Edie asked.

They were sitting at a small metal table in the room that was barely big enough to hold it and the three chairs. Kappy settled down next to Edie and across from Jimmy. It was good to see his face again.

"I'm okay," Jimmy said. But Kappy could tell he was putting on a brave face for his sister. "Heather, that's the girl at the front desk, she brings me stuff."

Edie frowned. "What kind of stuff?"

"She brought me a coloring book and some colored pencils and a box of graham crackers. Stuff like that."

Edie visibly relaxed. "Did you remember to tell her thank you?"

"*Jah.* Of course I did." He scratched his neck around the collar of his orange jumpsuit. "I don't like these clothes," he complained. "And I don't think the bishop would like them, either."

His sister reached across the table and squeezed his fingers reassuringly. "The bishop understands. This is a special circumstance."

Jimmy gave an exaggerated nod. "And they took my call necklace away."

"It's okay. They'll give it back when you get out of here," Edie said. "You don't need it right now."

"*Jah.* I guess not." He frowned.

Edie leaned forward in her seat, grabbing both of Jimmy's hands and tugging on his fingers to gain his full attention. "Listen, Jimmy. I need to talk to you about something important."

He dipped his chin in another exaggerated nod, his cowlick bobbing with the motion.

"Look at me," Edie commanded. "Look in my eyes."

Jimmy did as instructed.

"Can you tell us about the morning that *Mamm* died?"

He closed his eyes as if shutting her out. "I don't want to think about that."

"I know it's hard. It's hard for me, too, but I'm trying to get you out of here. And in order to do that, I need to know about that morning."

He blew out a gusty breath, then started shaking his head. "No, no, no," he chanted.

"Jimmy!" Edie tugged on his fingers once more. "Look at me. This is important."

Jimmy reluctantly opened his eyes.

"You have to tell me what happened that day."

Kappy could almost see the wheels turning in Jimmy's brain. "We got up that morning like we always do," Jimmy said. "We ate breakfast. *Mamm* made pancakes with honey. They were so good."

"*Mamm*'s pancakes are good," Edie agreed.

"But you don't like them with honey," Jimmy said.

"That's not important right now," Edie explained. "After pancakes, then what happened?"

"Then we went outside to feed the dogs and scoop the poop."

Edie smiled a little sadly to herself. "Yes, got to scoop the poop. What happened after that?"

"I fed the ducks and the rabbits and the gerbils. And we got the puppies and everybody else fresh water."

"So it was a normal day. Is that what you're saying?" Edie asked.

"Every day is beautiful," Jimmy said.

"Yes, it is," Edie agreed.

Kappy nodded. If only more people felt like Jimmy. "When did you come to my house?" she asked.

A pale pink stain crept into Jimmy's cheeks. "Just after lunch. *Mamm* wanted me to paint the doghouses. She said she had someone important coming over and she wanted everything to look extra special."

Edie caught Kappy's gaze. Maybe this was the clue they were looking for.

"Who was coming over, Jimmy?" Edie asked.

"I don't know. Just someone special."

"And *Mamm* didn't say his name?"

"No, just that he was important and special and everything had to look perfect."

"Okay," Edie said. "So you painted the doghouses. Then what happened?"

"I had a bunch of paint left over, so I took it over to Kappy's house and painted her front door."

"Did *Mamm* know you left the house?"

Jimmy shook his head.

It was just as Kappy thought. He snuck over while no one was looking and painted her door.

"Why did you paint Kappy's door?" Edie asked.

That flush of pink reappeared to color Jimmy's face. "I like her."

"I like her, too. But I didn't paint her door," Edie said.

Jimmy heaved a big sigh. "She and Hiram had just broken up. And I like her. So I wanted . . ."

"What did you want, Jimmy?" Kappy asked.

"I wanted all the guys to know that she is single now. If everyone knows that, maybe she can find a new boyfriend. One better than Hiram."

"And that's why you painted my door blue?" Kappy asked. "Jimmy, you know as well as I do the whole blue-door saying is just a myth."

He nodded. "*Jah,* but what if one of the guys believes it? People believe myths all the time. If they believe and see her door . . ." He trailed off again.

His friendship and devotion were touching. "*Danki,*" Kappy murmured, unable to say anything else.

"So you painted Kappy's door, then what?" Edie asked.

Jimmy shook his head. "No, no, no," he chanted once again.

"Jimmy," Kappy said. She laid one hand on his arm to gain his attention. "When you got back to the barn, is that when you found your *mamm?*"

Tears rose in his big gray eyes, tears so sad they nearly broke Kappy's heart.

"Stay with me here, Jimmy." Edie ran her thumbs across the back of Jimmy's hands. He gave a small squeeze in return. "Did you see anything on the way back home?"

"Anything?" he asked.

"How about anything unusual?" Edie qualified. "Like a strange car?"

"An unfamiliar buggy?" Kappy added. "Someone walking down the road?"

She almost asked about a woman in red or a man in a blue or green shirt, but she knew better than to put ideas in his head.

"I don't remember." He frowned as if the thought process was making his head hurt. "I don't remember."

"It's okay," Edie said, her voice reassuring. "But if you do remember or if you think about the name of who was coming to visit, you write it down with your coloring pencils, okay?"

Jimmy nodded. "*Jah*. Okay."

"And it would be good if you could remember," Kappy added.

"It's very important," Edie said.

"Very important," Jimmy parroted.

A soft knock sounded at the door only a split second before it opened and a uniformed deputy stepped inside. She was no bigger than Kappy herself but she had a tough look about her eyes.

"Time's up."

"You have to go?" Jimmy asked.

Edie squeezed his fingers. "I'm afraid so. But I'll come back. Real soon, okay?"

"Do you want us to bring you anything?" Kappy asked.

"No. That's okay. Heather gives me anything I need."

Kappy shot him a quick smile. Thank heaven for Heather.

"I'm just saying," Edie protested on the way home. "*That's* who you need to find. This mysterious, important person who was visiting *Mamm* just before she died."

"And I'm just saying that we need a little more to go on than someone who's important." Jack held up two fingers, curling them down as he said the word *important*. It must have meant something because Edie stared at him, mouth open in shock.

"This is a big deal. I've come to you with the clue," Edie continued.

"Sweetheart, if you think that's a clue, it's a good thing that you're not in law enforcement."

"Then what would you call it?" Edie asked in a huff. She sat back in her seat and crossed her arms over her chest, glaring at Jack's profile as he drove.

Kappy slumped back against the seat. Being confined in

the small space of the car with the two of them was not exactly safe traveling. Whenever they got together the atmosphere turned electric.

"I call it a rumor. I call it hearsay. I call it the ramblings of a simple mind."

"Jimmy may be simple," Edie started, "but he's aware of what's going on around him. He knows what *Mamm* said before she died."

"That may be," Jack said. "But important people don't exactly write that on their business card. Without that, we have no way of knowing who this important person is."

Kappy leaned forward, close to Edie. "Or if they own a blue shirt or a green shirt or maybe even a red dress."

"Would you be serious?" she hissed.

Kappy shrugged and sat back in place. This whole ordeal had been a wild-goose chase from the get-go. Not that it made getting Jimmy out of jail any less urgent. But they didn't have a lot to go on and each clue they found seemed to muddy the waters rather than give clear direction.

"That important someone is Carlton Brewer, the younger," Edie said with a self-satisfied nod.

"Why are you so sure of that?" Jack asked.

They were almost home and for that Kappy was grateful. Too long in the car with Jack and Edie was not a good idea.

"I saw it in her appointment book."

Jack slammed on the brakes and swerved, taking the first turn off the road. Dust flew as they pulled into a graveled lane. Edie and Kappy were thrown against their seat belts as he braked and shoved the car into park. Jack turned, arm braced across the back of the seat as he pinned her with a hard stare. "You have her appointment book and you haven't turned it over to the sheriff?" It was mostly a question.

Edie gave a small cough and adjusted her shoulder strap. "It was in her office. The deputies came and took fingerprints and whatnot. I figured if they left it they didn't want it."

Jack closed his eyes and exhaled out his nose. Kappy had

the feeling he was angry, maybe even counting to ten or twenty to get his ire under control. "When we get to your house I want that book."

Edie shrugged. "Whatever you say."

Edie and Jack managed not to argue anymore on the remainder of the trip back to Ruth's house.

They stopped first at Kappy's so she could feed Elmer, then on a hunch, she put him on his leash and led him back to the car. Now he squirmed on her lap, trying to lick her face as if he hadn't seen her in years.

"Are there more of them?" Edie stared out the window at the multitude of people crammed into the three feet on either side of the lane. A few still sat in lawn chairs and were forced to move back from the sides of the road as Jack came through.

"I thought they would have given up by now," Kappy said, staring out her own window. Well, what she could see of it over Elmer's head.

As if the protesters realized the owner of the so-called puppy mill was in the car, they began their chanting anew, pumping their signs up and down, their faces angry. For the most part, the two policemen still on the scene had managed to keep the crowd peaceful, but to Kappy it looked as if it was a slippery slope from where they stood to an out-and-out riot.

"Can you make them go home?" Kappy asked. The whole situation was unnerving.

"Afraid not," Jack said. "As long as they're peaceful, and they're not on private property, they have the right to assemble and protest."

"I was afraid you were going to say that," Kappy said, hating the way the protesters marched behind the car, shouting their slogans and flashing their signs.

"Sorry to have to do this." He pulled the car off the road and into the yard, somehow nudging the protesters apart. Then he drove to the back door and parked on the grass. That was when Kappy noticed a third police car waiting there along with a uniformed deputy standing guard at the porch.

"Three policemen?" Edie asked. "Are we in that much danger?"

The protesters started around the side of the house after the car. But they took one look at the policeman standing there and held their ground. They shouted and chanted, but didn't come any farther.

"It's better to be cautious than sorry," Jack said, and Kappy couldn't help but agree. The officer came forward and opened the back door for Edie. Kappy slid out on the same side, keeping Elmer in her arms for safety. Jack strode up the porch steps and into the house as if it belonged to him.

"Where's he going?" Edie asked.

The officer gave a grim nod. "He's just making sure no one got in the house while you were away."

"In the house?" Edie's expression turned to startled. "You think some of them might come into the house?" She swung her attention to Kappy.

"Hard to say, ma'am," the officer said. "But anything is possible."

Edie looped her arm through Kappy's and directed her toward the house. "You're definitely staying here tonight."

Chapter 13

Jack stayed just long enough to look through the house and make sure no protesters were lying in wait.

"I suppose you are going to want to see your brother again tomorrow."

That wasn't even close to a question.

Edie propped her hands on her hips and tilted her nose to the ceiling. She gave a derisive sniff. "Of course. I suppose you'll come out to get us again."

Jack flashed her a quick smile that Kappy noticed didn't quite reach his dark eyes. "It would be my pleasure."

Somehow she got the feeling he didn't quite mean those words. Bah! *Englisch!* They never said what they meant and they never meant what they said. She wasn't sure how they knew what anybody was going to do with the way they double-talked, avoided subjects, and antagonized one another. Or maybe that was just Edie and Jack.

He got halfway to the door before he stopped and turned back around. "Where's that appointment book?"

Edie flounced into the living room where she retrieved the book off the coffee table. Several other volumes were stacked there.

"What's all that?" he asked, waving a hand in the general direction.

"Here's her appointment book." Edie pressed the book toward him, bumping the edge against his trim midriff.

"I repeat, what is all that?"

Edie tossed a look over her shoulder at the many ledgers stacked on the coffee table. "That? Just some stuff of *Mamm*'s."

Jack accepted the appointment ledger from Edie, then edged around her and into the living room proper.

"What kind of stuff?" He plopped down on the couch like he wasn't going to leave for a long, long time.

"Boring stuff, really," Edie said. "You wouldn't be interested."

Kappy swung her attention from one of them to the other, though she was starting to feel a bit dizzy from whipping her head around so much. What was it with these two?

"Humor me," Jack said.

"Breeding schedules, shot records, dog family trees," Edie said. "Boring stuff."

He lightly fingered the pages of one of the open books. "Actually, I find it quite interesting." He pulled the book closer, running a finger down the page as he examined it. "Looking for clues?"

"What?" Edie's high-pitched response was not confidence-inspiring.

"I'll take that as a yes."

Edie seemed to wilt under Jack's dark stare. Kappy had to consciously stay in place or she would go over and offer her friend physical support.

"I can't let my brother stay in jail any longer than necessary, and if the police aren't going to search for clues, I am."

Jack leaned back and gestured toward the many volumes on the coffee table. "How can they search for clues if you are withholding evidence?"

Edie opened her mouth, then closed it again. She opened it once more, but ended up closing it before the words came out. She resembled a fish that had been thrown up on the bank of a creek, unable to do more than gasp for air as she searched for a solution.

This time Kappy did move. She stood next to her friend and wrapped one arm around her waist, offering whatever strength Edie could siphon from her.

"Take it," Edie said. "Take all of it, if you think it'll help."

"Do you have a bag or a box?"

Edie nodded as Jack stood. She untangled herself from Kappy's embrace and fetched the box from the other side of the couch. She set it on the coffee table and took a step back as Jack began to stack the ledgers inside. She crossed one arm over her middle while she chewed on the thumb of the other hand.

"You're doing the right thing," Jack said, as he gathered the last of the books.

Edie merely nodded while Kappy stood by.

"I'll return these as soon as we are finished with the investigation." Jack nodded at each of them in turn, then let himself out the back door.

"I certainly hope so."

It took Kappy a moment to realize Edie was talking about doing the right thing and not about getting the books back.

"Stand aside! I tell you, I'm welcome here."

Kappy looked up from the seed catalog to meet Edie's gaze.

After Jack left, the pair had sat down in the living room, doing their best to ignore the commotion continuing around them.

Elmer ran to the back door, barking like the devil himself was waiting.

The crowd outside didn't look like it was going anywhere anytime soon, which meant she wasn't, either.

She stood and tossed the catalog onto her vacated seat. She should've picked up her sewing as well. She might not be quite as bored as Edie without television, but empty hours were just that, empty hours.

"Edith Peachey!" a man called from outside. "Tell this *Englischer* to let me in."

"Oh, *now* he wants to talk to me." Edie rolled her eyes.

"Is that . . ."

"Yup. That would be our friendly neighbor, Jay Glick."

So much for boredom.

Edie and Kappy made their way to the back door. Kappy scooped up Elmer. Edie wrenched open the door just as the uniformed deputy nudged Jay back into the yard.

Jay caught sight of her and flapped his arms like a wayward bird. "Edie, I need to talk to you. Tell this man I'm welcome in your house."

A mischievous gleam lit Edie's eyes. She crossed her arms and shifted her weight to one leg. "I thought you weren't speaking to me, Jay Glick."

Elmer wriggled and whined to get down. At least he had stopped barking. Maybe because he could see his mark. Kappy kissed the top of his head.

"Now, Edie, let's not be touchy. I have a business proposition for you."

"I'm sorry," Edie said. She didn't sound the least bit remorseful. "But I can't have a business transaction with you. You know, because I'm shunned and all."

"Let's don't be hasty." Jay flashed her an enormous smile.

Kappy took a step back, somehow managing to keep her hold on the squirming beagle. Her breath was gone. Maybe it was because she had never seen Jay actually smile. Or maybe it was the sheer size of it alone. Whatever it was, the action seemed somewhat sinister.

"There are ways around these things, Edie."

She gave him a quick smile of her own. "Only if the parties involved are willing to overlook such things."

Jay nodded. "That's what I'm talking about. I'm ready to forget the technicalities."

Edie grabbed ahold of the edge of the door, her expression unreadable. "Well, I'm not." She shut the door on Jay's continued protest. Then she covered her mouth and giggled behind her hand. "That felt good." She leaned against the door, eyes sparkling.

Kappy chuckled and let Elmer loose. He ran to the door barking with all his puppy might. "I bet it did. But it wasn't very charitable of you."

Edie straightened and headed back to the living room. "It might not be," she said, "but I enjoyed every minute of it."

"Do you think Jack will actually be able to find some clues in *Mamm*'s books?"

Kappy smoothed her fingers over Elmer's silky ears, then raised her gaze to Edie. "That is what he's trained to do, *jah?*"

"*Jah*," Edie said, then shook her head. "I mean, yeah. But somebody graduated at the bottom of the class."

Kappy frowned. "I'm not sure what you mean."

"It means just because he's a cop doesn't mean he's any good. It's not like we're on *NCIS* or anything."

"I know I don't know what that means."

Edie stood with a frustrated growl and started for the kitchen. "It's a television show," she explained. "I'm hungry. Are you hungry?"

Kappy checked the clock above the mantle. It was almost time for supper. "I suppose," she said. "Do you really want me to stay tonight?"

"Of course I do." Her voice grew faint as she left the living room for the kitchen. "I don't want to face these people by myself."

Kappy stood and followed Edie into the kitchen. "You don't have to face them. We're avoiding them, remember?"

Edie turned from examining the contents of the pantry. "I want you to stay. Okay? Is that what you want to hear?"

Was it? Kappy couldn't remember a time when anybody had invited her to just sit around and talk. Hang out, as the *Englisch* said.

Don't get yourself all excited. She only wants you because you're one of the few people who will actually talk to her in this town.

"Why do you suppose Jay Glick wants this land so bad?" Kappy mused.

Edie pulled a jar of peanut butter and a loaf of bread from the pantry. "Strawberry or grape?" she asked. "I wouldn't say he wants it that bad."

"No jelly. But I would love some honey if you have it." Kappy eased down into one of the kitchen chairs and propped her chin in her hand. "He wants it bad enough that he's willing to talk to you while you're under the *Bann*."

Edie made a face at the mention of the word *honey*, then took the jar from the pantry. She gave a small shrug. "Suit yourself."

"You don't think so?"

She shrugged and grabbed a butter knife from the silverware drawer before joining Kappy at the table. "I don't know. He's going to have to break the *Ordnung* eventually if he wants to buy the land from me."

Kappy cocked her head to one side as Edie began smearing peanut butter on one side of the bread. "Are you really thinking about selling?"

Edie lifted one shoulder, the gesture looking more like she was shaking off flies than actually shrugging. "I don't know. I mean, what am I going to do with it?"

"Same thing that your mother did." She watched as Edie started smearing the jelly on the other side of the bread.

"What? Raise dogs?" She smashed the two sides of her sandwich together, then pushed the jar of peanut butter and the knife across the table to Kappy.

"Among other things. She leases the farmland, you know."

Kappy raised the peanut-butter-and-jelly-covered knife, turning it this way and that before she got up, grabbed a paper towel, and wiped it clean with one swipe.

"I don't know," Edie said. She took another bite of her sandwich and chewed thoughtfully. "I mean, I'm not sure I can keep up with all that stuff. I've looked at *Mamm*'s ledgers. That was a whole bunch of records."

Kappy returned to her seat and reached for the bread. "You don't have to keep the same records she did. I would say most people don't. I'm just asking."

"I don't know," Edie said. "I don't think I can stay in a town where nobody will talk to me." Her expression turned down with concern. "No offense, Kappy."

Kappy looked up from making her sandwich. "Why would I take offense to that?"

Edie gave another of those rippling shrugs. "No reason. Just that I know a lot of people . . . Well, what I mean to say is . . ."

What Edie didn't want to say was that Kappy was odd and everyone in Blue Sky knew it. That didn't mean people wouldn't talk to her. Or did it? She only knew what she knew.

Maybe it was better to just change the subject. "What about Jimmy?"

"What about him?"

"He'll never survive in the *Englisch* world."

Edie stopped. Kappy knew she spoke the truth. Jimmy needed the beauty and the simplicity of an Amish life as much as Edie needed to escape from it. "I don't know. He's pretty resilient."

"Would you listen to yourself?" Kappy took a bite of her sandwich and waited for Edie to come to her senses.

Edie straightened her spine and braced her elbows on the table. "I don't have to decide this now. I need to be worried about who killed *Mamm*. Everything else can be decided later." Mind made up, she gave a quick nod. But it was far from settled and they both knew it.

*   *   *

"I've got an idea," Kappy said just before bed.

"About who killed *Mamm?*" Edie's excitement withered as Kappy shook her head.

"About the car."

"What car?"

Kappy sighed. "Your car."

"What about it?"

"We get one of the deputies outside right now to move it over to Jay Glick's house. Then when we want to go somewhere we can just walk over there, get the car, and leave."

"We could park it at your house."

Kappy shook her head. "There are too many protesters between here and my house. But no one's behind."

Edie seemed to mull it over. "What about Jay wanting to buy my land?"

"If you're going to move, you have to sell it to somebody."

Edie nodded in a *That's true* sort of way.

"And the chance of selling it to him will be what motivates him to let us park there."

"Motivates?" Edie asked.

Kappy gave a small shrug. "I have a word-a-day calendar. It was on last week."

"Do you really think it will work?"

"We'll never know unless we try."

Edie checked the clock. It was almost nine. "You think he's still awake?"

"There's only one way to find out."

Edie slipped on her flip-flops and together they walked out the back door. There was still a deputy in the backyard, though if Kappy was remembering correctly, there had been a shift change since that afternoon.

Edie let the screen door slam behind her, the motion coinciding with the deputy's as he slapped the back of his neck. Obviously, the mosquitoes were already bothering him. Arms crossed, he leaned his rear against the front of his car, and even in the dusky light, she could tell he wished he was someplace else.

He caught sight of them and straightened. "What are you doing out here?" he asked once they got close enough he could talk without yelling.

"We want you to take my car and park it at Jay Glick's house," Edie said.

The deputy frowned. Unlike the men in the front, he didn't wear a traditional policeman's uniform. He had on those battle pants that looked like he was in the army and a knit shirt that stretched across his ample middle. "Who's Jay Glick?"

"He's the neighbor who lives right back there."

"I don't have authorization to move your car."

"Really?" Edie batted her lashes at the man. "You seem like the kind of man who's in charge. You aren't in charge?"

He blustered a bit. "I didn't say that."

"I need a man who can make a decision," Edie said.

Kappy resisted the urge to take a step back. How the words managed to sound like a challenge and a proposition all at the same time was beyond her. Seemed like Edie had picked up a few things in the *Englisch* world.

"Tell me what you want again," he said.

Edie took a step closer to the man. He straightened but didn't retreat. Kappy wasn't sure if that was a good or bad sign.

"I just want you to take my car—you know, the red one in the front—and move it to my neighbor's house. That way when I need to leave and go get things—you know, like groceries and stuff—I won't have to bother people as busy as you and Jack Jones."

He turned and indicated the house just on the other side of the field. "That neighbor?"

Edie smiled. "That's right. If you leave my car there for me, then tomorrow I can go visit my poor brother in jail."

Okay, now she was laying it on a bit thick. But it seemed she had the deputy hanging on her every word.

"I don't see why not," he said. "I mean, we weren't told to keep you in the house."

Edie nodded. "That's right."

"And if I'm not supposed to keep you in the house, then it stands to reason that you're free to leave."

"Right again." She held the keys out to the man. One more bat of her eyelashes was all it took. He snatched the keys from her grasp and started around the front of the house.

Edie raised one hand in the air. Her grin was a mile wide, her eyes expectant.

"What?" Kappy asked.

"High-five me."

Kappy just stared at her. That wasn't on her word-a-day calendar.

Edie grabbed Kappy's hand and smacked it against her own. "High-five. It's like saying good job."

"Oh," Kappy said. "I got it." She had seen *Englischers* in town do that but never quite understood what it meant. And having that moment with Edie . . . Well, it gave her a strange feeling of happiness and trepidation.

They shared a quick smile.

"Come on," Edie said. "Let's go talk to Jay and tell him about our plan."

Darkness had fallen by the time they made their way to the Glick house. Only the soft glow of the kerosene lamps burning inside gave them any direction.

"At least we know he's still awake," Edie said, indicating the yellow lights.

"Go knock on his door," Kappy said.

"You go knock on his door," Edie countered.

"It's your car."

"It was your idea."

"So you could go see your brother."

Edie shook her head. "He's not going to talk to me."

Kappy was about to point out that Jay seemed pretty will-

ing to talk to her that afternoon when Edie planted one hand
in the middle of her back and pushed her toward the door.

"Just go," Edie urged. "He likes you better than me."

Kappy stumbled, caught herself, then made her way up the
porch steps. She could protest and say that no one felt Jay
Glick liked them, but she figured Edie was right. If he didn't
refuse to talk to Edie because of the *Bann,* he would certainly
refuse based on the fact that she had shut the door in his face
that afternoon.

She took a fortifying breath and raised her hand to knock.

The door was wrenched open under her knuckles. She
took a step back.

"What are you doing on my porch at this time of night?"
Jay Glick trapped her with his hard stare.

"Um, well, I . . . See, I was hoping that you would let me
park Edie's car in your driveway. What with all the protesters, we can't get out to visit Jimmy in jail."

"You driving an *Englisch* car, girl?"

"No. See, I mean, Edie would drive the car and park here.
I would just ride with her to keep her company. You know."

Jay continued to stare at her. Then he swung his gaze past
her to the yard where Edie waited. Kappy turned just as Edie
waggled her fingers in a semblance of a wave.

"Bah," he said.

But he didn't have time for any more as the deputy pulled
Edie's car into the driveway.

"Don't you think it would've been a good idea to ask me
first?"

Kappy gave him the sweetest smile she could muster. "Actually, I was banking on you being a good neighbor and sharing the land."

Land. That seemed to be the magic word. Once she said it,
Jay's demeanor shifted.

"Well, okay then. I guess it'll be okay if you parked here
for a couple of days. How long are you planning on having
those protesters?"

"I would be more than happy if they left tomorrow," Kappy said. "But Detective Jones says as long as they aren't causing any problems, they have the right to protest."

Jay gave a sympathetic nod.

"Jay? Who's out there?"

He turned as Anna Mae bustled up behind him. "Kappy King and . . . the neighbor."

"Here we go again," Edie scoffed.

"Why, Kappy. You can't stand out there all night. Come on in here." Anna Mae waved her into the house. Kappy cast one look over her shoulder, caught between the neighbors' hospitality and the friend she was leaving behind.

"Don't mind me." Edie crossed her arms and frowned as Kappy was led inside.

The interior of the Glick house was much like all the Amish houses in the valley. At least most of them. Kappy could say that her house was a mite different, but the same thing could be said about her. The same thing *was* said about her. But Jay and Anna Mae's was filled with plain furniture, floors covered in dull linoleum, with dark green shades on the windows.

"Would you like a piece of pie?" Anna Mae led her toward the kitchen table. Joshua and Jeremiah were already seated there eating a healthy portion of their own. They were the two youngest of the four Glick boys. One day Jeremiah would inherit the farm while Joshua worked odd jobs around the community to make a living.

"I really can't stay," Kappy explained.

"Nonsense." Anna Mae bustled over to the cabinet and started pulling down dishes. "You have to try a piece of this pie. It's a brand-new recipe."

Though Anna Mae made the best shoofly pie in the valley, the owner of the title of all-time best pie maker belonged to Alma Miller, the bishop's wife. Yet that didn't stop the friendly and the not-so-friendly competition that went on year-round.

"I really should be getting back home."

"One little piece of pie won't hurt," Anna Mae insisted with a bright smile.

"Leave the woman be, Annie," Jay said.

Her husband's harsh words did not dim the twinkle in her eyes or take one ounce of rosy color from her plump cheeks. "I'll just get you a piece to go, *jah?*"

"That would be great, Anna Mae," Kappy said. "I'd really appreciate that."

She hovered at the edge of the kitchen, completely uncomfortable with the situation. Up until a few days ago she hadn't set foot in anyone else's house in longer than she could remember. She'd only been invited into the homes of those who still held church in their houses instead of in their barn or bonus room. Now she seemed to be welcomed all over. The sensation was a little unnerving.

"I did find one farm over near New Wilmington," Joshua said. Obviously, he had picked up the conversation she had interrupted when she came in.

"New Wilmington?" Anna Mae half turned, the shock on her face apparent. "That's so far away."

"*Jah.* I know. But what choice do I have?"

"Well, you can choose to wait and see if you can find anything closer." Her piece said, Anna Mae turned back to dishing up pie.

Joshua dropped his head, his disappointment clear. "How can I ask Susannah to marry me if I don't have anyplace to live?"

Kappy felt like she shouldn't be hearing this conversation, but she was stuck there until Anna Mae made her to-go plate.

"The Lord will provide," Anna Mae said with more confidence than her shoulders indicated. "Here you are." She turned around, holding out a foil-covered plate to Kappy.

"*Danki,*" Kappy murmured. "And thank you for letting us leave Edie's car here."

Anna Mae only smiled in response.

"Has the daughter decided what she's going to do with her farm?" Jay asked.

"Not that I know of." Kappy started for the door. "Sorry I have to leave so soon, but I really need to be getting back." It was an outright lie, but she felt confident the Lord would forgive her. Just this once.

"I'll walk you out." Anna Mae trailed behind her all the way to the door. "I put an extra piece of pie in there." She lowered her voice to where only Kappy could hear. "You know, for the daughter."

"The daughter thanks you," Kappy returned. What could she say, really? They wanted to buy the land that now rightfully belonged to Edie, but both of them were reluctant to even speak her name.

Anna Mae beamed at her once more as Kappy thankfully slipped out the door.

She wished she had thought to bring a flashlight. It was going to be slow going walking back to Ruth's house in the dark. She was sure by now Edie had already made it home.

"It's about time."

Kappy's heart nearly jumped out of her body. She pressed a hand to her chest as if to keep it in place. "Edie! You scared me! What are you doing out here?"

"I wasn't exactly invited in."

"I thought you would have gone home already."

"I couldn't very well leave you here." Edie stood from her perch on the porch steps and dusted off the seat of her lime-green shorts.

She could have. But for some reason Kappy was glad that she hadn't. Walking back to the house in the dark would be much more tolerable with a little company.

"So did they say anything?" Edie asked as she fell into step with Kappy. She pressed her thumb to her cellphone and a bright light came from it.

"Did your phone turn into a flashlight?"

"Nah. Flashlight app."

Whatever that meant.

"So what did they say?" They started across the fields between the houses.

"Jay asked about the land, and Anna Mae gave us some pie."

"Us?"

"*Jah*. She cut you a slice as well."

"I guess they want the land pretty bad, huh?"

Kappy scoffed. "Be serious. They're just being neighborly."

"I don't know," Edie said. "A *Bann* is no light matter."

"*Jah?* Well, neither is Anna Mae's pie."

Edie laughed. "Is she still trying to win the pie competition?"

"Every year. Her and Frannie Lehman, but Alma Miller is still the champion."

They walked in silence for a few moments. Kappy was lost in thoughts about how change was slow to come to Blue Sky. She wondered if Edie thought the same thing.

"Do you really think Jay saw a man in green running across the fields?" Edie finally asked.

"It was blue. He said he saw a man wearing blue. Nathaniel saw a man wearing green."

"Whatever color he was wearing," Edie said, "do you think he really saw someone?"

"Why would he lie?"

"I don't know. I mean, if he saw someone running through the fields, they would have been running away from Ruth's house and toward the Glicks'."

"Right," Kappy said slowly, the ideas continuing to form. "They could have stopped at his house."

"Maybe hid out in the barn."

"Then it would stand to reason that he knew the man. Maybe he's even covering for him."

"That's entirely possible," Edie said. They arrived back at

the house. Edie gave a small wave to the deputy stationed out back.

"I guess because he's still here, that means the protesters are, too."

"Probably."

"I wonder how long before they get bored and give up."

"I don't know," Edie said as they let themselves in the back door. "But I hope it comes sooner instead of later."

Chapter 14

Apparently, Jack had gotten Kappy permanently added to the list of visitors who could come in and see Jimmy. Heather waved them both back and buzzed one of the deputy guards to inform him they were there.

Now they sat in the same room as they had before, no closer to getting Jimmy out of jail than they had been when they started.

"Jimmy," Edie began, "did you have any time to think about the name of *Mamm*'s special visitor?"

"I thought about it all night." He looked as if he'd been up for days. Dark circles underlined his bloodshot eyes. His mouth turned down at the corners, an expression that was unusual for the happy-go-lucky Jimmy.

Edie wore a pinched look as well. This whole ordeal was taking its toll.

"What about before that day?" Kappy asked.

Edie swung her attention to Kappy and pinned her with a sharp gaze. The question wasn't on their list of things they had agreed to ask Jimmy, but the idea had just occurred to her.

"Did she have any visitors before that day? Visitors she called important?"

"I don't remember." A whine had crept into his voice. He was getting frustrated, that much was obvious.

But Edie pressed on. "What about somebody she argued with?"

Jimmy shook his head, his eyes closed. Then he stopped mid-shake. "There was Johnny." He opened his eyes and peered at them, first Kappy and then his sister.

"Who's Johnny?" Edie asked.

Jimmy shrugged. "Just Johnny."

"And she argued with him?" Edie asked.

Kappy sat back in her seat. She folded her arms and re-sisted the urge to jump in the questioning. She didn't want Jimmy to feel overwhelmed.

"All the time."

"Okay, Jimmy. Now listen. This is important. What did they argue about?"

Jimmy's soft gray gaze turned serious. "All sorts of things. But mostly the land and the puppies."

Edie glanced back at Kappy, then she faced front. "What about the puppies?"

"I don't know. I don't like arguing. When they started that, I would climb into the hayloft and cover my ears."

"Did they argue often?" Edie asked.

"They argued enough," Jimmy replied.

"What's enough?" his sister asked.

"Enough that I don't like him coming around anymore." Jimmy crossed his arms and stuck out his lower lip as if to emphasize his words.

"Did he come around much?"

"Enough," was all Jimmy said.

Kappy and Edie exchanged another look. "Did they argue every time?"

Jimmy didn't have time to answer. The short female deputy from the previous day opened the door before he could respond. "Time's up."

Jimmy's expression fell. "You have to go?"

"But I'll come back. You'll be okay until then?" Edie asked as Kappy stood.

Jimmy nodded bravely. "*Jah*. They are treating me good."

Edie gave him a trembling smile. "I'll have you out of here in no time," she said, but Kappy had to wonder if she was trying to convince him or herself.

"What about this Johnny person?" Kappy asked as they headed for Ruth's.

"I don't know. I didn't see anything about a Johnny in her appointment book. Or her schedule." From time to time Ruth had contracted others to help her with various chores and projects. "Now I can't check further since Jack has the books."

"It's so frustrating," Kappy said.

"Maybe we should stop by and talk to Carlton Brewer again," Edie suggested.

"Why? So he has reason to call the sheriff on us, and we can get locked up like Jimmy?"

Edie pounded one fist against the steering wheel. "I just don't get it. We found all these wonderful clues, and yet we still can't figure out who killed *Mamm*."

"I wouldn't go that far."

Edie cast her a sideways glance. "If we can't solve it, we can't solve it."

"No, about the clues." The clues they had found were pitiful at best. Pitiful and impossible to track down.

"I just can't help but think we're overlooking something."

"Like what?" Kappy asked.

Edie blew her bangs out of her face. "If I knew I wouldn't be overlooking it."

Kappy gave a quick nod. "Right."

They drove in silence for a moment, and as she had when she was a child, Kappy withdrew into herself. Who was this mysterious Johnny, and why was he arguing with Ruth? And about what?

"Maybe his real name isn't Johnny," Edie said.

"Why would his name not be Johnny?"

"Just hear me out." Edie turned the car onto School Yard Road. Almost home. "Maybe we didn't see his name anywhere because Johnny is a nickname. You know how the Amish like their nicknames."

That was true. There were a few names the Amish seemed to use a lot more than others. It was common for more than one person in a church district to be named the same thing, even more so for a community. Eventually, nicknames popped up to help distinguish one Ben Miller from the next.

"Just never heard of Johnny for just a nickname. Isn't that a name-name?"

"It's a nickname," Edie said, "if his name is Jonathan and he only allows his close friends to call him Johnny."

"What if his name is Johnny?" Kappy countered.

"Work with me here," Edie groused under her breath. "There has to be something we're missing."

"Maybe," Kappy murmured in return. "The only John is John David Peight, right?"

"That's the only one I remember." She drove past the lane that led to Ruth's and around the bend to Jay Glick's house.

Edie put the car in park and cut the engine. She sat there for a moment, hands still curved around the steering wheel, eyes straight ahead.

Kappy stopped with one hand on the door, reluctant to get out if Edie was going to remain inside.

"I can't imagine John David Peight allowing anyone to call him Johnny," Edie said.

Kappy had to agree. There was something inherently elegant about the man. As if he had been a high-born *Englischer* who converted to Anabaptist on a calculated whim. Though with a name like Peight, she knew that not to be the case. Still . . .

"No," Kappy said. "I can't imagine anybody calling him anything other than John David."

"Which leads us right back to another dead end." Edie got out of the car and Kappy followed suit.

The Glicks were nowhere around as they crossed the yard and headed through the cornfield. And for that Kappy was grateful. She had too much on her mind today to have to deal with Jay Glick on top of it all.

Edie fell quiet as they crossed into Ruth's backyard.

The protesters were still out, though if Kappy wasn't mistaken, it looked as if their number had been cut in half. Those with milk crates and lawn chairs to sit on had perched on the side of the road, their signs braced against the ground. Some were still walking and chanting, but for the most part it seemed as if the largest portion of the protest was over.

"Something's gotta give," Edie said. "But what?"

"Where have you been?" Jack Jones hustled down the back porch steps and over to them. "I've been waiting for you for over an hour."

"Really?" Edie asked. "Why?"

Jack propped his hands on his hips and glared. With his swarthy appearance and dark eyes, Kappy had to admit he was more than just a little intimidating. "Because you asked me to pick you up and take you to see your brother this morning."

Edie shrugged. "You should've called first."

"I should have called—" The detective laughed, but the sound held no humor. None at all.

"You have my number, right?" Edie slung the strap of her gigantic yellow bag over one shoulder as if she hadn't a care in the world.

"I have your number." The words were somewhere between a statement and a question, though Kappy couldn't figure out which one held more weight.

"As part of the investigation. You do still have my number? At least I hope you do."

"I have your number." This time the words sounded more confident. "I just didn't expect you to be out gallivanting around."

Edie tossed her hair over one shoulder, then skipped up the steps. "Gallivanting? Who says that these days?"

"I do." He followed her up the stairs, leaving Kappy no choice but to tag along behind.

"You never answered my question."

Edie beelined for the refrigerator, taking out a pitcher of water to pour herself a drink. "Not that it's any of your concern, but we went to see Jimmy today."

Kappy propped one hip against the center kitchen island and watched the two of them. She wanted to keep a sharp watch in case other things became airborne.

"Wasn't I supposed to take you to see Jimmy?"

Edie poured something to drink and gave a small shrug. "I thought this would save you the trouble." She took a quick sip.

"Well, it cost me more trouble than it should have. I've been sitting here for over an hour."

Edie rinsed her glass and set it in the dish drainer. "You've already said that."

"I've been waiting for over an hour. There. I said it again."

"Do you want to discuss that," Edie asked, "or do you want to know what I found out this morning?"

"That depends," Jack said. "How good is it?"

"Pretty good," Edie responded. "It seems that Ruth was supposed to meet with somebody named Johnny right before she died."

"It seems?" he asked. "Or it really happened? None of that was in her appointment book."

"He's right," Kappy said. "Jimmy didn't say who the someone important was."

Edie shook her head. "I think the someone important and Johnny are the same person."

"You have no proof of that." Kappy could see the disappointment on Edie's face.

Perhaps Jack identified it as well. "Take it easy, Edie. I know you want your brother out of jail, but we are doing everything to make sure he's well taken care of."

"My brother wouldn't be in jail if it weren't for you."

He held up both hands in a gesture of surrender. "Can you talk some sense into her?" he asked Kappy.

"I'm not sure anyone can."

Jack shook his head. "I'm out. If you find any real clues give me a call." Without even a glance in Edie's direction, he stalked out the back door.

Edie stared after him as if she expected him to turn cartwheels on his way out.

"Do you still think he's cute?" Kappy asked.

Edie dropped her head into her hands. "Unfortunately, yes."

A loud knock sounded sometime after lunch.

"Now who could that be?" Edie tossed her magazine onto the coffee table and headed for the front door.

Elmer jumped down from his resting place on the couch and followed behind Edie, barking all the way.

"Maybe it's Jack, come back for round two," Kappy suggested.

"Jack always goes to the back door."

"Good point."

The knock sounded again. Louder this time.

Edie jerked it open without looking through the peephole to see who was on the other side. Elmer continued to bark.

"Hiram. How nice to see you. What do you want?"

"Is Kappy here?"

She was on her feet in a second.

"Watch out," Edie warned. "You don't want to get caught talking to me. That would be bad for a man in your position."

"I'm here." Kappy went to stand next to Edie.

"I would like to talk to you, Kappy." He stepped over the threshold, reaching for her hand as he entered the house.

Elmer continued to bark, but backed up with each step Hiram took forward. Some watchdog.

"Come on in," Edie said, moving to the side as Hiram nudged past her. Like she had any choice but to let him in.

"How did you find me?" Kappy asked.

"I went by your house and saw your sign. It wasn't hard to figure out that you'd be here." He cast a glaring look at Edie.

"It's sweet of you to stop by, but why are you here?" Kappy needed to remind him that they had broken up. It seemed he was still having trouble remembering that little fact.

He looked to Edie, then turned his attention back to Kappy. "Can we talk alone?"

"Don't mind me." Edie held her hands up. "I'm just furniture, remember?"

"Sure . . ." Kappy dragged out the one word until it held nearly four syllables. "Let's go out back."

"Please tell me there aren't protesters there."

Kappy shook her head. "They're all in the front."

"Yes, it's good to see you, too. I know it has been forever." Edie held the imaginary conversation with herself as Kappy scooped Elmer into her arms and walked Hiram to the back door.

"Cute puppy. Is that one of Ruth's?"

"He was. He's mine now."

Hiram nearly tripped on his way down the steps. "Why is your dog at Edie's?"

"It's easier to care for him when he's with me."

"Yo-yoou're staying here?" Hiram sputtered.

Kappy set Elmer in the grass. He immediately ran toward the pens, barking at his brothers and sisters and fellow beagles. "For a while."

"And your horse?"

"Is at home." She had been sneaking down to care for June Bug each day, Maybe it was time to put her in the barn with Ruth's horses. "What do you want to talk about, Hiram?" Kappy fell into step beside him.

"It wasn't hard for me to find you, you know."

Kappy frowned. "I wasn't hiding."

He led her toward the bench Ruth had placed under her

large apple tree. "It's all over town that you're running around with Edie Peachey."

"*Jah*. I suppose it is."

"She's under the *Bann*." Hiram settled down on the bench and Kappy reluctantly joined him there.

"I'm well aware of that," she said. "And I believe we've had this conversation before."

"You shouldn't be talking to her," he said. "Much less riding around in a car with her and questioning upstanding members of our community."

Hadn't they already covered this as well? Wait . . . What was he talking about? The only person they had truly questioned was . . . "Are you talking about Carlton Brewer?"

"He is a well-respected businessman in the valley. I find it hard to believe that you would feel the need to question a man like that about Ruth's murder."

Kappy jumped to her feet. "I have to do something. The police aren't doing anything."

"They arrested Jimmy."

Kappy resisted the urge to growl in frustration. "You know as well as I do that Jimmy Peachey is not capable of murder."

Hiram shook his head sadly. "Unfortunately, everyone is capable of murder. The Bible is full of stories of people pushed too far."

"That's not the case here." This conversation was growing tiresome. "The police have all but abandoned this investigation."

"Sit down, Kappy. There's no need to get this upset."

"There's every need to get upset," she said. "An innocent man is in jail. And if that's not enough, he needs special care. He just lost his *mamm*, his sister has finally returned to Blue Sky, and he's locked away without any support or love. That's plenty enough for me to get upset about."

Hiram either recognized how passionate she was about the subject or decided that it wasn't worth pursuing. "Jack Jones is investigating."

"If he thinks someone else is guilty, then they need to let Jimmy go."

"That may well be," Hiram said. "But not having anyone in jail and a murderer on the loose is not good for the community."

Kappy turned and eyed him critically. "You sound like a sod."

Hurt flashed in his eyes. "That was a mean thing to say. Or maybe it was a compliment. I may be thinking like an *Englischer,* but it's for the good of Blue Sky."

"I'm just looking after Jimmy."

"I talked to Samuel Miller."

"You talked to my bishop?"

Hiram nodded. "He's not happy with you running around all over with Edie Peachey. He said I should come talk some sense into you."

Kappy wasn't sure which part of that information to address first. "I'm running around all over with Edie, as you put it, to help get Jimmy—a fine member of my church district—out of jail. I don't care if she's under the *Bann* or not."

"Samuel Miller does."

"And furthermore, I do not need sense talked into me. I have all my faculties. I know exactly what I'm doing. I'm trying to find a murderer."

That brought Hiram to his feet. "That's just it, Kappy. You can't go around accusing upstanding members of the *Englisch* community of murder."

"So we're back to Carlton Brewer again."

"It's a serious matter, Kappy."

"I didn't accuse him of anything." She had merely *asked* him what he was doing at that time.

"Carlton Brewer didn't take it that way."

"Then maybe he is guilty."

Hiram threw his hands in the air, then slapped them against his pant legs. "See! That's the kind of talk I mean. You can't go around saying things like that."

"Noted," Kappy said. "I will no longer go around saying things like that." Why was everyone so touchy?

"You don't need to be going around with Edie Peachey at all. It's not good for your standing in the community."

Kappy nodded, the truth suddenly so very clear. "Now I see what's going on here."

Hiram frowned. "What are you talking about?"

"This has nothing to do with Edie and everything to do with you."

He scoffed. "Quit making excuses, Kappy."

"I don't need to make excuses, Hiram. We don't belong together. For a while I thought we did. I was mistaken. The quicker you realize that, the better off we'll both be."

"Your reasons for breaking up with me are weak," he said. "I understand that you're having some doubts. It's only natural. But you and I both know we are meant to be together. Why fight the inevitable?" He reached for her hands, and Kappy took a step back. It wasn't fair. How he could touch her and send her mind into a tailspin. She needed her wits about her if she was going to hold her ground. "Don't, Hiram."

She whistled for Elmer, but he was off chasing butterflies on the other side of the horse corral. He stopped, one paw in the air as he waited for the next command. "Come here, Elmer." She whistled again and he took off running, his ears flapping as he sped through the grass. She and Hiram would never make it. That much was obvious. But she would have Elmer. At least for a time.

"You can't run from this, Kappy."

"I'm not running," she said. Elmer arrived and she scooped him up into her arms. "I'm facing reality." And that reality was that Hiram would never love her the way he had loved Laverna.

"You and I are just too different. Good-bye, Hiram." She turned without another word and walked back to the house.

Chapter 15

"I've been thinking about this Johnny character," Edie said a couple of hours later.

She hadn't asked any questions of Kappy when she came back in the house, her eyes swimming with tears. She just shot her a sympathetic smile and went about her business. It was one of the things that Kappy liked about Edie. If she had tried to give her a hug and console her, Kappy would've fallen completely apart. As it was, just her friend's presence was enough support for her to swallow back the tears and continue with the day.

"What about him?"

They were standing in the kitchen eating a mid-afternoon snack of carrot sticks and hummus. Kappy hadn't been entirely sure about eating mashed chickpeas, but it wasn't half bad.

"Granted, I didn't get to look through all of *Mamm*'s books. But the only person that this Johnny character could be is John David Peight."

"And if he is Johnny, and if what Jimmy told us is true and they argued a lot, then it could very well be that he's the murderer."

Edie pointed a carrot stick in Kappy's direction. "Exactly."

"Are you thinking what I'm thinking?" Kappy asked.

"I am if you're thinking we should go pay John David Peight a visit."

Of all the suspects they had, and there weren't many, he seemed to be the one with the most motive. Plus, he owned a green shirt and he was in competition with Ruth.

"That's exactly what I'm thinking."

"Let me get my purse."

Kappy put the hummus away and stored the carrot sticks in the vegetable drawer in the refrigerator. By the time she was finished, Edie had returned, keys in hand.

"Why did you change clothes?"

Edie looked down at herself. "I thought this looked more professional."

Kappy didn't know the first thing about *Englisch* fashion, but she was fairly certain that skintight, stretchy black pants and a too-big shirt that said WORKOUT QUEEN didn't fall into the category of professional.

Edie tugged on her shirt, pulling it back into place. It had a tendency to fall off one shoulder. "You could do with a new outfit as well." Edie gave a pointed nod toward Kappy's dress.

So there were a few stains around the bottom and a small tear along the hem of her apron. She was still dressed according to the *Ordnung*. She shouldn't have to change.

Their gazes locked. Kappy stared at Edie. Edie stared at Kappy. Neither one moved for what seemed like several minutes. She really shouldn't have to change. Her clothes might not be the cleanest. But she'd been doing things all day in them. And they were a sight better than what Edie had on. At least, Kappy thought they were.

They continued to stare at each other.

Finally, Kappy threw her hands in the air. "Fine. We'll go get your car. You can stop by my house and I'll find something better to wear. Okay? I need to see about June Bug anyway."

Edie grinned. "I'll make a fashionista out of you yet."

There was that word again. Perhaps she should submit it to the word-a-day-calendar people. It might be a good addition to next year's calendar.

The crowd of protesters had thinned, and only one deputy remained, keeping the line at the front of the house.

Kappy and Edie started across the yard and into the fields, on their way to Jay Glick's house.

"I'll be glad when all these protesters give up and find someone else to pester. I mean, somewhere out there is a real puppy mill that needs to be shut down and instead they're here bothering us."

"True dat," Kappy said.

Edie stopped. "What did you just say?"

Kappy shrugged. "I heard somebody say it in town."

"Don't say it again." Edie started up once more.

Kappy trailed behind her. "Okay, I guess."

"Why do you suppose Joshua Glick wants to farm so bad?"

"What makes you ask?"

Edie pointed to where Jay and his son Jeremiah were working in the fields. Two large Belgians pulled their mower, leaving a trail of hay behind. "It's a lot of work," she said. "A lot of hard work. A man can break his back working like that."

"You've been living with the *Englisch* too long." Kappy smiled to take the sting from her words. But it was true. Edie had lost that Amish sense of value. She had lost that knowledge of what it felt like to work at home, be self-sufficient, connect with the land and God, and make a living all at the same time.

"I suppose," she said. "It just looks like a big hassle."

"It might be," Kappy agreed. "But he wants to marry Susannah Miller."

"The Bishop Sam's daughter?"

"The very one."

Edie shook her head. "He's going to need a big farm."

Samuel Miller was very protective of his only daughter. Even with as long as Edie had been away, she remembered.

"I know," Kappy said. "I feel sorry for him."

"Me, too." Edie shook her head. "Can you imagine having the bishop for a father-in-law?" She shuddered.

Anna Mae was hanging wash on the line when they came through the yard. Thankfully, she didn't drop her basket and hustle over for a chat. She just gave them a wave and kept pinning up clothes.

That was fine with Kappy. She was anxious to get over and talk to John David Peight. She wasn't exactly convinced that he was the Johnny that Jimmy had been telling them about, but he might hold some sort of clues as to who might want to harm Ruth.

Kappy heard the buzz of a saw as they walked past the work building. Jeremiah might be out helping his father in the fields, but Joshua seemed to be working an odd job for someone. Perhaps building a chicken coop, a rabbit hutch, or even a set of steps or a ramp for someone's home.

He seemed to make a decent enough living at it, but Kappy knew a decent living wouldn't be enough for Samuel Miller's daughter. It was a shame, really. After the conversation she had overheard the night before, she had come to realize how scarce farmland had really become in the valley. Especially if Joshua was thinking about moving all the way to New Wilmington, though she knew that would never come to pass. Samuel Miller would not allow his daughter to move so far away. That just wasn't happening.

Edie waited inside the car while Kappy went in her house and hurriedly changed clothes. She smoothed her hands down her clean dress and apron. It did feel good to put on something a little nicer. After all, it wasn't every day she was part of a murder investigation, and she supposed it would be wise to look her best.

And that meant fixing her hair as well. She unpinned her prayer *kapp* and set it gently on the counter. Unlike some of the Amish women in Pennsylvania, the women of the valley wore the same prayer *kapps* as the women in Lancaster County. It appeared as if their covering was a heart they wore on the back of their heads.

She didn't have time to take her hair completely down and re-fix it. But she undid what damage she could with a dab of baby lotion on both sides of her part. Unlike the women in Lancaster, the women of Blue Sky and the Big Valley didn't twist the sides of their hair before putting it into a bob. As far as Kappy was concerned, it was much nicer to not have to worry about such a small detail. And it was a lot easier to fix when the wind took hold.

She studied herself critically for a moment, then, satisfied with her appearance, she rushed back out to the car.

"When we get there, you'll have to do all the talking," Edie reminded her.

"Didn't he talk to you the other day?"

"He did, but I don't think he will now that he probably knows I'm under the *Bann*."

"I don't know," Kappy said. "Something about him is different." She determined it to be an elegance, but there was something unique about John David Peight. It wasn't that he was extremely handsome. He was good-looking enough, she supposed. He was not too tall and not really short; he wasn't fat nor skinny. But there was an air about him that seemed to set him apart. She wasn't even sure if he was aware of it. But it was almost as if he was among the Amish but not one of them.

"You don't suppose—" Edie slammed on the brakes and swerved to the side of the road, first throwing Kappy forward and then to the side. Her head conked against the passenger-side window. "Ow," Kappy said. "If you're going to drive like that, I'm not riding with you anymore."

"Sorry," Edie said. "But I have a thought."

"You have thoughts about trying to kill both of us?"

Edie shook her head. "No, no, no, just listen. He is different, right?"

Kappy rubbed her head in the spot where it had connected with the window. "I thought we had agreed on that."

"The question is how different."

She knew she hadn't hit her head that hard, but Kappy was having trouble keeping up with this conversation. "I don't understand."

"Just how different is he?"

"Would you explain that, please?"

"What if John David Peight is an *Englischer,* and he's wanted for murder somewhere else, so he's hiding out here. And he almost blew his cover because he murdered my mother!"

"Did you hit your head, too?"

"Kappy, I'm serious! Think about it. We've never had any trouble in Blue Sky before. Have we?"

"No," Kappy said slowly.

"Now all of a sudden he's here and there's a murder. See the connection?"

"Sort of. I mean, it could be the truth, but it seems a little far-fetched." Rats, she should have used *plausible.* It might have been last month's word, but it was still fun to use it.

"Not any more far-fetched than the idea that a woman was killed in her own barn and her only son has been accused of the crime."

"You got me there," Kappy said.

Edie grinned, though it wasn't an expression of happiness but more of triumph.

"I knew it," she said. She put the car back in gear and pulled onto the roadway. "I knew it." She thumped one hand against the steering wheel.

"I wouldn't start counting chickens if I were you," Kappy said. "John David Peight might be just as innocent as Jimmy."

They finished the rest of the drive in silence. Kappy hoped Edie was seriously considering what she'd said. John David might be completely innocent. But one thought kept coming back to Kappy over and over: He was the only one with a motive. If he put Ruth out of business, then he would have all her customers for himself, as well as any future ones. He would be the only hound dog breeder in the area.

"Just look at that sign," Edie said. "There's a word for your calendar. *Ostentatious*. That sign is ostentatious."

Kappy didn't need her dictionary to figure out what that meant. The sign in the yard in front of John David Peight's house was unlike any other Amish sign Kappy had seen. The others were hand-painted or made with letters bought from the bulk goods store. They were white and plain with black letters. They were no-nonsense signs.

But this sign was a pale yellow color with navy-blue letters that curved this way and that as if some artist had drawn them. And he'd been more concerned with the direction of the letters than he had been with the message they were getting across. It was showy, the exact opposite of plain.

"See?" Edie said. "Things like that. That's why I think he's *Englisch*."

It made sense to Kappy as well, but wasn't a man considered innocent until he was found guilty? Even if the charge was being *Englisch?* "Maybe he's just fancy."

Kappy had heard tales of the fancy Amish, with solar panel electricity, hardwood floors, and all sorts of propane-powered appliances. If John David was one of those fancy Amish, maybe if he had moved up here from Lancaster, she could see him wanting a sign like that. Well, kind of.

"Look at his yard!" Edie said. "Name me one Amish house in the valley that looks like this."

She couldn't do it. No one else had green grass like carpet or a stone walkway lined with petunias to rival those Nathaniel grew.

"It must take a lot of money to keep it like this," Edie said.

A lot of money meant a lot of dogs and a lot of dogs meant no competition.

"I don't know," Kappy said. They got out of the car and started toward the house. She was reluctant to hang the man already. But it was looking more and more like he was a murderer. Heaven forgive her, but she had wanted it to be Carl-ton Brewer. She kind of liked John David Peight. He seemed like a good man, caring and understanding. Carlton Brewer seemed only interested in himself. *Jah,* it would've been much easier for her if Carlton had been guilty.

"Go on up and knock," Edie said, nodding toward the door.

Suddenly, Kappy's mouth went dry, her palms grew wet, and her heart thumped painfully in her chest. Was she about to confront Ruth's murderer? It had been different when he came out to the house. He wasn't a suspect then. Now he was a sus-pect. Practically their only suspect. Definitely their only sus-pect with a motive. And a good motive at that.

She sucked in a deep breath to calm her nerves. If this was what it took to get Jimmy out of jail, then she needed to be strong for him.

She raised her hand and knocked on the door. There was no answering sound of shuffling feet or a call out that he was on his way. Nothing. She waited a moment more.

"Knock again." Edie danced in place, her flip-flops slap-ping against the heels of her feet. She was as agitated as Kappy.

Kappy knocked again, but she knew. John David Peight wasn't home. Or if he was at home, he wasn't in his house. Legs shaking, she turned around and descended the porch steps.

"Maybe we should check around back," Edie said.

"That's what I was afraid you were going to say," Kappy replied.

"Are you scared?" Edie asked.

"You're not?"

"It's not that," Edie said. "You just always seem so calm and collected. Nothing seems to ruffle you."

Kappy shook her head. "Trust me. I get ruffled."

The sound of barking dogs greeted them as they rounded the corner of the house.

"This is different," Edie said, her gaze taking in the details of John David's setup. Whereas Ruth had converted a large horse corral into a safe zone for her dogs, John David seemed to prefer them indoors. A converted hay barn housed the baying hounds. Kappy could see him in the center of the barn, water hose in hand and rubber boots on his feet as he sprayed the concrete clean.

"I need to get me a pair of those," Edie said.

"Muck boots?"

"They're a sight better than these, don't you think?" She held out one flip-flop for Kappy to see.

"Definitely."

Whether it was their voices or he happened to catch sight of them, John David gave them a wave. He cupped one hand over his mouth as he continued to spray the barn floor. "Just give me a minute. I'll be right there." He smiled at them and then turned back to his work.

It wasn't the smile of a greedy man. Or a man who was overly competitive. It was a smile between friends, and Kappy's doubts raised their heads once more.

A few minutes later, John David rolled up the water hose, then came out of the barn toward them.

He looked mighty different today than he had the day he came visiting. His quiet smile was the same and his caring eyes, but his clothes . . . Definitely work clothes. His blue shirt was smeared with mud and his one suspender looked like it had been mauled by one of the dogs. His black pants also showed traces of mud and wear, at least down to the tops of his boots. He had his pant legs tucked inside to keep them dry.

"Edie, Kappy, so good to see you."

He reached out to shake both their hands. Edie shifted her weight to one leg and propped a hand on the opposite hip. "How is it you don't mind talking to me?"

John David waved away her concern. "I wouldn't feel right shunning you. I wasn't a member of the community when you committed your infraction. And your mother used to talk about you so much. It's like I practically know you."

Tears rose in Edie's brown eyes. "My mother talked about me to you?"

John David nodded. "All the time. She was very proud of you."

"But she—"

"Your mother was a good woman through and through. But she was an Amish woman. And she followed her *Ordnung* to the letter. But I have a feeling if she could have gone back and done it again, she would've found a way around your *Bann*."

Edie visibly swallowed. "Thank you for telling me that."

"I should have told you the other day, but I was in shock. I had just heard the news."

"It was a bit shocking," Kappy agreed.

"What brings you out today?" John David took a rag from the back pocket of his pants and blotted his forehead.

"We were hoping you might help us," Edie said. She had managed to pull herself back together and was all business once more.

"Help with what?"

"We're trying to find out who killed Ruth," Kappy said.

He sadly shook his head. "Ruth didn't have any enemies. I can't imagine anyone wanting to hurt her, in any way."

"That's just the thing," Edie said. "We were talking to my brother and he said *Mamm* used to argue a lot with a man named Johnny. You wouldn't happen to know who this Johnny is, would you?"

Kappy had to hand it to Edie. She had stepped up and laid it all out. And without the slightest bit of tremble in her voice. That was bravery at its finest.

John David laughed. The sound seemed apologetic. "Of course I know him. I'm Johnny."

Chapter 16

A dozen or so questions immediately galloped through Kappy's thoughts.

"You're Johnny?" Apparently, the hinge on Edie's jaw had malfunctioned. She couldn't seem to keep it closed. "You're Johnny?"

"Why are you so surprised?"

Edie shook her head.

"If you're Johnny, why did you introduce yourself as John David?"

"I, uh, visited with Ruth often." He cleared his throat. "I thought Jimmy might relate to the name better. Why?"

Edie found her voice once again. "You don't seem like the kind that goes for nicknames."

John David gave a tiny shrug.

"So why were you arguing with Ruth?" Suddenly, she wished Edie had called Jack Jones before they drove out here. They were all alone with John David Peight, the mysterious Johnny, the one man who had a motive to kill Ruth. What would stop him from killing both of them if they revealed they knew his secret?

A stain of pink colored John David's face. He gave another apologetic smile, and wiped the rag across the back of his neck. "She wouldn't marry me."

"What?!" Edie screeched.

Kappy had to admit it was the last answer she would've expected. "Because you wanted to merge your two dog-breeding businesses."

"Because I loved her."

"Wait, wait, wait." Edie held her hands in the air to stop any more words from being spoken. "Hold on a minute here. You and my mother?"

"I know that might be difficult to hear, since we don't really know each other, but it's the truth. I loved Ruth and wanted her to marry me."

Kappy squinted at him, trying to decide if he was telling the truth. "Then why were you arguing?"

"Ruth has been . . . was on her own for so long," John David said. "I think she was afraid of giving up freedoms. Of course she said it was Jimmy. That he would be confused. But I think we got along just fine."

Edie shook her head as if she were still trying to get a handle on what John David was saying. "You and my mother?"

John David nodded. "Would you like to come in and have a cup of coffee? It's a little awkward, talking about this in the middle of the yard."

Edie turned to Kappy. "Can I talk to you for a moment, please?" she asked. "Over there." She pointed to a spot about fifteen feet away. Close enough that they could watch John David, yet far enough away that he wouldn't hear what they were saying.

He seemed to understand. "Go ahead. I'll stay right here."

Edie dragged Kappy over to the spot she had indicated. "Do you believe him?" She lowered her voice to a whisper.

Kappy looked back at John David. He had his hands parked on his hips, his gaze trained on some distant point across a nearby field. "We don't have any reason not to."

"But we don't have any reason to believe what he says is true. There's no proof. Just his word."

"What about Jimmy?"

Edie shook her head. "I think he would've already said

something if he had known about it. I think they kept it from him."

"That makes sense, especially if Ruth was certain he would be confused by the relationship."

"So do we believe him or not?" Edie asked.

"We believe him," Kappy said. She recognized the look in his eyes when he said Ruth's name. He got the same sorrowful look that Hiram got when he mentioned Laverna. It was obvious John David had loved Ruth just as Hiram had loved Laverna.

"Are you sure?"

"Pretty sure."

"Only pretty sure?"

"Very sure."

Edie nodded. "Okay. You want to go in and have a cup coffee?"

"Only if you want to," Kappy said.

"Okay." Edie started back to where John David waited. "Your offer for a cup of coffee sounds wonderful, but can we get a rain check?"

He smiled and Kappy couldn't help but notice that the action was on the sad side. "Of course. You and Jimmy are welcome here anytime."

"That's very generous of you. Thank you. But first we have to get Jimmy out of jail." Edie pressed her lips together. Kappy wasn't sure if she was trying to keep herself from saying more or keep tears from falling.

"I don't know," Edie said as they drove up School Yard Road. "Something about it just doesn't sit right with me."

"Because you're uncomfortable with the thought of your *mamm* having a boyfriend?" Kappy asked.

"No . . . Maybe . . . I don't know." Edie drove past both their driveways then back around to where the Glicks lived. She parked the car in their designated spot and they got out. "See?" Edie pointed to Jay and Jeremiah still out in the field working. "They'll be out there all day. And they'll be out there all day tomorrow. And the day after that, and the day after that, so forth and so on."

"So farming isn't for everyone. Where would we be without them?"

"True dat," Edie said.

"Don't say that," Kappy replied as they started across the yard.

A flash of black and tan sped in front of them.

"Was that Elmer?" Edie asked.

"He should be in his kennel." Her footsteps quickened.

Up ahead was another beagle. And another. And another.

"Oh my gosh," Edie exclaimed. "The dogs are loose."

They both took off running at the same time.

"I shut the gate this morning," Edie said as she scrambled after one of the running dogs. They seemed to think it was a big game and dashed out of her reach as soon as she drew near. "I know I shut the gate this morning."

"Then how did they get out?" Kappy asked.

"I don't know," Edie said. "But it wasn't because I left the gate open."

Kappy dashed after one of the puppies. She scooped it into her arms and it wriggled against her hold, trying its best to lick her face as she went after another. "This isn't working."

Edie stopped. Some of the dogs kept running, going in big circles around her. Others simply watched, ready to start the game the minute she moved. "What should we do?"

"Your mother has some leashes hanging up in her office. Remember? On the far wall."

Edie nodded. "You think I should get those?"

"It is our only hope of catching them all." And they needed to catch them fast. They were tearing through the fields, knocking down the stacks of hay that Jay and Jeremiah had worked so hard to create that very morning. As if they needed another reason for the Glicks to be angry with the Peacheys.

Edie sprinted to the house, a few of the dogs following behind thinking the game had changed. She returned a few moments later, out of breath and clutching a fistful of leashes. "I
caught two on the way back."

"Good," Kappy said. "Only thirty more to go."

It took the better part of the early evening to catch the
dogs. Finally, Kappy lay down in the middle of the yard and
let the dogs come to her. She might have been wearing one of
her best dresses, but it was important to gather up the dogs
as soon as possible. They were too vulnerable out in the
world, and she was afraid one would wander into the road
and get hit by a car. That was the last thing they needed, with
the animal-rights activists protesting in front and murder
charges still hovering over Jimmy's head.

"Did we get them all?" Edie asked.

"We're still missing two." But they couldn't continue to
scour the valley. "That'll have to do for now."

Edie nodded. "Maybe they'll turn up later."

"Maybe," Kappy murmured.

"Come on," Edie said. "I'll buy you some supper and we
can talk about what we should do now."

Kappy was almost too tired to walk back across the field
separating Ruth's house from the Glicks'. But the promise of
food was enough to keep her moving. They hopped into the
car and headed back toward Belleview.

The aroma inside Frank's Original Italian Pizza was enough
to make Kappy's stomach growl and her mouth water. The
smell was a tantalizing combination of yeast, oregano, and gar-
lic. They slid into a booth and waited for someone to come
take their order.

"Tantalizing," she repeated softly to herself.

"Was that on your word-a-day calendar?" Edie asked.

Heat immediately rose into Kappy's cheeks. "*Jah,* from a
couple of months ago."

Their conversation stalled as the young man approached

the table. He handed them menus, took their drink orders, and disappeared back into the kitchen.

"What made you buy such a thing?" Edie asked.

Kappy gave a quick shrug. "I don't know. It sounded like a lot of fun, you know. Learn a new word every day."

"I hadn't thought about it much, actually," Edie said. "Do you use the words often?"

"Sometimes, I guess."

The young man slid their iced teas in front of them and pulled out his order pad. "What'll you have?"

Edie shook her head. "We haven't had the chance to look at the menu."

"Sorry," he said. "Do you need a few more minutes?"

"We're getting pizza, right?" Edie asked.

"Fine by me."

"What do you want on it?" the young man asked, pencil poised above his order pad.

"Cheese only," Edie said at the same time Kappy said, "Everything."

They looked at each other and laughed.

The young man frowned. "Half cheese, half everything?"

"That would be good," Kappy said.

"I'll have it right out to you." He disappeared back into the kitchen.

"Hey," Edie said. "What did the Zen Buddhist say to the hot dog vendor?"

Kappy frowned. "I don't know."

"Make me one with everything." She sat back in her chair laughing.

"I don't get it," Kappy said.

"Because you ordered your pizza with everything . . . Never mind."

"Are you ready to talk about what happened today?"

Edie shook her head. "I'm not sure I'll ever be ready to talk about that."

"Is it hard for you to believe that your mom would have a boyfriend?"

"No. I guess not. I mean, she was a good woman. People loved being around her." She tore the end off the wrapping around her straw. She didn't put the straw in her drink, just starting tearing the paper, leaving little bits of confetti all over the table. "I mean, he's handsome and all."

"*Jah*. I agree with that."

Edie sat up a little straighter in the booth. "Speaking of handsome . . . You and Hiram?"

"I already told you: That's over."

"Somebody needs to tell him that."

"Are you volunteering?"

"Not hardly."

"What about Jack Jones?" If she could be put in the hot seat, so could Edie.

Edie shook her head. "I mean, he's cute and all, but he's just so . . . cop-ish."

"He seems very caring to me. He reopened the investigation, and he's making sure that Jimmy is taken care of in jail. That seems like a good thing to me."

Edie propped her chin in her hand and stared out the window. "Maybe." Then she seemed to snap out of her trance. "Let's talk about your word-a-day calendar more."

"Why, because you don't want to talk about Jack Jones?" Kappy pinned her with a look. "You want to talk about Hiram Lapp?"

"Today's word was *facetious*," Kappy said.

Edie laughed. "That about sums up this conversation." And talking drew to an end as their waiter brought out their pizza.

"You know what this means, right?" Kappy asked as they drove home from supper.

"What?"

"We were with John David when the puppies were let loose."

Edie pressed her lips together in a stern frown. "So you think he can't be guilty?"

"I'm pretty sure that's what I'm saying." Aside from the fact that he had declared his love for Ruth Peachey, how could he be in two places at one time?

"What if he hired somebody to do it?"

Kappy shook her head, her prayer *kapp* strings brushing her shoulders with the motion. "He didn't know we were coming today."

"Maybe it was just a coincidence."

"Why do you want him to be guilty so bad?" Kappy asked.

"Why do you want him to be innocent?"

Kappy sank a little deeper into the passenger seat of Edie's car. "I like the idea of him being in love with your mother. I know it's silly and romantic of me, but I think if they had been given a chance, they would've made a beautiful couple."

Edie exhaled like a balloon losing all its air. "Maybe. Probably."

They would never know now.

Edie pulled her car into the spot by Jay Glick's farm.

"How long are you planning on parking there, Kappy?" Jay called from the porch. Had he been waiting for them to return home?

Kappy didn't bother to correct him. She wasn't parking anywhere.

"Just a couple of years," Edie sassed.

He might not be acknowledging her words, but he could still hear them. He frowned.

"I wish I had an answer for that, Jay," Kappy said. "Maybe in a couple more days all the drama will die down over the puppies, and things will go back to normal."

Jay rocked back and forth in his rocking chair. "Bah," he said, waving one hand as if swatting her words away.

"One of these days," Edie said as they walked across the fields.

"You've just got to ignore him," Kappy said.

"And I expect you to pay for all the damage your dogs did," he called after them.

Neither one bothered to turn around.

"What in the world?" Edie's words were barely more than a whisper.

Then Kappy saw it. Hundreds of birds littered the backyard. Live birds, thank heavens. But Kappy had never seen so many birds together in one place in all her life.

Edie stumbled. "It's like that movie."

"What movie?"

Edie shook her head. "You don't want to know. But there were these birds . . ."

"What are they doing here?"

"I don't know."

But the closer they got to the barn, the clearer everything became. The five big tubs containing their animal food had been dumped in the backyard. The canisters had been tipped over and rolled around, spreading the food throughout the grass.

"All the dog food," Edie said. "All the duck food, all the gerbil food, all the rabbit food. It's all gone."

"How much is it going to cost to replace all that?" Kappy asked.

Edie looked near tears. "A lot. Besides the expense of the food, there's the delivery charge." She looked around her at the many birds.

"Do you think we should chase the birds away?" But any birds they disturbed simply fluttered around to another spot before touching down to dine once more.

This time tears did fall. They rolled down her cheeks as Edie shook her head. "Who would do all this?"

Only one cop was stationed out front. Was it any wonder that someone had slipped past?

"I'm just saying our visitors out front."

"But why? They wasted all their food. How do they expect me to feed all these animals?"

"I think the goal is to make this so hard on you that you give up breeding and find the puppies good homes."

"I'm not even a dog breeder."

It was true. She had inherited the situation and she was the one left to resolve it.

"What will we feed them in the morning?"

"Let's head over to the Super Saver," Kappy said. "Maybe the co-op can deliver food in the afternoon. But at least they'll eat in the morning."

It took another hour to get back to Edie's car, drive to the store, and buy dog food, but Edie was determined not to walk across Jay Glick's field anymore.

She pulled up the lane that led to Ruth's house. "Look at them." Only about twenty or thirty protesters remained on the sides of the lane. Even then, the zeal had gone out of their protest. Some still held their signs, while others had driven them into the ground and sat down next to them to rest.

"I think they're about to give up," Edie said.

"I hope so."

There were so few left that the deputy had gone, leaving Kappy and Edie to fend for themselves.

But the protesters didn't harass them as they parked the car and got out. Edie popped the trunk, and they removed two of the large bags of dog food and carried them toward the barn. They also bought a bag of dried corn. Surely they could make do with that until the proper food arrived.

"What's that?" Edie pointed to the back of the house.

Someone had painted them a message in big red letters.
YOUR NOT WELKUMM H—
"Who would—" Kappy started.
"There!" Edie pointed. Across the field between Ruth's and Martha's houses was a man in a green shirt. And he was running as if the devil himself were chasing him.

Chapter 17

Without a word, Kappy and Edie took off across the yard toward the man. But he had too much of a head start on them. A hundred or so birds took to the air as the women ran across the field.

Kappy got no farther than the edge of the Peacheys' cornfield before the stitch in her side took over. She pressed one hand to it, limping and out of breath.

Edie ran for a few more minutes, even in those flip-flops, but she still couldn't catch him. Maybe she was the Workout Queen after all. And maybe if she had had on some decent shoes she would've caught him.

And then what?

And then nothing. They might have known who he was. They might not have. They might've been able to get Jack Jones out there. They might not have.

Edie was still out of breath when she got back to Kappy. "Two things," she said. She held up two fingers in illustration. "We know the man is Amish." She sucked in a deep breath.

"What's the second thing?"

Edie bent over at the waist, trying to catch her breath. "I forget."

Together they limped back toward the barn. A few of the

birds had settled back in the grass, looking for any remains of the pet food.

It was dark when they finally got the dogs fed, gave them fresh water, fed all the other animals, and managed to get back into the house.

"I'm going to call Jack Jones." Edie pulled her cell phone from her purse.

"You *what?*" Jack's words were so loud, Kappy could hear them across the room.

"We went over to talk to John David Peight," Edie explained. They settled down in the living room as Edie related her story to Jack. Kappy just was happy to be able to sit down for a while. It seemed like they'd been running across these fields forever.

"He's on his way." Edie tapped her phone off and set it on the end table. She leaned her head back against the couch and closed her eyes. "What a day."

Kappy would love nothing more than to crawl into the guest bed and sleep until lunchtime tomorrow. Yet she was certain they would be up for hours filling out police reports and giving statements.

In record time Jack Jones was pounding on the front door.

Edie pushed up from her seat and made her way stiffly to answer it. "Hang on. I'm coming."

Elmer climbed into Kappy's lap and promptly fell asleep, his long ears draped across Kappy's leg.

"Was anyone hurt?" Jack asked as he rushed into the house.

Edie shut the door behind them. "Nice to see you, too, Jack."

"I'm serious." He whirled around to pin her with a stare.

"We're all fine," Edie said. "But sore and tired."

"Why are you sore?"

"I unloaded a hundred pounds of pet food, then chased a man through three fields."

"Wearing flip-flops," Kappy added.

Jack shook his head. "You should have never chased him. You know how dangerous that was?"

"He was Amish," Edie explained.

"And possibly the same man who killed your mother." He shook his head in exasperation.

Edie sat back in her seat. "Oh." The one word was small. "Take me to see the vandalism."

Edie turned on the couch and stretched out lengthwise. She waved a hand toward the back door. "I haven't moved it. Everything's around back."

"Just stay right here. No bother, I can find it myself." Jack made his way to the kitchen and out the back door.

He returned a few moments later, a can of spray paint held by two fingers of one gloved hand. "He spelled *welcome* wrong."

"It's Dutch." Edie didn't bother to open her eyes as she spoke.

"Where did you get gloves?" Kappy asked. It might not have been the most pressing question, but what did he do? Walk around with a pocket full of them?

"Do you have a paper sack?" Jack asked.

"In the kitchen," Kappy and Edie said at the same time.

Kappy propped her feet on the coffee table. Elmer stirred just a bit, then started snoring once again.

"Don't get up," Jack said. "Really. I can get it myself."

"Good man," Edie replied.

Jack returned a few moments later. In one hand, he held a brown paper sack that presumably contained the can of spray paint. "Why did you have to unload hundreds of pounds of dog food?"

"Just one hundred," Edie clarified.

Jack shifted in place. "Okay, why did you have to lift one hundred pounds of dog food?"

"Because somebody dumped all of ours out," Kappy answered.

"Dumped it out?"

"Scattered it everywhere," Edie said, eyes still closed.

"When was this?"

"This afternoon when we got back from visiting with John David Peight."

"About that," Jack started, "you cannot go around questioning people."

"Yeah, yeah," Edie said.

"I'm serious."

"We have to do something," Kappy said. "The protesters are leaving, but things around here are getting worse."

"I know it looks bad, but the paint on the house is common vandalism. The problem with the feed is probably a prank. In case it's not, you have to be careful. You have to leave it up to us. We are professionals, after all."

"If you're so professional, why am I still missing two dogs?" Edie said.

"What does that have to do with anything?"

"Someone let all the dogs out," Kappy explained.

"I swear, Jack, if you start singing . . ." Edie said.

"I might have, if this wasn't so serious."

Kappy could only imagine Edie was referencing some sort of *Englisch* song because she had no idea what letting dogs out and singing had to do with each other. Honestly, she was a little too tired to care tonight. She rubbed Elmer's ear between her thumb and her forefinger, loving the silky feel. He seemed to like it as well and released a shuddering puppy sigh in his sleep.

"If this is so serious, then you need to catch this guy," Edie said.

"And let Jimmy out of jail," Kappy added.

"That's not up to me," Jack said. "The DA thinks we have enough evidence to try him. If that's the case, he'll have to stay in jail until—"

"Until what?" Edie pushed herself up into a sitting position, most likely tired of Jack towering over her.

"Until we catch the real killer."

Edie stood, turned him around, and marched him toward the door, both her hands planted in the center of his back as she urged him forward.

"What are you waiting for? Get out there and get the killer before he knocks down the mailboxes or sets the house on fire."

"Whoa," Jack said. "We don't know that the killer is also our vandal."

"But it's possible, right?" Edie asked.

"Anything is possible."

And that was what they were counting on.

As expected, Kappy and Edie spent the better part of the night filling out police reports, making statements, and trying to explain to the uniformed officers what had happened.

They were told repeatedly how lucky they were that they hadn't come home sooner and caught the vandal before he got away.

"It's almost like whoever's doing this knows when we're not here," Edie said the next morning.

As soon as the officers left, they had gone to bed, but Kappy had been so tired she didn't rest well. She would love nothing more than to take a couple hours' nap immediately, if not sooner. But they had too much to do. Aside from needing to replenish all the pet food on the farm, Kappy was very behind in her sewing. All this running around and trying to solve a murder was taking its toll on her inventory. And she promised herself she would devote the afternoon to sewing *kapps*.

"Maybe it's one of the protesters," Kappy said.

"None of the protesters are Amish."

"Maybe one of the protesters is calling someone or radioing them or something and telling them that we're leaving."

Edie thought about it a moment. "I don't think that's it. We've been leaving out the back and walking across Jay Glick's yard to get our car. The protesters are in the front. How would they know when we left?"

Well, it sounded like a good idea. But somehow they were finding out when Kappy and Edie were gone and that was when they made their move.

"Maybe one of us should stay here," Kappy suggested.

Edie shook her head. "I need you to go with me in case someone Amish won't talk to me."

"Good point." Besides, Kappy wasn't looking forward to being left behind at Ruth's house.

"Maybe we could set a trap for them." Edie's brown eyes lit with excitement.

"What kind of trap?"

"We'll make a big show out of leaving," Edie said. "But instead of going to town, we'll drive around, park at Jay's house, then walk across the fields."

"I am so tired of walking across the fields," Kappy said.

"It's the only way this will work," Edie said. "Chin up, Buttercup."

Kappy stared at her blankly.

"It means 'Deal with it.'"

"Then what?" Kappy asked.

"Then we hide and watch to see who comes."

"Just watch?"

Edie held up her phone. "We take pictures."

Edie and Kappy stepped out onto the front porch an hour or so later. They both carried their purses as part of the cover.

"How long do you think we'll be gone?" Kappy asked in an over-loud voice.

Edie locked the door. "You're a terrible actress, you know that?" she whispered.

"I'm doing the best I can," Kappy whispered in return.

"Only about an hour or so," Edie said, her voice raised to carry across the yard.

"Never make fun of my acting skills," Kappy whispered. "Yours are just as bad."

"Yeah," Edie said as they walked to the car. "It might take even longer than that. We have to get the critter food and arrange for it all to be delivered."

"*Jah,* we will be lucky if that takes less than an hour for sure. Maybe even two."

"Not too thick," Edie coached.

They got in the car and pulled out, waving to a couple of the protesters as they drove by.

"Do you think we should go toward town?" Kappy asked. "What if whoever's coming doesn't see us and thinks that we didn't leave?"

Edie shook her head. "They could be coming from either direction. Let's just drive over to Jay's and get in place in case they come quickly."

Kappy's heart was pounding in her chest by the time they pulled into Jay Glick's driveway. Edie parked her car on the side, as had been agreed upon, and the two got out.

"Back again, are you?" Jay Glick came out of the barn. "When you didn't leave your car here last night, I figured that mess was over."

"We just need to leave it here for an hour or so," Edie said.

Jay trained his gaze on Kappy. "Are you going to leave that here all afternoon?"

"Only for about an hour," Kappy said.

Edie rolled her eyes. "Honestly," she growled.

"See that you don't leave it here longer than that." He turned on his heel and disappeared back into the dim interior of his barn.

"One of these days," Edie said as they started across the fields. "One of these days I'm going to give that man a piece of my mind."

Kappy smiled. "Go right ahead," she said. "He won't be listening."

They made their way to the edge of the cornfield and pushed between the stalks about three rows in and four plants down. With any luck the thick stalks would hide them from view, or perhaps their culprit would be in such a hurry he wouldn't notice a flash of blue or yellow in the middle of the cornfield.

"How long do we have to wait here?" Kappy said.

"Just an hour," Edie said. "We said we would be back then, so if he doesn't come within an hour we know he's not coming after that."

Kappy nodded. "Right."

But an hour sitting in the cornfield with nothing to do but stare at the back of the Peacheys' house was more boring than Kappy could've ever imagined.

Edie wanted to play video games on her phone but knew that if she did and she ran the battery down, they wouldn't be able to take pictures should the vandal show up today. So they sat and watched birds peck at bugs and the clouds blow across the sky. They listened to the cornstalks rustle in the breeze. For Kappy it was a special kind of torture.

"How long have we been sitting here?" she asked.

Edie checked her phone. "Fifteen minutes."

"Fifteen minutes? Are you serious?"

"Unfortunately, yes."

The minutes ticked by like hours, maybe even days. Kappy was sure she'd aged a month just sitting and staring at the back door.

Finally, Edie called time.

"I guess he's not coming today," she said. Her disappointment was palpable.

"I guess not," Kappy replied. "Wait. Are you saying we're going to have to do this again tomorrow?"

"I don't see why not."

Kappy bit back her sigh. "Fantastic."

Edie gave her a hand up from their sitting position amid the rows of corn. "Sarcasm is not a good look for you."

"Neither is sitting in a cornfield," Kappy said.

"Jimmy doesn't look good in orange," Edie said.

"Point taken." Together they walked back to Edie's car and drove to the co-op.

Jack called later that same afternoon. "Do you want the good news or the bad news?" he asked.

Edie had put him on speakerphone so Kappy could hear the conversation as well. They had gone to the co-op and bought all the things they needed with a promise of delivery the next day. Then they swung by the jail to visit with Jimmy. Kappy could only imagine how hard it was for Edie to go every day, see her brother, and know that she couldn't do anything to help him. Or that she was doing everything she could and it wasn't quite enough. But Jimmy appeared none the worse for wear. Heather evidently had been treating him very well, even sneaking him in a couple of grape Popsicles, his favorite.

"I want the good news first."

"We were able to lift a good set of prints off the paint can."

"That's awesome," Edie said.

Kappy shook her head and mouthed, *Don't say that.*

Edie shot her a look. "What's the bad news?"

"They don't match anyone."

"I told you, he was Amish," Edie said.

"So you did."

"What about the paint can? Can we track down the store where he bought the paint?"

"Edie, this isn't television. That paint is sold in every hardware store, Walmart, Target, and art-supply shop in the country."

"And?"

"And there's no way of knowing where he got the paint. It's just too broad of a clue."

Edie plopped back on the couch, then sat up straight. "So you admit it is a clue?"

"It's evidence, Edie. We're doing everything with it we can."

Chapter 18

Kappy and Edie finished feeding the dogs somewhere around eight thirty the next morning. They were both still exhausted from the day before, but chores went on. Always.

"Good morning."

They both turned as Jack Jones came around the side of the house. He had a leash in each hand, a beagle at the end of both.

"You found them." Edie rushed to greet him, dropping to her knees in front of the two dogs, Daisy and Lulu, a mother-daughter team Ruth had used for breeding. Daisy had gotten on up in years and hadn't been bred in a couple of cycles, Lulu taking her place in the lineup. They were two of Kappy's favorites. Edie's, too.

Kappy trailed behind Edie, glad to see the dogs return.

"Mama is so glad to have you home," Edie gushed. She rubbed the dogs behind the ears, let them lick her face, and laughed as they danced around. It seemed they were just as happy to be home.

Jack handed the leashes to Edie. "And in other news, there's only a handful of protesters out front this morning. They look worn-out. I have a feeling by this afternoon you will be HABID free."

Kappy's wide grin matched Edie's. "That is good news," Edie said.

"How did you find them?" Kappy asked.

Jack jerked one thumb over his shoulder. "I was over talking to Nathaniel. He found them but hadn't had a chance to bring them back over."

Thank heaven for good neighbors.

"I guess I should be going." He seemed reluctant to leave. "Got lots of investigating to do still."

Edie nodded. "Thanks again."

Jack smiled, and Kappy wondered how at eight thirty in the morning the man still had five o'clock shadow. His beard must grow in immediately after he shaved it. "My pleasure." He turned as if to walk away, then stopped and whirled around. "One other thing," he said, "when you get ready to go see Jimmy today, let me know. I'll be the one taking you over there."

Edie's happy expression fell. "What? Why?"

"The sheriff feels it would be . . . better that way."

Edie propped her hands on her hips, and Kappy winced. She knew what was coming next. "Better? He's just trying to keep tabs on us."

"It would be better to not have to worry about you while I'm trying to conduct this investigation."

"Maybe if you gave the investigation top priority, I wouldn't have to be doing all the work for you."

Kappy would've never thought it possible, but Jack Jones's eyes darkened. "I'll be by to pick you up around noon."

Edie stomped around the rest of the morning. The delivery truck arrived from the co-op, and the driver, along with another employee, graciously unloaded the large canisters of food. They even placed them in the barn where they had previously been.

"You want us to take the other cans away?" the Mennonite driver asked.

"We recycle them," his young helper explained.

"Yeah, sure," Edie said. "That would be great."

The man nodded. "It'll take you a while to get through this food, but when we come back out we'll take these canisters, too."

Edie opened her mouth to respond, then shut it instead. "That would be good. Thanks." She signed their invoice, then they climbed back into the truck and disappeared down the road.

"Does that mean you're thinking about staying?" Kappy asked.

Edie shook her head. "I don't know. I can't go anywhere until Jimmy's home, you know?"

Guilt stabbed through Kappy. She shouldn't have even asked, but she'd sort of gotten used to having Edie underfoot and jumping in her car and running all over the valley. She was just trying to prepare herself for the time when life in Blue Sky went back to normal.

"The thing that gets me the most," Edie mused, "is we're no further now than we were when all this started."

"True dat," Kappy said.

Edie shot her a look.

Kappy flashed an innocent smile. She had to say something to break up the heavy turn of the conversation. It was true they were no further than when they had started. They had scoured the valley, talked to people, found clues, and run their own type of investigation. But all they were left with was an Amish man in a green shirt and the red button that had no value at all.

What had happened to their previous optimism?

"You don't suppose that more than one person is responsible?" Edie asked. "I mean, all this time we've been looking for one person, right?"

"Go on," Kappy urged.

"Well, what if we can't find one person because there's really *not* just one person?"

"Are you saying that more than one person killed your mother?"

Edie shook her head. "No, I think one person is responsible for that. But what if another person is responsible for the dogs and another person is responsible for the food being scattered around and another person is responsible for the spray-painted message?"

Kappy thought about it a moment. "I don't know. I guess it could be true. But why would so many people target Ruth all at the same time?"

"I don't know."

"And it didn't seem that Ruth had any problems before now. If she did, she certainly didn't write about it in her daily journal."

Edie blew her bangs out of her face with a frustrated growl. "It was just an idea."

And that was where they had ended up. Searching for far-fetched ideas in order to figure out how to get her brother out of jail. If it wasn't so important, Kappy had a feeling Edie would've given up long ago. But it was important. Jimmy was doing okay now that he was in the county jail, separated from the rest of the prisoners, and given preferential treatment by staff. What happened if they couldn't free him? What happened if he was tried, convicted, and sent to prison? He would be all alone then. Kappy swallowed hard. A large lump clogged her throat.

She looked up and met Edie's gaze and saw her own fears reflected there.

"We have to get him out of jail, Kappy," Edie said. "We just have to."

"I have half a mind not to be ready when he comes," Edie said somewhere around eleven thirty.

Kappy didn't need to ask who she was talking about. It was obvious. Jack Jones. "And what exactly would that prove?"

Edie continued to apply mascara, leaning toward the mirror, eyes and mouth both wide open. "It's just . . . that he . . .

needs to know . . . that I'm not . . . at his beck and call," she said between brushstrokes.

"I see." Well, not really.

"I mean, what is the deal? That I'm sitting right here waiting on him to come and get me?"

All this doublespeak was making Kappy's head hurt. "Since he told you he was coming at twelve I would say yes, but I have a feeling that's the wrong answer."

From downstairs a loud knock sounded at the front door. "That must be him," Kappy said.

Edie took one last look at herself in the mirror. She fluffed her hair, smooshed her lips together, then pranced from the bathroom.

Kappy was left to follow behind. "Are you wearing that?" she asked as they walked down the stairs.

Edie stopped at the bottom and looked down at herself. She had on the yellow pants again along with a purple-and-silver top that sparkled like jewels. Actually, it was made of tiny little disks that seemed to be sewn to the entire garment. Kappy wanted to touch one just to see what it felt like. But she kept her hands to herself.

"What's wrong with what I'm wearing? Is that what you're wearing?"

Kappy glanced down at her blue dress and black apron. This was one of her favorite dresses. The blue was darker than most and mixed with a little green. It was the color of the ocean, or at least the ocean she had seen in pictures in books.

"What's wrong with what I'm wearing?"

"Nothing." Edie's voice was filled with innocence.

Kappy rolled her eyes. "You're saying that to make me feel like I'm dressed inappropriately. Everything I'm wearing goes right along with the *Ordnung*."

"I think you're trying to make me feel like *I'm* dressed inappropriately."

Kappy frowned. "I don't know what's appropriate for *En-*

glisch dress. I thought you just might want to wear something a little more conservative."

"I ran away from conservative, remember?"

"True d—"

Edie whirled on her as a knock on the front door started
again. "Don't say it."

If Jack thought Edie's outfit was unusual, he didn't say so.
He didn't register the tiniest bit of shock in his expression as
he caught sight of her. Kappy knew. She was watching.

Jack filled the drive to the jail with constant chatter. Kappy
had a feeling he was doing it just to keep Edie thinking that
they were working on the case. He told them they had no
suspects to check out and they were cross-referencing the fingerprints with some database. Kappy didn't understand half
of it, but it seemed to satisfy Edie.

He opened Kappy's door and she slid out as he did the same
for Edie. But at that very moment, clouds moved in front of
the sun and Kappy shivered. It wasn't cold, just ominous. Like
a bad omen of things to come. "I'll be in my office when you
two are done. Just come down the hall and get me. I'll take
you back to the house."

Surprisingly enough, Edie didn't comment. She gave him a
small nod and the three of them walked into the sheriff's office.

As during the previous visits, they took Edie and Kappy
into a small room to wait on Jimmy. He came in a little bit
later, but unlike the times before, his ankles were shackled together and his wrists were handcuffed at his front. He shuffled in, escorted by a large dark-skinned deputy. The man's
sheer size intimidated Kappy, but Edie had no such reservations. She was on her feet in a second. "Why is he trussed up
like a Christmas turkey?"

"You'll have to talk to the evening shift. He was like this
when I came in." His voice was deep like the croak of a bull-
frog.

For a moment Kappy thought Edie was going to say more,

but instead she turned her attention to Jimmy and the deputy left the room.

"What happened?" she asked as she helped him to the chair.

"I got upset."

That was when Kappy noticed it. A small cut in his hairline. It might've been short but it appeared deep. Whoever had doctored it had used one of those Steri-Strips to hold the two sides together.

Edie's fingers fluttered to the wound. "Who did this to you?" Her voice was soft but threaded with steel.

"Nobody," Jimmy said.

Edie leaned forward and clasped his hands in her own. "Jimmy, you don't have to lie for them. Tell me who did this so I can talk to Jack. They can't treat you like this."

Jimmy glanced at their hands, then turned his attention to the wall. He seemed reluctant to meet her gaze. "Nobody," he said again.

"Jimmy?"

He pulled his hands from hers. "I said nobody!" He raised his voice to a shout. It echoed off the walls of the tiny room.

Edie drew back, obviously stunned.

"Are you okay?" Kappy asked, her gaze trained on the young man.

He didn't look up but merely nodded. "I'm okay."

Edie caught her gaze, her eyes filled with hurt.

They had talked about all the things they wanted to ask Jimmy today, but none of that seemed important now that he was hurt, most likely at the hands of those who held him captive. It was heartbreaking.

"I did it myself."

Edie turned back to her brother. "What?"

He cleared his throat and said a little louder, "I did it myself. I hit my head against the wall."

"It's not necessary to protect them," Kappy said gently. Maybe it would be different coming from her.

But Jimmy shook his head. "No. I did it myself. I got mad and I hit my head against the wall. Nobody did anything except clean up the blood."

Kappy's stomach fell. They needed to get him out of here as quickly as possible. Jail was a terrible enough place, but for somebody like Jimmy . . . He couldn't understand what was going on. She could only imagine how overwhelmed he felt.

"Can you tell me something, Jimmy?" Edie started. "Was Johnny there the day that *Mamm* died?"

"No. I already told you somebody important was coming."

"And that somebody important was not Johnny?" Edie clarified.

"She never said who it was."

"And you didn't see them?" Edie asked.

Jimmy shook his head. "I left. I went over to Kappy's to paint her door. I thought it would be a good gesture." Tears welled in his soft gray eyes. "If I hadn't done that *Mamm* might still be alive, *jah?*"

She might be. Or they could both be dead. The thought sent shivers down Kappy's spine.

"You can't think like that, Jimmy. It'll make you bonkers."

"I'm already bonkers."

Edie stiffened. "Who told you that?"

His sadness deepened right before their eyes. "You did."

Edie reached for his hands once again, gently squeezing them to get his attention. "Look in my eyes," she said.

He did as she asked.

"I was wrong."

Jimmy nodded. "If you say so."

"I do. I was very wrong about that and I was wrong to say that. Will you forgive me?"

It was as though the sun came out to wash away the rain. His smile beamed, outshining his tears. "You were only fifteen."

"I don't remember."

"*Mamm* sent us to the barn to milk the cow and gather the eggs. I dropped one and tried to put it back together so *Mamm* wouldn't know. You said I was bonkers."

Edie had said it but couldn't remember and Jimmy remembered every detail. Strange how the things people say to one another can mean nothing to one and the world to another.

"I was wrong," Edie said again. "You're perfect. Just the way you are."

Jimmy grinned. "Just the way God made me."

"Just the way."

After their visit, Kappy and Edie met Jack in his office.

"Sit down," he said, indicating the two chairs in front of his desk.

Kappy did as he asked, then immediately shot to her feet when Edie shook her head. "No. You told us you would take us home when we're ready. I'm ready."

"I need to talk to you about something. Sit." His voice rang with authority.

Kappy immediately perched on the edge of the chair, though Edie did so with great reluctance.

"Did he tell you what happened last night?" Jack asked.

"Jimmy?"

"No, the Pope. Of course Jimmy."

"He said he got mad and hit his head. But I feel like he's covering for someone."

"Anytime an inmate gets hurt a report has to be written. There were several witnesses. And all their stories match."

"What happened exactly?" Kappy asked.

"It seems he asked for a peanut butter sandwich after he had already been served dinner. Because he had a tray, he was refused and that sent him over the edge."

"What was for supper?" Edie asked.

"Spaghetti."

"That's a problem. He doesn't like to eat red food."

"Red food?"

"That's right," Edie said. "He won't eat tomatoes, strawberries, or cherries. He doesn't like red gummy bears or any red candy, for that matter. If it's red, he won't eat it."

"What about strawberry jam?"

"If the color is dark enough he doesn't notice, especially if it's inside a biscuit. If you're going to serve him toast, I would go with grape."

"I see." But his tone indicated anything but.

As much as Kappy cared for Jimmy, it was a hard concept to understand.

"Your best bet is brown food."

"Like chocolate pudding?"

"Beige, really. Like graham crackers."

"Why beige?"

"How would I know?"

"The sheriff is asking that you write some of this down so we don't have this problem in the future. We can't have him hurting himself over spaghetti."

"You could let him out, and I could take him home. Then you won't have to worry about it at all."

Jack pressed the clipboard and a pen toward her. "If it was up to me, he would've been out of here on day two."

After Edie recorded all of Jimmy's quirks that she could remember, Jack escorted them out to his car.

"I guess it's a miracle this hadn't happened before now," Edie said.

"Definitely." But Kappy knew Edie was thinking the same thing she was. They needed to get Jimmy out of jail. Not only that, he needed to be back home with someone who understood him, who loved him like his sister.

And after that, then what?

Edie still hadn't made up her mind about staying in Blue Sky, and the longer she took to make her decision, the more Kappy became convinced that she was heading out as soon as possible.

She would have to take Jimmy with her. There was no way he could run the farm by himself. He was able to do the chores and keep up with the work itself, but the business end of it was beyond him. And because of that, it wouldn't be long before the whole thing collapsed around him.

Kappy would have to say extra prayers tonight, not only that they would release Jimmy soon but also that he would be able to make it in the *Englisch* world. She could only hope that since he would be with Edie, he would be okay. She could only pray.

Jack turned the car down School Yard Road and drove toward Ruth's driveway. A utility truck was parked on the side of the road, but as they turned up the driveway one thing was abundantly clear. The protesters were gone!

Edie raised her hands in the air. "Hallelujah. They found someone else to bother."

Kappy laughed. It was good to know that the protesters were gone, even though it didn't take them one inch closer to finding out who killed Ruth.

"Who's that?" Jack pointed toward the back of the property.

Two men wearing safety vests and carrying some type of equipment seemed to be setting up on the other side of the barn.

"I don't know." Edie slid out of the car and started over to where the men worked.

Kappy and Jack followed behind.

"What?" Edie exclaimed.

Kappy hadn't heard the question, but whatever it was, Edie hadn't liked the answer.

"Here's the paperwork." One man handed her a thick document attached to a clipboard while the other continued to unload his equipment.

He set up a tripod with what looked like a camera. Not that Kappy knew much about cameras, but she had seen a couple in town.

Edie flipped through the documents, then handed them to Kappy. "Read this. I can't see a thing without my glasses."

"Then why aren't you wearing them?" Jack asked.

Edie shot him a glaring look.

Kappy scanned the first sheet and then the next. It took until page five for her to truly understand what was going on. "You're land surveyors."

One man nodded. "That's right."

"But why are you here?" Edie asked.

"Let me see that," Jack said.

Kappy passed him the clipboard.

"We had a complaint about your barn. One of your neighbors is complaining that it is actually on his property. We've come out to assess the situation and to let you know if the barn must be moved."

"Moved?" Edie repeated.

"How does a person move a barn?" Kappy asked.

"You don't," Jack said. "You tear it down."

"That's right."

"And then build it someplace else?" Kappy asked.

"Right again." The man with the red hard hat snapped his fingers as if they should win a prize.

"But . . ."

"Don't you Amish build barns for each other all the time?"

"Do I look Amish?" Edie held her arms out to her sides as if to prove her point.

"No, but she does." He nodded his head toward Kappy.

Edie looked helplessly at Jack. "If they tear down my barn, what am I going to do with my puppies?"

"Don't worry about that yet. Let's see what happens first."

The three of them sat on the back porch steps and watched the surveyors work.

"Who would do this?" Edie said. Tears thickened her voice.

"Someone who wants you to leave," Jack replied.

"But why?" Edie asked. "What did I do to anyone? I've been gone for years."

It was true. Edie had been gone long enough that the world had turned without her. Blue Sky had moved on. Even her old boyfriend had married another. Kappy saw them at church every other week, and he seemed very happy with his new bride and baby girl. As far as she knew, he held no ill will against Edie.

"So the question remains: Who wants you to leave and why?" Jack clarified.

Kappy glanced up at the red letters scrawled across the back of the house. They would have to get some paint and cover it soon. May even have to paint the entire house to cover it up. It was a shame, such senseless hate. What would drive a person to such lengths?

Greed? Money?

Love?

She shook her head, trying to clear her thoughts. The men were measuring off distances. They walked from the edge of Jay Glick's cornfield to the far wall of the barn.

Was Jay claiming some of that land as his own? He had been after Ruth's farm from the start, but such a small strip wouldn't matter all that much when it came down to farming.

"Except that without a barn you would be out of business."

Edie roused out of her thoughts. "What?"

"It's not so much the land, but if you have to tear down your barn and rebuild—"

"Who's going to rebuild for me? No one in this town even talks to me except for you."

"Exactly." It was all becoming very clear now. "You would have to rebuild, but you wouldn't be able to rebuild, which would mean you would sell your farm."

"Is it crazy that I actually understand that?" Edie frowned. "I would either have to give the puppies away or sell them."

Jack studied her intently.

"Do you think the protesters did this? And that's why they left today?"

"It's possible," Kappy said. "But . . ."

"But what?" Edie asked.

"The animal-rights activists don't truly profit from putting you out of business. Unless you count their satisfaction that one more puppy breeder is off the map. But who would stand to gain if you were pushed out of business and forced to sell your farm?"

She knew the exact moment when Edie understood. Her eyes grew wide, and she jumped to her feet.

"Jay Glick."

"Where do you think you're going?" Jack chased behind them as Edie and Kappy started across the field. This was one time she wouldn't mind running across the field. She had a couple of questions for Jay Glick.

"We're going to talk to the neighbor," Edie called over her shoulder.

"You can't go talk to him alone. What if he's dangerous? We need backup."

Edie turned around, still walking backward as she hollered across the field. "Then call for some."

Kappy could clearly see the exasperation on Jack's face, then he turned and stalked toward the front of the house.

She and Edie quickened their steps. They had some questions for Jay Glick. Starting with, *Where were you when Ruth was murdered?*

"Have you got this?" Edie asked.

"I've no idea what I'm doing," Kappy said. Then she stopped, as surely as if someone had poured glue in the grass and stuck her feet to it. "What if he truly is the murderer?"

Edie backtracked and grabbed her hand. "Then he needs to be behind bars, and Jimmy needs to be home."

Kappy shook her head, resisting Edie's tugs. "Seriously, though. If he killed Ruth . . ."

"That's why we have to go now. He doesn't know we're

coming. It's the element of surprise. And it works every time."

"Really?"

Edie tugged Kappy out of place and hustled her through the fields. "It's on all the cop television shows."

"And they're real?"

"Well, no, but evidence is evidence."

Kappy wasn't sure what that meant, but Edie was determined to question Jay Glick. And dangerous or not, she couldn't let her friend do that alone.

"I wonder where he is."

Kappy gazed around them. "I don't see him in the field."

"It's too early for supper."

"Maybe he's in the workshop."

But the last thing she wanted to do was walk into the dim, converted barn and confront a man who might or might not be a killer. "Maybe we should wait on Jack."

Edie shook her head. "Maybe Jack should hurry up."

Anna Mae bustled out of the house. She held a laundry basket propped on one hip, and let the screen door slam behind her. *Thwack.*

Kappy nearly jumped out of her skin.

"Oh, it's Kappy King and . . . the neighbor."

"Oh pul-lease," Edie said. "Where's Jay? We need to talk to him."

"What brings you out today, Kappy King?"

Anna Mae made her way casually over to the laundry line and hummed a little under her breath as she began to work.

"I was hoping I could ask Jay about something."

"Oh, *jah?*" She pulled the hanging bag of clothespins closer and grabbed the first garment off the top of the basket.

"I want to know where he was when Ruth Peachey was murdered."

The garment Anna Mae held fluttered to the ground. She snatched it up but didn't try to hang it back on the line. "He's . . . he's not here."

Kappy's eyes narrowed. "Where is he?"

Anna Mae's normally rosy cheeks turned beet-red. "Well, not here."

"Maybe over at the County Assessor's office paying someone to come over and tell Edie that her barn is in the wrong spot?"

"What does something like that cost anyway?" Edie asked.

Anna Mae's hands trembled as she tried once more to get the garment to the line. "I have no idea what you're talking about."

"I think you do," Kappy said.

"What is going on out here?" The screen door slammed again, this time behind Jay himself.

Edie rushed over to greet him at the bottom of the steps. "Where were you the day my mother was murdered?"

"I swear these mountains create such an echo, it's almost impossible to hear a thing," Jay groused.

It was a lie. The mountains didn't create any kind of echo. He just wanted to pretend he didn't hear Edie, and he was running out of excuses. Soon he would be down to simply ignoring her.

"Where were you the day Ruth Peachey was murdered?" Kappy asked.

"Not that it's any of your business, but I was over at the co-op picking up a new blade for my mower. Hit a rock, I did."

Edie propped her hands on her hips. "If you weren't here, how could you have seen a man in a blue shirt running across the fields?"

"I never said I saw a man in a blue shirt." He must have forgotten he wasn't speaking to Edie the Shunned.

"Your wife said you did."

"I don't have to answer that."

Anna Mae must have had enough. She abandoned her half-full laundry basket and pushed past Jay and into the house.

"When Detective Jones gets here, you'll have to answer all that and more."

"You told us last time that you were here all day when *Mamm* was killed. Your stories don't match."

He might have been trying to ignore Edie, but there was no escaping the truth. Caught in his own lie, he dashed down the steps and ran through the field.

The cornstalks were well over Kappy's head, but she couldn't let him get away. She plunged into the field behind him.

"Wait for me," Edie yelled, her footsteps pounding behind them.

"Go get Jack," Kappy called.

"I'm a better runner than you. You go get Jack."

She couldn't argue with that logic. She might have a head start on Edie, but with her longer stride, Edie would make up that time in just a few seconds.

"Okay. Fine." Kappy stopped running and pressed a hand to her throbbing side.

"Now's the moment to see if all that time on the treadmill will pay off."

Kappy wasn't sure what that meant, but didn't ask as she turned and ran for the house. They needed Jack's help and they needed it five minutes ago.

"Jack! Jack!" Kappy ran as fast as she could, which admittedly wasn't nearly fast enough.

He met her halfway across the yard. "Backup's on its way. Where's Edie?"

Kappy sucked in a big gulp of air. "She's chasing Jay Glick through a cornfield."

"She *what?*" He didn't even wait for her reply. He simply took off in the direction Kappy had pointed.

"It's him," Kappy called after Jack. "Jay killed Ruth." She pressed a hand to the stitch at her side. She would have to get in better shape if she was going to run through cornfields after killers. Not that it was likely to ever happen again.

One last gulp of air and she jogged after Jack.

She could hear them all stomping around in the field, but the sound seemed to be coming from all around her. Maybe because four separate people were running through the field, or maybe it was just a weird echo caused by the tall stalks. Whatever it was, she couldn't tell where anyone was. And she wanted so badly to help.

She eased into the field, once again listening to see if she could determine anyone's real location. The sound could be coming from straight ahead. Or not. It could be Edie, Jay, or Jack. She had no way of knowing. It was beyond eerie being surrounded by corn on all sides, kind of like a corn maze except the stalks were green and there was no clear path. Oh, and there was a killer hiding somewhere inside.

She would have never imagined Jay Glick to have done something like that. She couldn't wrap her mind around it. True, he was a bitter man, cranky, or as her Aunt Hettie would say, a curmudgeon. But she would have never suspected him a murderer.

She whirled around as a sound came from the right. It was closer than she had realized. "Edie?" She wanted to yell, but she kept her voice at a whispering level. If Edie was close, she didn't want to alert anyone else to the fact.

Where was the backup? Then again, how would they know that everyone had run into a cornfield? They were on their own.

"Edie?" This time just a little bit louder.

She heard a yelp. Of surprise or pain, she wasn't sure. Only that it was Edie's voice.

"Edie?" She headed in that direction, uttering a small prayer that Jack had found Edie and not Jay.

There was a brief thrashing sound, then everything went still. Kappy could only hope that if she went straight ahead she would eventually find Edie. What condition she would be in was anybody's guess. If Jay was brazen enough to kill Ruth for the land, what would stop him from harming Edie?

And there she was, her unlikely friend, slumped over in the middle of the cornfield.

"Edie?" But she didn't move. "Please, Lord, let her be okay."

She fought through stalks to get to Edie's side. She had a big gash in her forehead, similar to the one Jimmy had inflicted upon himself.

"Great," Kappy said, even as tears welled in her eyes. "You and Jimmy will have matching scars." But that would be all right as long as she would be okay.

She held two fingers under Edie's nose to make sure she was still breathing. She was! Good news. The bad news was there was no way Kappy could get her out of the cornfield by herself.

"You stay right here. I'm going to get Jack." Hopefully, by the time she found the detective, backup would be there, Jay would be arrested, and everything would be over and done.

She stood next to Edie and stomped down the nearest cornstalks. Instead of avoiding them, she walked over them, pressing them down as she went, leaving a trail back to her friend. It was Jay Glick's corn and the least he could sacrifice after everything he'd put their family through.

She had twisted and turned when she'd run into the cornfield, and now she had no idea how deep she was among the stalks. Surely, it wouldn't be long before she came to the path that ran between the fields.

"What in the world are you doing?"

Kappy stomped one last cornstalk and came face-to-face with Jay Glick.

Chapter 19

"You!"

"Me," he sneered. "Out of my way, girl."

He tried to push past her, but Kappy was small and quick. She ran around in front of him, holding her hands out like she had seen the kids do in the martial arts studio in town.

"I know karate, Jay Glick. My hands are lethal weapons." It was perhaps the biggest lie she had ever told. But somehow it came out without even the slightest tremble in her voice.

"I don't believe you." But he stopped in place.

"I suggest you don't test me," she said. "Are you really going to chance it?"

He gave her a once-over, then a small nod. "I think I will." He started toward her, and Kappy was shocked by the meanness in his expression. It was do-or-die time. Time to back up her words, regardless of the fact that they were nothing but lies.

"Don't make me hurt you." She took two steps backward.

"You couldn't hurt a flea."

Really, if she was going to prove her claim, now was the time. She gathered her courage and said a quick prayer.

He took another step toward her.

Kappy closed her eyes and swung, a blind karate chop. There was a wheezing sound and then nothing.

She opened her eyes. The stunned expression on Jay's face

was near comical. He seemed frozen in place. He held both of his hands to his throat, and it didn't look like he was breathing. The moment suspended between them. Should she hit him again? *Could* she hit him again? She had merely lucked out the first time.

He squeaked in another breath, then he went down like a sack of potatoes.

"I did it," she whispered in awe. She had never hit another human being in her entire life, much less karate-chopped one. And yet whatever she had done had worked. Maybe her hands truly were lethal weapons.

She held them out in front of her, turning them this way and that as Jay lay on the ground in the path between the two fields.

No, her hands looked like they always had.

He must have managed to get some air into his lungs. He pushed himself to his hands and knees, then his air wheezed in and out like each breath was more painful than the last. "I'll get you," he rasped.

Kappy dropped her hands back to her sides. Could she do it again? Could she physically harm another human being? Then she remembered Jimmy in jail and Hiram's words that people could do almost anything if pushed too far. The answer was yes. Yes, she could do it again if need be. But she wasn't proud of the action at all.

"I suggest you stay right where you are, Jay Glick."

He lifted his head to look at her. Tears ran down his cheeks, but she figured they were from pain and not any remorse that he had for his evil deeds.

"You don't want me to have to hurt you again."

Who said that? It surely wasn't Kappy King, mild-mannered *kapp* maker in Blue Sky, Pennsylvania. Or maybe it was.

"Edie? Kappy?"

Jack.

"Over here," she called over one shoulder. She never took her gaze off Jay. And he never took his eyes off her hands.

She raised them back into her karate position, just to be on the safe side. That seemed to hold him in place.

Who knew?

"I fought Jay Glick."

"You *what?*"

She didn't have time to answer as Jack pushed through stalks of corn to stand at her side. His eyes widened as he took in her karate stance, then he turned to Jay. A large bruise had already started forming on his throat. His eyes were still watering.

"What did you do?"

Kappy smiled. "Only what I had to."

From there everything happened so fast it seemed to occur in a blur of sound and color. Jay Glick was arrested for the murder of Ruth Peachey. One of the uniformed officers who came as backup took him away in one of the sheriff's cars. Kappy led Jack back to where Edie was lying in the cornstalks. He lightly slapped each cheek just enough to stir her awake.

"Why didn't I think of that?" she asked no one in particular.

Jack helped Edie to her feet and they got on each side of her and walked her from the cornfield.

"Tell me again what happened." Edie held up a bag of frozen peas to her forehead. Thankfully, the bleeding had stopped, and though Jack insisted on taking her to the hospital, Edie dug in her heels and equally insisted that she wasn't going anywhere.

"The best we can figure," Jack started, "is Jay wanted to buy some land from your mother and she refused to sell. They got into an argument. He pushed her; she hit her head and died."

"So it wasn't really murder?" Edie asked.

"I'm sure the district attorney will take it down to manslaughter."

"Was he the important person who was coming over?" Edie asked.

Jack shrugged. "Hard to say."

"But he'll still go to prison, right?" Kappy asked. "He hit Edie in the head with a rock. He could have killed her, too."

"Not to mention all the trouble he caused." After Jay had been handcuffed, he seemed to lose a great deal of his starch. He confessed to calling the animal welfare inspectors as well as HABID. Once the activist group thought the Peacheys were running a puppy mill, everything fell into place. But Edie was stubborn and wouldn't take the not-so-subtle hint. That was when he resorted to out-and-out vandalism. He spray-painted the message on the house, let the puppies loose, and even scattered their animal feed as a way to hurt their business and their confidence.

Edie had settled on the couch, while Kappy had claimed her spot in the rocking chair. Elmer had curled up on her lap as he liked to do, and even with the crazy events of the day, a sense of contentment came across Kappy.

"And all this simply because he wanted his son to have his own farm." Jack shook his head.

"It's a big deal," Kappy said. She had heard the Glicks talking about how Joshua was going to have to move if he wanted to get married and have a farm of his own. *Englisch* families might live spread out all over the place, but it was important for Amish families to remain close. They needed one another as much as they needed the community.

"I can hardly believe that happened here," Edie said. "Blue Sky used to be such a peaceful place."

"It still is," Jack said. "For the most part. It's certainly nothing like Philadelphia or Pittsburgh."

It wasn't like a murderer had been roaming the back roads of Blue Sky. Ruth had died, yes, but as the result of a terrible accident.

"True dat," Kappy said.

Edie closed her eyes. "Don't say that."

"If Jay is arrested, then can't Jimmy come home?"

Jack nodded.

"Don't just stand there," Edie said. "Go get my baby brother."

"Sorry. Doesn't quite work that way. But tomorrow we'll have the judge sign the order and he'll be released."

"Tomorrow."

One more night in jail, then Jimmy was coming home. After that, who knew? She certainly didn't think Edie would stay in Blue Sky any longer than necessary.

The judge signed the order first thing the next day, and Jimmy was released. He came out wearing his regular clothes, the clothes he'd had on at his mother's funeral. On his feet he wore a pair of orange rubber slides. He held his black boots in his hand and smiled when he caught sight of Kappy and his sister waiting there for him. "Look," he said. He pointed down at his shoes. "They said I could keep them."

Kappy rolled her eyes, then gave a small chuckle. "Now he has worse shoes than you do."

Edie nudged her in the ribs with her elbow, but didn't take her eyes off her brother. "Are you ready to go home?"

Jimmy nodded.

Heather came around the tall desk. "Wait a second." She disappeared into the break room and came out a few moments later, a whole box of grape ice pops in her hand. "You take these home."

Jimmy's eyes grew wide. "All of them?"

Heather smiled prettily. "All of them," she said. "But you can't eat them all at one time."

"Right," Jimmy said. "I'll get a bellyache if I do that."

Heather smiled. "That's right. And you don't want a bellyache." She squeezed Edie's hand and went back around the desk.

Together they walked out of the sheriff's office. Jimmy stopped just outside the door and raised his face to the sun.

He closed his eyes and let the warm rays wash over him. "It feels good to be outside," he said. "That's the worst part of jail. You can't go outside."

"I'm sorry you had to go through all this," Kappy said.

"Me, too," Edie added.

"It's okay," Jimmy said. "It's not your fault."

He set his feet in motion, and they walked to Edie's car.

"And look." He reached in under his shirt and fished out his alert necklace. "You were right. They gave me my call necklace back. That's how I know I don't have to worry."

"If I have anything to say about it, you will never have to worry about anything again," Edie promised.

"Can you just drop me off at my house?" Kappy asked when Edie turned onto School Yard Road.

"Why?" Edie caught Kappy's gaze in the rearview mirror. Kappy had offered to ride in the back, allowing Jimmy to have the coveted place of honor in the passenger seat.

"I have a lot of sewing to catch up on. Those *kapps* aren't going to make themselves, you know."

Edie nodded. "If that's what you want."

"Perfect. *Danki.*" Kappy turned and looked at the window.

It was far from perfect. But it was what it was. It had been an interesting couple of weeks, but now that time was over. Jimmy was out of jail. Edie would make a decision on what to do with Ruth's farm. And she would go back to being odd-ball Kappy King.

Like it or not, her real life was back.

She couldn't say she actually *wanted* to go home . . . alone . . . but at least she had Elmer.

Who was at Edie's house.

"On second thought, I left Elmer at your house."

Edie turned down the driveway leading to Kappy's. "Me and Jimmy can walk him down later. That way you can get a jump start on your *kapps.*"

"*Kapps.* Right."

Edie pulled to a stop, but left the car running.

Kappy grabbed her purse and opened the door, stopping to lightly touch Jimmy's shoulder. "I'm glad you're home, Jimmy."

He half turned in his seat. "I'm glad I'm home, too, Kappy."

She gave him a quick smile, and somehow managed to fight back her tears.

"I hope you're not mad about your door," Jimmy said.

The tears that threatened clogged her throat. She gave a small cough to clear it. "I love my door," she said. "And I'm thinking of leaving it that color."

The smile on Jimmy's face was worth any teasing she would receive about her door. She would keep it that color forever.

She got out of the car and waved good-bye as Edie backed down the drive. It was another beautiful Pennsylvania day, so why did she feel so melancholy? It was one word from her word-a-day calendar she'd hoped never to use. Yet here she was.

She let herself into her house, kicked off her shoes, and headed for her sewing basket.

"Kappy! Kappy! Kappy!"

Kappy jumped at the pounding on her front door and pricked her finger with her needle. Thankfully, she didn't get any blood on the delicate organdy *kapp*.

Was that Jimmy?

She flung her sewing to the side and jumped to her feet. Then she raced to the door and wrenched it open. "Jimmy? What's wrong?"

He tugged at her hand. "You have to come quick! The dogs are out!"

"What? Again?"

Jimmy continued to pull her out the door. "Edie said to get you. We need help! Please, Kappy!"

"I'll be right there. Just give me my arm back so I can put my shoes on."

He gave her a sheepish grin and released her hand. "Okay. But you are coming, right?"

"I'm coming," she said, stuffing her feet into her shoes.

Her agreement must have satisfied Jimmy, for the urgency was gone now.

"Don't we need to hurry?" she asked.

"Oh. Right. Let's go." He grabbed her hand and pulled her down the porch steps.

"Jimmy," she exclaimed. "You're going to pull my arm out of socket if you don't stop."

He immediately released her and rubbed her shoulder. "I'm sorry. But you need to hurry. Edie says."

So much for a boring, peaceful, typical-Kappy afternoon. She'd gotten two *kapps* made and was working on the third when Jimmy knocked on the door.

"Hurry!" Jimmy skipped on ahead, stopping every few steps to remind her to come quickly.

"I'm coming as fast as I can." Who in the world would have let the dogs out? Or maybe she was still in mystery-solving mode. "You didn't leave the gate open, did you?"

Jimmy shook his head in an exaggerated way that would've made Kappy dizzy. "No. You must always shut the gate when you're done with the dogs. You shut the gate when you go in, and you shut the gate when you come out. That's a rule."

They had to have gotten out somehow. And with Jay Glick behind bars, who could be responsible for this round of excitement?

"Come on," Jimmy urged. He shot her that irresistible grin of his. He sure was happy to have the dogs out. Or maybe he was just happy to be out of jail. She knew when she got to the house that Edie wouldn't be nearly as happy about the turn of events.

Jimmy ran up the short drive. Kappy watched him go, expecting him to be chased by dogs all the way to the porch. But there were no pups running around the front yard.

"Jimmy," she called. "You said the dogs were out."

He ran up the porch steps and wrenched open the front door. "They're in here." He motioned for her to join him, then dashed inside.

They were in the house? How was that even possible?

Or maybe just a few of them had somehow gotten in. There were still some in the pen. She could see their wagging tails as she made her way up the porch steps.

She inched cautiously inside, expecting a friendly "attack by a dog" at any moment.

"Surprise!"

She jumped back as people seem to pop out of everywhere. Edie jumped up from behind the sofa. Hiram stepped out from the kitchen, and Jack came out from behind the rocking chair.

Jimmy jumped up and down in place, clapping his hands in excitement. "It's a surprise party!"

Kappy slapped one hand over her heart. "What for?"

"Because we can!" Edie said with a smile.

Kappy shook her head. "I don't understand."

"Well," Edie said, "we're having a party because the real murderer was found, and Jimmy is now back home where he belongs."

"And I wanted to have a surprise party. I read about it in a book while I was in the slammer."

In the slammer?

Kappy shook her head and chuckled. "It's a very nice surprise party." And she felt honored to be a part of it. "I guess it's also a going-away party."

Jimmy grinned, his eyes sparkling like jewels in his face. "Nope."

It took a moment for his words to sink in. No? It wasn't a going-away party?

Jimmy bounced on his toes once more. "That's the surprise! Edie's staying!"

"What?" she asked. "In Blue Sky?"

Edie nodded, happiness and excitement lighting up her face. "For a while anyway."

"Cut the cake! Cut the cake! Cut the cake!" Jimmy chanted.

Jack chuckled. "I'll get it." He ducked into the kitchen, leaving Kappy to stare after him.

"What's he doing here?" she asked Edie in a quick whisper.

"I invited him." She gave a quick shrug as if it were no big deal, lightly fingering the red button hanging from a cord around her neck. The clue that wasn't a clue at all.

"Oh, *jah?*"

"Stop." She lightly tapped Kappy on the arm. "It's nothing."

"That's what they all say."

Edie wasn't able to respond as Jack came back into the room carrying a white sheet cake. On the top *Welcome home, Edie and Jimmy* was written in letters made of blue icing.

Kappy leaned in close. "I thought you didn't like blue."

Edie shrugged again. "Jimmy does."

"Uh-huh."

"Can I cut it?" Jimmy asked. He grabbed a plastic knife and begin hacking away at the party cake.

"Hiram is here," Edie said.

Kappy was well aware. "Oh, really?" She shot Edie an innocent look.

"I know you saw him."

"Just why is he here anyway?" Kappy asked, dropping any pretense that she wasn't aware of his presence.

"Jimmy wanted to invite him. I think he feels bad about your door."

"I meant what I said. I love my door."

Edie leaned in close. "Do you love it enough to leave it blue even after you and Hiram get back together?"

Kappy's heart gave a hard thump in her chest. "Hiram and I are not getting back together."

"All I'm saying is if he wants to talk, you should give him a chance."

"Bu—" Kappy started.

Edie just gave her a look and sashayed away.

The last thing Kappy wanted to do was talk to Hiram. She had been strong and held her position these last couple of weeks, but her resolve was thin. And she wasn't sure how long she could keep it up. The best thing to do was to avoid him altogether. That was exactly what she did as they ate cake and drank punch and made plans for Edie and Jimmy's future in Blue Sky.

Kappy was thrilled that her newfound friend was staying. She knew in her heart that Edie would never give up her *Englisch* ways, but Jimmy needed to remain Amish. He needed the support and understanding he got from his community and his church.

Yet the miracle of it all was that somehow Edie had fallen in love with the farm. She had fallen in love with the dogs, and the ducks, and the gerbils, and she wanted to continue her mother's business. Kappy knew she had a long way to go, but with all of the meticulous records that Ruth had kept, Edie had a better chance than most.

Sometime after three, Kappy knew it was time to be getting back home. She found Elmer's leash and whistled for the pup.

But her stomach dropped when Hiram stood as well.

"Let me walk you home," he said.

Kappy didn't miss the nudge Jimmy gave his sister.

She had been royally set up.

"That's not necessary," she said as politely as possible. "But *danki* anyway."

"I think it's entirely necessary." Hiram shook hands with Jack and Jimmy, and even tipped his hat toward Edie. She might be under the *Bann*, but he saw her value as a member of the community even if she wasn't a part of the church any longer.

Kappy led Elmer down the porch steps and across the yard at a brisk pace. The best thing to do was to get this over with as quickly as possible. When would Hiram realize that she meant what she said? That they weren't meant for each other, and they couldn't get over their differences?

"I want another chance." His words were so softly spoken that the wind almost immediately carried them away. She turned to see if he had spoken them at all.

Only the expectant look on his face let her know that the words were there.

"Why are you doing this to me?" Kappy asked.

Elmer stopped to sniff at a particularly interesting rock, giving Kappy no choice but to stop as well. Really, the tiny pup was as strong as a mule when he set his mind to it.

"I'm doing this because I know we were meant to be to-gether," Hiram said. "But I can't prove it if you won't give me a chance."

Heaven help her, she wanted to give him another chance. But she was so concerned about her own heart that fear had her shaking her head.

"Just hear me out," Hiram said.

They began walking once again as Elmer took off after a butterfly.

"I did everything wrong with you. I forgot you haven't been married before. I jumped steps, and I shouldn't have done that. I want to go back—if you let me—and start over. We'll take it slow this time. And when you're ready, we'll talk about getting married. Not a moment before."

Kappy shook her head. She wanted to tell him the real rea-son, that she didn't believe he could ever love her the way he loved Laverna, but the words wouldn't come. And even if she spoke them, would they change anything? They surely wouldn't change his feelings for another. "I don't know, Hiram."

He took her hands into his own, Elmer's leash tangling with their fingers. "Just promise me you'll think about it. Can you do that much?"

What could she do but nod? "I'll think about it." They were almost to her drive. Hiram stopped and picked a bunch of bachelor buttons, presenting her with the purple flowers as if he had given her the moon.

Together they walked up the porch steps. She stopped at the front door.

"Think about it," Hiram said. He traced the line of her prayer *kapp* where it lay against her hair. "Promise me."

"I promise."

He smiled and made his way back across the yard. She watched him until he disappeared down the road.

She couldn't say that thinking about it would change even one thing, but she had to do that for him. After all, it was a new day in Blue Sky. And on a new day anything could happen.

Please turn the page for an exciting sneak peek of
Amy Lillard's next Amish mystery

KAPPY KING AND THE PICKLE KAPER

coming soon wherever print and e-books are sold!

A car horn honked outside. Well, *honked* was a kind word. It was more like the driver pressed the wheel and didn't stop.

"I'm coming!" Kappy called, though there was no way Edie could hear her.

She let Elmer, her beagle pup, out the back door. "And stay in the yard this time," she called, but the puppy didn't even break his stride.

The day before, Kappy had filled in all the holes that Elmer had dug, even the ones around the small fence that she and Edie had put up to keep Elmer from roaming across the valley. The dog liked to dig. And get out of the yard. Hopefully, today he would behave, but she wasn't counting on it.

Kathryn King, otherwise known as Kappy since as long as anyone could remember, grabbed her purse, checked her prayer *kapp* in the mirror in the living room, then locked the door behind her.

Finally, Edie took her hand off the horn and silence filled the air. For about a second and a half.

"Kappy, would you hurry? You know how Jimmy gets when I'm late to pick him up."

Kappy grumbled to herself and hustled to the car. "Is it my fault that you're late picking me up?"

Edie barely made sure the door was closed before putting

the car in reverse to back out of the drive. "You were supposed to be ready."

"I was ready. Fifteen minutes ago."

Edie waved away her protests. "It's okay." She turned the car onto the main road and headed toward the Peachey Bait Shop.

"Tell me again why you thought Jimmy should go to work at Mose's shop."

"He needs to get out more. I worry about him. I mean, the only time he goes anywhere is church." She shrugged, her off-the-shoulder top slipping a little farther down her arm. "And sometimes to the grocery store. He needs to socialize."

"I'm not sure working at the bait shop can be considered socializing."

Edie cast her an exasperated look. "It's a start."

"*Jah*." Kappy turned to face front, the glare of the sun off Edie's bright pink outfit almost more than her eyes could take.

If anyone saw her, they would never know that Edie Peachey had once been Amish. Or that she had only recently returned to take care of her special-needs brother. Edie looked carefree, bohemian even. At least Kappy thought that was the word. Or maybe it was *eclectic*. That one was on her word-a-day calendar and she knew it applied.

Edie seemed to wear whatever was at hand. Kappy wasn't sure if the clothes actually went together or not, but one thing was certain: Edie didn't dress like the other *Englisch* women Kappy knew. Not that she knew that many.

"It gets him out of the house a couple of days a week. And I think it gives him a sense of importance."

"He can't get that from taking care of the puppies?"

After her mother died, Edie had inherited more than the care of her brother. She had also gained her mother's beagle-breeding business. For a while, it seemed as if Edie would return to her life among the *Englisch,* but after working side by side with Kappy to uncover the truth behind her mother's death, Edie had decided to stay. For a time, at least. She hadn't wanted to take Jimmy away from his friends and support system. Not after just losing their mother. But Kappy wondered if Edie was as unhappy with the *Englisch* as she had been with the Amish. Not that Edie would ever admit such a thing.

"No," Edie finally said. "Taking care of the puppies is not a challenge for him. This way he's learning all about bait and fishing poles and a whole bunch of other sportsman things like that."

Kappy nodded. "I see. So this is about a father figure."

Edie sent her a shocked look. "Of course not."

Then why would Mose, who had a fifteen-year-old son who helped him, need the help of a twenty-something special-needs man?

Unless he was just doing this as a favor to Edie. Back in the day, Mose had been a part of their youth group. And those ties were strong. "So how did you get Mose to talk to you?"

Edie sniffed. "He didn't actually talk to me." She gave another of those shirt-slipping shrugs. "Jimmy went in and talked to him."

"Alone?"

"I was with him, of course."

"Of course," Kappy murmured, hiding her smile. All that meant was Edie had been behind Jimmy feeding him lines while Mose pretended she wasn't there. Oh, the joys of being shunned.

And Edie was shunned. She had joined the church then left the Amish. Now she was back and unwilling to join the church. But at least she was providing a steady home for her brother. In light of his trouble after their mother's murder, Kappy was glad that Edie had decided to stay.

"What in the world?" Edie slowed the car, drawing Kappy's attention to the road. Normally, she didn't like to watch where they were going. Edie's driving was a little . . . well, scary. She drove too fast as far as Kappy was concerned and seemed to

take too many chances on the road. Anytime Kappy said anything, Edie scoffed and laughed, leaving Kappy to pretend that
they weren't hurtling down the road in a dangerous car with
an inattentive driver. No, that wasn't the case as all.

A line of cars stretched in front of them as far as Kappy
could see. They all had their back lights on, *brake lights* she
thought they were called, indicating that they had all stopped
for something. Hardly any traffic came from the other direction, and Kappy wondered if the two were connected. Were
there cars backed up on the other side of the road, just farther down and out of sight?

"What's happened?" Kappy asked.

Edie stuck her head out the window and looked ahead. "I
don't know. An accident, I guess." She reached for the radio
knob, then pulled back with a sigh. "I guess we can't listen to
the traffic report and see if there's any news."

"Not until you have that bulb replaced," Kappy returned.

"Fuse," Edie corrected.

"Right."

The radio in Edie's car had gone out not long ago. And
though Kappy didn't know two cents' worth about the details, she knew that it wouldn't work.

Edie hung her head out the car window once more. "I can't
see anything but cars," she complained. "A whole bunch of
cars." She gave the steering wheel a quick pound. "We are
going to be so late."

But being late wasn't the real problem. It was how Jimmy
would react to the fact that they were late that was poten-
tially troublesome.

"Maybe he'll be okay," Kappy murmured. She was trying
to be encouraging, but Edie just shook her head.

"You weren't with me the last time." She shook her head
some more. "He was not happy."

"Maybe you should leave a little earlier," Kappy suggested.

"Like I have any control over this." She waved a hand toward the long line of cars.

True, with this sort of delay there was no way anyone was getting anywhere on time for a while.

"Why don't you call Mose and tell him? Maybe if he prepares Jimmy, it won't be such a surprise to his system."

Edie tossed her an appreciative look. "Hey. That's not a half-bad idea." She fished her phone out of her purse and pulled up the number, setting the phone to call before she tossed it to Kappy. "You tell him."

Kappy frowned, but couldn't say anything as Mose picked up the phone at his bait shop.

They inched forward as Kappy explained the situation to Mose. The man was more than happy to help. Kappy promised to be there as soon as possible, then handed the phone back to Edie.

"Thanks," Edie said, and pushed on the screen, effectively hanging up.

"With any luck that will help him."

Edie nodded. "With any luck," she repeated. Though Kappy knew what she was thinking. They were backed up so badly, it was going to be a while before they got past and on the other side of whatever had happened.

"I really hope no one's hurt," Kappy murmured. She hadn't planned on being gone this long. At the speed they were going and the fact that they would have to most likely take an alternate route back home, they could be gone over an hour. She said a quick prayer that God would help direct Elmer's mischievous puppy steps so that he would stay in the yard today and not dig his way out.

Then she immediately felt a little guilty. With all the problems in the world, she shouldn't take up God's time with her dog's bad habits.

"I think we're moving a little faster now," Edie said, but

Kappy couldn't tell. "I wish I knew what was going on up there."

"I don't know," Kappy murmured. With the way traffic was lined up and the number of cars barely inching forward, Kappy had a feeling whatever was ahead of them was pretty bad indeed.

But Edie was getting impatient. Kappy had grown used to most of Edie's *Englisch* habits, but her urge to just . . . go was not one of them.

"We'll get there soon enough."

Edie shot her a look. "You sound like my mother when you say things like that."

Kappy sniffed and smoothed her hand over her apron. "I'll take that as a compliment."

Edie laughed, shook her head, and turned her attention back to the road. "I really do think we're moving better now."

Not knowing how else to respond, Kappy nodded.

"Look." Edie pointed to a spot up ahead.

Kappy saw the flashing lights of multiple emergency vehicles, but not what they were attending. Kappy counted three police cars, a fire truck, and two ambulances. "That looks serious."

Oddly enough, the cars were moving a bit quicker, slowed only by the other drivers craning their heads around to see everything of the accident.

And Kappy was certain of that now. This was definitely an accident.

"Maybe one of those big trucks turned over," she said.

"Maybe," Edie murmured, still trying to see what was in front of them.

Finally, they got close enough to see.

The yellow buggy was almost unrecognizable. Just the sight of it made Kappy gasp. That and the acrid smell of vinegar that rent the air. The buggy was turned over onto one side and off in the ditch. The back wheel that was up in the air was cracked in half, tilted like one of those crazy rides at the county fair. The buggy itself . . . well, Kappy only knew what it was because of its distinctive color.

"Holy cow," Edie breathed.

"You can say that again."

Only the gravity of the situation kept Edie from actually repeating it. Having traveled in carriages most of their lives, they both knew: Whoever had been in that carriage was hurt. Badly. If not—

"What is that smell?" Edie asked, pulling the wide neck of her shirt up to cover her mouth.

"Vinegar, I suppose." At least that was what it smelled like. But why would this particular spot in the road smell any different?

"From what?"

"Maybe the other vehicle was a vinegar truck?" Kappy speculated.

Edie rolled her eyes. "There is no such thing as a vinegar truck."

"How am I supposed to know?"

But Edie had moved on to other issues. "Is that glass on the road?" She pointed in front of them where something sparkled like a diamond in the sun.

"I guess." What else could it be?

"And . . ." Edie leaned over her steering wheel, squinting ahead of them as if that could help her see better. "Are those pickles?" She pointed.

Stacked on the side of the road were several wooden cases, their contents a mystery except for the jars and jars of pickles littered around. Some had been turned upright, but still others lay willy-nilly as if they had been tossed aside. Or flung out when the car or whatever it was rammed into the buggy. And not just any pickles, but the white church pickles Big Valley was known for. Kappy had never thought twice about the white pickles and the white cucumbers used to make them, but here with them lying all over the road and off in the grass, some in jars and others not . . . well, they were downright ghostly.

"That looks really bad," Kappy said. There was no horse to be seen. And no other car. Or even a vinegar truck. Edie had already knocked down Kappy's truck theory, which quickly explained why there wasn't one. The other car could have already been towed. And the horse . . . ? If the horse had managed to make it through the crash, someone could have already taken it to the large-animal vet clinic. But from the looks of the carriage . . .

"You don't think . . ." Edie turned wide eyes to Kappy.

"I don't know."

"Do you know who it belongs to?"

They were almost past now. Kappy turned in her seat to look behind them. Cars still lined the highway as far as she could see. Vinegar, pickles, wooden crates. "It has to be Jonah Esh."

Edie whirled around as if to get a better look.

"Turn around!" Kappy yelled. Edie's driving was bad enough without her being distracted by pickles and broken buggies.

"Jonah Esh is just a kid."

"He was a kid when you left. He's seventeen or eighteen now." If she was remembering right.

"And his family still makes pickles?"

"His mother has turned it into an empire," Kappy said with a quick nod.

"A pickle empire?" Edie asked.

"Something like that." Finally, they were through the wreckage. Kappy was glad. Just the sight of all those pickles and that broken carriage was enough to give her chills.

Lord, please take care of those involved. Heal them and watch over them. Amen.

As far as prayers went it was quick and to the point, but she figured the victims in the accident could use every prayer they could get.

The sentiment was proven as the emergency workers loaded a stretcher into the back of one of the ambulances. Kappy shivered.

"That was a lot of pickles." Edie glanced in her rearview mirror as if checking for pickles once again. They were a bit eerie-looking, almost ghostly white against the darkness of the road.

"*Jah*," Kappy whispered and faced front once again. She was beginning to get a little sick to her stomach turned around like that and moving at faster than a buggy pace. Or maybe it was the stench of vinegar.

"I'm sure what happened will be all over the valley by dark."

"Maybe," Kappy said. She closed her eyes, almost haunted by the sight of the stretcher being loaded into the ambulance, pickles lying all over the place, and the strong smell of vinegar. And the broken buggy. Don't forget that.

A thoughtful silence fell between them as they continued toward Mose Peachey's bait shop.

"We are never going to make it now." Edie flipped one hand at the dash clock. They should have been at the shop ten minutes ago and they had at least five minutes left before they arrived. Well, she *thought* anyway. She wasn't practiced at determining arrival times in cars.

"Maybe he'll be okay."

That was the thing about Jimmy. He was as sweet as they came, but things could set him off. Kappy wasn't sure why some things bothered him more than others, like why he wouldn't eat red foods, but he was trying. Ever since his mother died, things had been a little harder for him, but he was giving it a huge effort, for Edie's sake. Kappy was just glad that Edie had decided to stay in Blue Sky, allowing Jimmy to do the same.

Despite Jimmy's usually positive and amicable attitude, Kappy could tell that Edie was concerned. *Amicable*. That was another one from her word-a-day calendar. It meant friendly, and that was one word that fit Jimmy Peachey for sure.

"Oh, no." The car started to slow as Edie whispered the words.

"What?" Kappy glanced at the dashboard as if somehow she could determine the problem, but Edie wasn't staring at the car's gauges, she was looking ahead, at the bait shop's gravel parking lot.

Jimmy was out front, pacing back and forth, shaking his head. In his hands he held the fob on the alert necklace he wore in case of emergencies. Even from this distance, Kappy could tell that he wore a frown of worry.

Edie pulled the car into the lot, a little too quickly as far as Kappy was concerned, but she knew that Edie wanted to get to her brother as soon as possible. Edie might be a little flighty, but Kappy knew she loved Jimmy above all else.

She shoved the gearshift into park and hopped out of the car with it still running. "Jimmy. Hey, Jimmy."

He stopped pacing and lifted his head, pinning his sister with a hard gray stare. "Where have you been?"

"There was an accident on the highway. Are you ready to go home?"

"Accident?" His gaze swung wildly around as if making sure everything in their corner of the world was still intact.

"Yeah, of course." Edie's tone was offhanded. She was trying to downplay the emotions and get Jimmy into the car without a meltdown. Whether she would be successful or not still remained to be seen.

Jimmy held up the fob. "Do you know how many times I almost pushed this button? This one right here. Do you know?"

"You didn't push it, though, right?"

"Five times." He held up his fingers to emphasize his point.

"But you didn't?" Edie asked again.

"When *Mamm* . . . when *Mamm*, you told me that I needed

to push it. I thought I would have to push it again." Tears welled in his eyes, but whatever anger he had drained from him. "You worried me."

Edie reached for him, then remembering he didn't like to be touched, she lowered her hands to her sides. "I know. And I'm sorry."

"I thought you were . . . I almost pushed the button five times."

"I know. But I'm here now. Are you ready to go home?"

He looked from his sister to where Kappy waited in the car. "Now?"

Edie smiled with apparent relief. "Yes. Now."

Jimmy nodded. "*Jah*. Okay." He started toward the car, then stopped and captured the alert fob in his grasp once again. "But next time you're late, I'm pushing it. How else is anyone going to know if something happens to you?"